PUSHING THE LIMITS

The convict took a step forward, and Callie shrank back automatically. But he only extended one shackled arm far enough to offer the return of her wrap and shift.

"You might want to put these on. It's been a good long while since I've had a woman, and there's no sense pushing the limits of my control."

Callie couldn't have agreed more. Taking the clothing, she half stood and shrugged them over her damp body as quickly as possible, showing as little flesh as she could manage. She stood in the middle of a foot of water, holding the hem of her gown up to keep it from getting wet. The man offered a hand to help her, but despite the chivalry of the gesture, she refused to touch him.

Semingly unperturbed by her rejection, he retracted the proferred hand and instead stooped to spread the earlier missing towel on the floor beside the tub. The thick iron chains rattled with every move he made.

She had one foot on the towel, the other lifted to step the rest of the way out of the bath, when his next words froze her in place.

"Why don't we make this short and sweet for everyone involved? Just tell me where the boy is, and I'll be on my way."

Other *Leisure* books by Heidi Betts:
WALKER'S WIDOW
ALMOST A LADY
CINNAMON AND ROSES
A PROMISE OF ROSES

CALLIE'S CONVICT

HEIDI BETTS

LEISURE BOOKS NEW YORK CITY

A LEISURE BOOK®

July 2002

Published by

Dorchester Publishing Co., Inc.
276 Fifth Avenue
New York, NY 10001

ISBN 0-8439-5030-7

The name "Leisure Books" and the stylized "L" with design are
trademarks of Dorchester Publishing Co., Inc.

Printed in the United States of America.

Visit us on the web at www.dorchesterpub.com.

This book is dedicated to the thousands of innocent men, women, and children who lost their lives in the September 11, 2001 attacks on the World Trade Center in New York City and The Pentagon in Washington, D.C.

For those aboard all four hijacked flights, who so bravely tried to warn us that the planes had been taken over, and in some cases even tried to prevent what was about to happen.

For the legions of firefighters, police officers, rescue workers, and volunteers who rushed to the scenes, risking their lives to save others.

For my fellow Americans who gave their time and resources and even their very blood, coming together once again to show just how strong a nation the United States can be.

And for the families of all the loved ones who were taken from us that day. As I was writing this book, I prayed for you and want you now to know that your sons, your daughters, your husbands, wives, sisters, brothers, friends, grandchildren, and countrymen will never be forgotten.

God bless you all.

May the road rise up to meet you,
May the wind be always at your back.
May the sun shine warmly upon your face,
The rains fall soft upon your fields.
And until we meet again,
May God hold you in the palm of His hand.

—An Old Gaelic Blessing

CALLIE'S
CONVICT

Prologue

Lily White hadn't been a whore all her life. In fact, if her parents' intentions by giving her such a name were any indication, she should have been a businessman's wife, a seamstress, maybe even a schoolmarm.

But the cards for Lily's destiny hadn't been dealt in such a tidy manner. Instead, her brother had died of snakebite on the trip from Ohio to Texas, and she'd been forced to complete the rest of the journey by wagon train on her own.

She and her brother had planned to buy a small plot of land to begin farming and raising cattle or sheep or some other form of livestock. But when she'd arrived in Purgatory, with no family to help her shoulder the burden, she'd

1

been forced to support herself by any means necessary.

That was why the name Lily White was now synonymous with the best sex a man could buy for two gold nuggets or seven pieces of silver.

No, Lily White hadn't been born a whore, but she'd certainly perfected the vocation.

Now, however, she was thinking of getting out of the business. She wanted a home and a family and a reputation that didn't cause proper women to cross the street when they saw her coming. She wanted a man to love her, and care for her, and stay in her bed long enough to actually sleep.

That man, she'd decided, was Wade Mason.

And there was only one small hitch in her plan: presently, Wade Mason was a guest of the Texas State Penitentiary at Hunstville.

Not that she had any intention of letting that stop her.

Her back ramrod straight, she perched on the hard seat of a worn wooden chair outside the warden's office. She'd been waiting nearly twenty minutes for the man to make an appearance so she could appeal to him to let her see Wade.

She knew prisoners weren't normally allowed visitors, but Lily was nothing if not persuasive. By the time she finished convincing Warden Luckett to approve her request, he would likely be willing to grant her anything she wanted.

Just then, the door opened and Warden Luckett emerged, his dark blue suit impeccably pressed, his black hair well and truly oiled. His equally slicked-down mustache was no thicker than the string tie at his throat.

"Miss White," he murmured pleasantly, stepping forward to take her proffered hand.

The grease from his pencil-thin mustache, which he must make a habit of stroking, left a stain on her brand-new ivory gloves, but Lily hid her annoyance. Her goal today was too important. If it cost her a fifty-cent pair of gloves, it was a small enough price to pay.

The long black feathers of her burgundy felt and velvetta hat fluttered as she inclined her head and lowered her lashes in a way that had sent hundreds of men before him slavering at her feet. "Warden Luckett. How gracious of you to agree to see me."

"My pleasure, my dear. Why don't you step into my office, and you can tell me about this urgent business that brings you to Hunstville."

Lily moved ahead of him, making sure to brush against him as she passed, twitching her hips back and forth in an exaggerated swaying motion beneath the narrow bustle of her low-cut walking dress. By now, she had the warden's full attention, just as she'd intended.

Taking a seat in front of his desk, she made a long drawn-out show of arranging her skirts and discarding her gloves while he moved around to take his chair.

For several minutes, Luckett didn't speak, focused instead on Lily's movements as she tugged material slightly away from each of the five fingers on her left hand, repeated the motions, and then removed the accoutrement altogether. She did the same with the right glove, smoothing both pieces over one knee before raising her eyes to meet the warden's intent gaze.

Of course, his gaze wasn't precisely on her face, but more in the region of her generous bosom.

When he caught her looking at him, Warden Luckett jerked up his head and cleared his throat, a flush of embarrassment climbing his neck. "Now, then," he began, stopping to clear his throat again, "what is it I can help you with, Miss White?"

"I'd like to see one of your prisoners," she said without preamble. "Wade Mason."

The warden frowned, marring his otherwise smooth brow. "I'm afraid that's impossible, Miss White. Visitors aren't allowed. These men are hardened criminals. They need to be punished, and allowing visitors is not a way to teach them the difference between freedom and incarceration."

Lily had known that, of course, but Warden Luckett's fervor on the subject did little to change her mind. "I realize it's a unique request, but it's very important that I speak with Wade. Our mother has . . . taken a turn for the worse."

Luckett's eyes narrowed. "You and Inmate Mason are related?" he asked, his voice tinged with surprise.

"He's my brother. White is my . . . late husband's name." The lie rolled easily off her tongue.

The warden's gaze flicked back to her chest, and then his features hardened. "I'm sorry, Mrs. White, I can't allow it."

Coming slowly to her feet, Lily cocked her head and gave him a pouty, sensual look. "Oh, but Warden Luckett, it's ever so important that I be allowed to see Wade."

She made her way around his desk. Luckett's chair squeaked as he twisted in her direction. Setting her gloves aside, she leaned close, spreading the sides of his jacket and reaching for the clasp of his belt. His head whipped down to her nimble fingers, watching with wide, round eyes, mouth agape.

"I would be willing to do just . . . *anything* if you'd give me a few minutes alone with my brother," she cooed, slipping the leather strap through its silver buckle. Once she had the belt and the top button of his pants loosened, she dropped to her knees and wiggled between his splayed legs.

"Oh, please, Warden Luckett," she whispered, fingering his rigid length. "Do say you'll sanction this one, itty-bitty request."

He opened his mouth, emitting nothing more than a strangled squeak. And then his head moved up and down, bobbing in tandem with his rock-hard organ.

Lily smiled sweetly and whispered, "Thank you." Then she lowered her head and paid him back for the favor he'd just granted.

Ten minutes later, a uniformed guard led Lily down a dank, narrow corridor that smelled of mildew and urine and . . . worse. Battered wooden cell doors with barred windows no larger than a human head lined the walls, and the sounds coming from behind those doors made Lily's skin crawl. Even in the middle of the day, the walkway was shadowed. The guard led with a burning torch, and she imagined any number of hideously dangerous criminals pacing and slobbering on the other side of those bars.

Another ten paces down the dark passage, the guard stopped, fitted the torch into a sconce on the wall, and pulled a wide ring of long metal keys from his belt.

"The warden says I should leave you with the prisoner for as long as you like, but I wouldn't dally if I was you. Mason's a mean one, he is."

He fitted the key into the lock, opening the heavy wooden portal with a creak.

"I'm sure I'll be fine," Lily told him, moving forward.

He held the door for her, waiting until she'd taken one step into the room. "All the same, I'll wait out here in casen you need me."

She nodded, letting her eyes adjust to the lighted interior of the cell. It wasn't much, just a sliver of daylight shining through the equally tiny barred window adjacent to the one in the door. And still she jumped when the door slammed behind her, the key once again grating in the lock, this time trapping *her* inside.

She couldn't see anything, wasn't even sure the guard had taken her to the correct cell. "Wade?"

A squeak met her ears, and she turned in the direction of a small cot resting against one wall, hidden in the shadows beneath the narrow strip of sunlight.

"Who is it?" a voice asked, cautious and unnecessarily gruff.

"Oh, Wade," she cooed, finally able to make out a man's form. She rushed forward and fell to her knees before him. "Wade, it's Lily." Tears came to her eyes when she ran her hands over his cheeks and found his face gaunt beneath a thick growth of beard. "Oh, Wade, I've missed you. What have they done to you?"

His laugh was harsh and bitter. "Treated me like a criminal, what else? What are you doing here, Lily? How did you convince them to let you in to see me?"

Sniffing back her tears, she smiled tremulously and rested her hands on his thighs. Thighs thinner than she remembered. If she'd known that bastard warden was starving Wade, she might have bitten him while she'd had his most delicate body part deep in her mouth.

"Don't worry about how I got in," she chided. "Just know that I'm here for you."

She lifted up on her knees, pressing a kiss to his mouth and running her hands over his chest and hips. His body immediately came alive, just as she'd known it would.

"Lily," he ground out, making a token effort to grab her wrists and still her wandering touch. "What are you doing?"

"It's been so long, Wade. Don't tell me you don't want me."

"It's hard not to want a woman when she's got her hand down your pants," he muttered. And it had been a long time. He hadn't been with Lily, or any other woman, in longer than he cared to remember. Prison wasn't exactly a prime place to find a swatch of calico to cuddle with.

Her hands dug into his prison-issue trousers, weighing and stroking, reminding him of all the things Lily used to do to him when he was a free man and he'd been paying for her time.

"Make love to me, Wade," she murmured. "Touch me the way you used to. I've missed you so."

The gentleman in him poked him in the ribs and told him to push her away, told him a man in his position would never use a woman in such a manner. Never mind that the woman had come to him. Never mind that she did this sort of thing for a living.

The beast in him was beyond rational thought, reaching, straining, ready to rut. And if he'd needed any further convincing, Lily's hand on his ballocks and mouth on the tip of his shaft wiped any further argument straight out of his mind.

"I hope you know what you're doing, Lily," he muttered gruffly. " 'Cause I'll be damned if I can turn you away."

Even in the dark of the cell, Wade saw her smile. "I know exactly what I'm doing, darling."

She rested her palms flat on his thighs and rose to her feet, then moved to the empty side of the cot and lay down, lifting her skirts to her waist. Open and willing and waiting, that was Lily. No niceties and no preliminaries, just straightforward sex. Which was exactly what he needed at the moment.

He'd never quite pictured Lily White as an angel before, but at the moment, he thought she might have been sent straight from heaven just to ease the ache that was throbbing through his body at the speed of a steam-driven locomotive.

Tearing at his shirt and jumping out of his pants, he quickly joined Lily on the narrow cot, covering her soft, sweet-smelling body with his own hard and sweaty one. He wished he'd been able to bathe before her visit, shave, and maybe rid himself of the lice and other vermin he was sure had taken up residence on various parts of his anatomy.

Because Lily seemed so eager, he wasted no time stroking or whispering or readying her for his entry. Lily had never needed coaxing, anyway, and she seemed exceptionally fervent today.

And so, with one quick thrust, he buried himself deep inside and began the rocking rhythm that would bring them both to completion.

Her fingers curled into his shoulders, his hands clutched her buttocks. A second later, Wade's body tensed as he spilled himself into her. It was over too soon, of course, but it had been a long time—too long—and when he lifted his head, Lily didn't seem disappointed. In fact, she looked quite pleased, smiling and licking her lips in a slow, sensual gesture that brought him back to hard, throbbing life when only moments ago he thought he'd never rise again.

"You all right?" he asked, shifting but not breaking their intimate link.

Burrowing her fingers in the hair at his temples, she sighed. "More than all right, darling. I'm perfectly lovely. I hope it will always be this way between us."

"They keep me in this hellhole much longer and I can guaran-damn-tee I'll always be this randy."

"You won't be here much longer, darling. Soon you'll be out of here and we can start our life together."

Rearing up on his elbows, Wade stared down at her, his brows knit in confusion. "What are you talking about, Lily?"

"As soon as I tell them the truth, tell them what I saw, they'll have to let you go. They won't keep an innocent man in prison, no matter what Brady Young says."

"You were there that night?" Wade demanded, his fingers digging into the soft flesh of Lily's upper arms. When she winced, he made himself loosen his hold, forced himself to breathe in and out, in and out, until his heart slowed to a near-normal beat.

"What did you see, Lily? Tell me what you saw."

"I saw everything, darling. I was there to visit Neville; he had me over once a week to warm his bed. When you arrived and he went out to meet you, I watched from the upstairs window." Her fingers trailed down his face, and the look in her eyes was dreamy, almost ethereal. "I'm sorry I

11

didn't say anything sooner, but I was frightened. Brady can be mean as a sidewinder when he's crossed. But as long as you're with me, I won't be afraid, darling. And you will be with me, just as soon as I can get you out of this place."

Wade's hands spasmed again into fists, and any desire skating across his skin evaporated, sending a chill along his spine. Pulling away from her, struggling back into his clothes, he stood above her and stared down at her prone form.

"I appreciate you stepping forward and telling the law what you saw, Lily. I wish you'd done it a mite sooner, but better late then never, I guess."

Half a year in prison and he was being *noble,* damn his soul. He wanted to shake her until her teeth rattled, wanted the last six months of his life back. But the thought of being released at all enabled him to set aside his anger and frustration and focus on the glowing dawn of his near future.

Freedom. Blessed freedom outside of this sickening cell, away from the thieves and murderers who surrounded him. Away from the warden who treated them all like dirt on the bottom of his shoe, and the guards who took sadistic pleasure in the prisoners' pain and suffering.

First he would bathe, then he would shave. Then he would kiss the ground Lily walked upon and spend the rest of his days trying to find a way to thank her for saving his life.

Then again, maybe Lily already had her reward figured out. His mind whipped back to the last thing she'd said and latched on, turning the statement over in his head.

He chose his words carefully, not wanting to upset or offend her. After all, she might very well hold the key to his cell in her dainty, long-fingered hand.

"What do you mean I'll be with you, Lily?" Had she arranged for him to work at the Painted Lady with her, maybe to watch out for the girls and keep the peace? It wasn't what he was used to, but since his land had been stolen out from under him, he might not have a choice. And at least it would give him something to do, some way to earn a little money until he could get his ranch back.

Lily smoothed her skirts and sat up, still wearing that all-knowing grin that was beginning to set off warning bells in his head.

"We'll be happy, Wade, I just know it. As soon as you're out of this awful place and Sheriff Walker makes Brady Young return the deed to your land, we'll marry and move there. I'll cook your meals and keep your house. And you can work the ranch just the way you always have. And maybe someday we'll even start a family." From the cot, she reached up to stroke his hair, oblivious to the filth that matted the dark strands together. "I'd like that, Wade. I'd like to have your babies."

"Babies?" His hand curled around her wrist, halting the slow progress of her fingers down his jaw. "Lily, I like you a lot, you know that. We've always been real good together. But I'm not going to marry you. I don't know if I'll ever marry anyone."

Where only a moment ago her hands had been soft and caressing, they now turned stiff and dangerous. Curling into fists, her nails raked one cheek, leaving welts, Wade was sure. Her smile vanished, replaced by a near-sneer.

"What's the matter, Wade, am I not good enough for you? Nothing more than a whore? You'll heave up and down on me, spend yourself inside me, but I'm not good enough to take up with permanently?"

"It's not like that, Lily. I don't want to hurt you, God knows I don't, but I don't love you. I'm not going to marry a woman I barely even know."

"Not even if that woman can get you out of prison? Isn't your freedom worth selling your soul to the devil by marrying me?" she snapped.

Wade considered that. There was nothing he wouldn't do to get out of this hell on earth. And if that meant marrying up with Lily, then he didn't suppose it was such a bad price to pay. But even if he did what she wanted, Lily would be the one to get hurt. He didn't love her, and no matter what she thought, he doubted he could truly make her happy.

What would happen down the road when the bubble holding her dream of happily-ever-after burst and reality set in? Lily's life was anything but perfect now, but he didn't want to play a part in making it worse, even if it meant denying her what she thought she wanted at the moment.

But was his honor and reluctance to hurt Lily worth spending even one more night in this rat-infested cesspool?

Before he had a chance to answer that question, Lily banged on the cell door and called for the guard.

"Lily, wait." He moved toward her, wanting her to stay, wanting to talk this out and see if they couldn't come to some sort of understanding. Surely there was a way to unruffle her feathers and still get him released from Huntsville.

If it was his one chance at freedom, then he'd marry her. They'd make each other miserable and she'd regret it by their first anniversary, but he would do it.

He touched her arm, tried to pull her around. But as he did, the cell door swung open and the ape of a guard shouldered his way in. As soon as he saw Wade's grimy hand on the clean, delicate material of Lily's gown, his face mottled and a growl of rage rolled up from his diaphragm.

"Get your hands off her!" he bellowed.

Wade's fingers fell away, but that didn't keep the guard from barreling forward and raining several hard thwacks on Wade's back and side with the long carved stick he carried for just such a purpose.

"Back against the wall, you mangy cur."

Despite the blows sending needles of pain through his already abused frame, Wade struggled to get Lily's attention. "Lily, please, wait. Don't leave like this."

She turned, watching the guard beat him, her lips turned up in smug satisfaction.

"Good-bye, Wade. And good luck." Then she turned and sauntered out of the cell.

"Lily! Don't leave me here. You're the only person who can save me, Lily!"

"Shut up, Mason," the guard ordered, delivering one last blow to Wade's midsection that doubled him over and nearly made him vomit. "The lady's finished with you, can't you tell?"

Gasping for breath, fighting to keep the bile from working its way up from his gut, Wade let out one last desperate scream.

"Lily!"

Chapter One

With the baby asleep upstairs and all the chores done for the day, Callie Quinn couldn't wait to slip into the hot, steaming tub that stood invitingly in the middle of the pantry.

She was exhausted, pure and simple. Looking after one little boy shouldn't be so hard, but when she also had to take care of her brother's share of running the farm, the added responsibility of seeing to the three-month-old pushed her just this side of having one foot in the grave.

But now the sun was down, Matthew was sleeping, and if luck was with her, he might give her a full hour of peace and solitude before screeching the roof off the house.

Slipping out of her ivory wrap and peeling the thin lawn of her shift from her weary, perspiration-damp body, she dipped one foot into the warm water and sighed in delight.

Oh, she'd been dreaming of this all evening. Five minutes of quiet abandon. A relaxing bath to wash off the dirt of the day. A few drops of lilac essence to scent the air and her skin, and remind her that there were moments like this to look forward to after a day of baking bread, feeding livestock, and tending the garden—all with a squirming baby balanced on one hip.

She sank farther into ecstasy, the water lapping at the sides of the metal tub as it rose to cover her breasts, her collarbone, her neck. Inhaling a breath and holding it, she slid all the way under the surface. Her hair felt like strands of silk running through her fingers as she floated there like a mermaid.

Even beneath the comforting cocoon of water, she heard a noise at the other side of the room. It seemed Matthew wouldn't be cooperating with her decadent plans, after all.

With a sigh that sent bubbles cascading through the bathwater, Callie resurfaced and sat up, running a hand over her face and hair.

She opened her eyes and reached for her wrap . . . and frowned. Her robe had been slung over the back of the chair just an arm's length away; she was sure of it. And her shift had been on the seat.

She really was working too hard if she'd begun to misplace things, she thought.

Turning in the other direction, she reached for the towel she'd left within reach . . . and found that, too, missing.

The corners of her mouth turned down even more. What was going on? Maybe she was losing her mind.

With an even more fatigued release of breath, she grabbed the sides of the tub and pushed herself to her feet. At least Matthew seemed to have quieted. She would check on him to be sure, but if he'd fallen back to sleep, then she fully intended to slip directly back into her bath.

From behind, she heard the scrape of a boot sole on the hardwood floor just before a deep, decidedly masculine voice murmured, "Very nice."

She swung around, a scream clawing its way up her throat.

"Very nice, indeed," the stranger added, letting his gaze steal down the length of her body.

With a squeak, she dropped back to the bottom of the tub, drawing her knees up to her chest and doing her best to cover herself with her hands and arms.

In the barest fraction of a second, she took in every detail of the man standing before her, not three feet away. His black hair, beard, and mustache were filthy and unkempt, his blue shirt and trousers equally soiled. The skin of his face and hands looked as if it hadn't been washed in a number of months, and she wondered what manner of creatures might be jumping around on his tall—at least six-foot—frame.

But it wasn't the unruly hair or unwashed flesh or even the thought of fleas and lice crawling about his body that sent a shiver down her spine.

It was the sight of heavy iron manacles weighing down his wrists and ankles that terrified her. And the realization that a man in shackles was not wearing them by choice. A man in shackles likely belonged in a prison cell somewhere, not in the middle of her pantry, holding her shift and robe in his unwashed hand.

The fact that she was naked and at a stranger's mercy didn't even cross Callie's mind. Instead, she thought of Matthew, helpless and vulnerable. She prayed he would remain quiet so this man never need know that an infant slept upstairs, but if necessary, Callie knew she would do whatever it took to protect the child.

And then she thought of her brother's pistol, loaded and waiting in her sewing basket. Nathan had left it for her to use as protection when he'd gone away, never really believing she would need it, she was sure.

Of course, her sewing basket was in the living room beside the wide, medallion-backed armchair she usually sat in to embroider or darn stockings while Matthew played or chewed his toes on a blanket in front of the hearth. If she could get away from this man long enough to reach the gun, she would have a way to protect herself and Matthew. If not . . .

If not, she didn't want to think about what this man who appeared to be an escaped convict might do to them.

Callie swallowed and realized suddenly that she'd opened her mouth but never gotten around to screaming. Not that it would have done much good. The house was a good mile from town, and isolated enough that they rarely got visitors without first extending an invitation.

"Who are you?" she asked, her voice both sharp and breathless at the same time.

"The name's Wade Mason, ma'am. I wouldn't normally intrude upon you like this, but I'm afraid I don't have much choice."

Wade Mason? Why did that name sound familiar?

And then it struck her. Her brother had been friends with a man by the name of Mason who ran a ranch on the other side of town. Or *had,* before he'd been convicted of murder and sent away to prison.

She also recalled her brother saying he didn't believe Wade Mason had committed the crime of which he'd been accused.

The disheveled man took a step forward, and

21

she shrank back automatically. But he only extended one shackled arm far enough to offer the return of her wrap and shift.

"You might want to put these on," he said in that deep, gravelly voice that put the fear of God into her bones. "It's been a good, long while since I've had a woman, and there's no sense pushing the limits of my control."

Callie couldn't have agreed more. She wanted to ask him to turn around but doubted it would do any good. Taking the clothes, she half stood and shrugged them over her damp body as quickly as possible, showing as little flesh as she could manage. And ignoring the likelihood that the material might now be hopping with the very same vermin that no doubt infested his person.

She stood in the middle of a good twelve inches of water, holding up the hem of her gown to keep it from getting wet. The man offered a hand to help her, but despite the chivalry of the gesture, she refused to touch him.

Seemingly unperturbed by her rejection, he retracted the proffered hand and instead stooped to spread the earlier missing towel on the floor beside the tub. The thick iron chains rattled with every move he made.

She had one foot on the towel, the other lifted to step the rest of the way out of the tub, when his next words froze her in place.

"Why don't we make this short and sweet for

everyone involved? Just tell me where the boy is, and I'll be on my way."

Wade Mason watched the woman's chest hitch as she stopped breathing, saw her spine snap whipcord straight.

When she spoke, her words were chips of ice, sharp and clipped and aimed directly at his skull. "I don't know what you're talking about."

Even if the stiffness of her body and the wariness in her eyes hadn't told him otherwise, he'd have known she was lying. There was only one family by the name of Quinn living in Purgatory, and since he'd had dealings with Nathan Quinn before being sent to prison, he knew this was their house. And the woman standing before him, smelling of flowers in bloom and sending red-hot pokers of desire through his groin, was Nathan's sister, Callie. The same Callie Quinn who was supposed to have his son.

"Don't lie to me, Callie," he said with just enough edge to make the words sound ominous. "I know who you are, and I know you have my son. Hand him over and I'll be on my way. Those bastards from Huntsville are right behind me, and I want to be well away from here before they close in."

She stood staring at him, weaving slightly, her mouth open and working but no sound coming out.

He closed the distance between them in two long strides, grabbing her arms and yanking her up against him. So close her breasts rubbed his chest through the thin material of her robe and sent shocks of desire through his system.

God, it had been a long time. And worse yet, the last time had been with Lily—which hadn't been so bad when it was actually happening but quickly turned into a day he thoroughly resented.

Bringing his train of thought back to the matter at hand, he let his fingers dig a little deeper into the soft flesh of her upper arms. "Where is he, Callie? I want my son."

He saw the change come over her features—the lift of her chin, the firming of her mouth, the hardening of her eyes—and felt her stiffen beneath his hold. Although the trepidation hadn't left her, she had gone from being frightened of him to not being frightened enough to keep from standing her ground.

"You can't have him," she snapped back, and Wade had no doubt she meant what she said.

"I don't know what Lily told you, but he's my son and I have every right to take him with me. Now tell me where he is."

"No father would risk his child's health and safety by taking him on the run. You may be a worthless felon, but Matthew shouldn't have to suffer for your crimes."

A flash of anger stole over him, making him

want to squeeze Callie's arms even tighter, maybe move his hands up and wrap them around her neck. That would put the fear back into her cold blue eyes.

And then sanity returned and his hold loosened. Taking a deep breath, he warned her, "You know nothing about the kind of man I am, or the real reason I was put away."

With his grip no longer anchoring her in place, she stepped away from him, once again putting distance between them. "Fair enough. But I do know Matthew is only three months old and you're running from the law. What do you intend to do with him if the authorities get too close? Hide him in the knot of a tree? Turn him over to someone who may or may not treat him properly?"

She was shaking her head, firming up her argument with the rigid stance of her shapely but not-much-over-five-feet-tall figure. "No. I don't care if you're his father. That only means you're the man Lily was with when she happened to be unlucky enough to get pregnant. She trusted me to care for him, protect him, and I'll be damned if you're going to take him away from me."

He studied her for a long minute, wondering if her hair was as soft as it looked, draped over one shoulder and still wet on the ends but beginning to dry at the top. Would she slap his hand away if he reached out to feel the loose strands?

Definitely.

"Those are strong words coming from a woman no bigger than a minute. You prepared to back them up?" he asked, sizing her up and realizing the top of her head just passed his chin. He could press a kiss to her forehead without leaning over, but that was about it.

Wade almost chuckled. He imagined she'd do a hell of a lot more than slap him if he tried to kiss her—on her forehead or anywhere else.

Her jaw rose another notch, and Wade found himself admiring her spunk. She might be little, she might be keeping him from his son, but she for damn sure had enough gumption for any three men combined.

"I'd guard Matthew with my life," she replied, her tone and stance giving him every reason to believe her.

She was the one person standing between him and his son, and yet her devotion relieved a great deal of the worry he'd harbored ever since learning he'd fathered a child.

Mail had been delivered to the prison about once a month, but only handed out to prisoners if Warden Luckett was in a generous mood. Knowing how much the prison officials despised him, it was a wonder Wade had received any posts at all. But even though Lily's letter had reached him, telling him that she'd given birth to a boy, and where he could find the child if he so desired, he hadn't known what kind of condition his son was in or how he was being cared for.

Now, he suspected the boy—Callie had called him Matthew—was being taken care of just fine. Better than fine, if this woman's mama-bear performance was any indication.

"I'm glad you feel that way," he said finally, "because you may just have to."

Chapter Two

Callie didn't know what to make of Wade's words. They sounded less like a threat than a warning. But against what or whom? She decided not to probe further now. For the time being, it was enough that he'd put a stop to his threats and intimidation . . . and his demands to take Matthew away.

The tension went out of his muscles and he looked suddenly not quite as towering as before. Much less menacing, that was for sure.

And regardless of the fact that he was an escaped convict, she was about to invite him to sit. Put on a pot of coffee for him, if he liked.

She hoped to heaven her brother was right, because otherwise, she had to be crazy to even think it. Maybe she'd been underwater too long.

Maybe she'd added too much lilac essence to her bath and it had begun to addle her brain.

Or maybe she simply felt sorry for him, a man who had never seen his son, a man who had been behind bars both when that child was conceived and born.

Callie didn't want to think too long on how the conception had come about in an institution such as Huntsville Penitentiary, but then, she was quite familiar with Lily's wild ideas and her penchant for carrying them out.

Looking at the man standing before her, though, she wondered what had fascinated Lily so much that she'd risked getting with child to be with him. Lily had been a prostitute too many years not to know how to avoid such things, Callie was well aware.

"I'd like to see my son," he said, in a much less demanding tone than his earlier requests. "And then, if you don't mind, I think I'll make use of that bathwater you've got handy."

Callie thought a good scrubbing was just what he needed. She wasn't sure it would make a dent in the filth that covered him, but it might be a start.

Her main concern, however, was still for Matthew. Drawing the material of her wrap more tightly around her, she looped her arms across her stomach and hugged herself to ward off a chill that had nothing to do with the evening temperature. "You won't try to take him away?" she asked.

The man stared at her for a moment, his gaze so intense, she almost looked away. But if she showed even a modicum of fear now, it might be just the opportunity he needed to run roughshod over her, and she couldn't risk the ground she'd gained so far.

"I won't try to take him away," he answered finally. "But I won't leave him, either, which means you're stuck with the both of us. At least for a while." His gaze lowered to the heavy iron shackles binding his wrists. In a low voice, he added, "I hope you know what you're getting into."

She didn't, but she was beginning to suspect it would be nothing good. An escaped convict in her house, likely a posse of lawmen not far behind him, and a child she would protect with her very life.

Callie supposed she should be grateful the stranger didn't appear to have anything more menacing than a bath on his mind. His main concern seemed to be for his son, not for the scantily dressed woman standing in front of him. For that, she was infinitely grateful.

"He's upstairs," she said, and began to lead the way. She heard the man move to follow, chains clanking and scraping along the floor with every step.

Pausing outside the room where Matthew napped, she opened the door a crack to peek inside, then turned to face his father. "He's sleeping," she whispered, "and I would much appreciate it if you wouldn't wake him. He'll be up on his own soon enough."

The man nodded and took hold of the iron links between his arms to keep them from jangling. As they moved forward, he was careful to slide his feet along the floor instead of lift them, thereby keeping the chain between his manacled legs from rattling, as well.

Callie led him to the hand-carved cradle in one corner, then stepped back to allow him a full view of his son. A part of her wanted to throw herself in front of Matthew. Protect him, keep him to herself. Which was entirely selfish, she knew, but she couldn't seem to help it.

From the moment Lily had entrusted this tiny child into her care, just days after his birth, Callie had taken the responsibility very seriously. She had never been married, never carried a child of her own. But none of that mattered when it came to Matthew; she couldn't love him more if he had come from her own womb.

And the truth of the matter was, she had never expected Matthew's father to come for him. Lily hadn't told her much about the man who had gotten her in the family way, merely that he was imprisoned in the Texas State Penitentiary at

Huntsville and would not be released anytime soon. Callie hadn't expected him to care that he'd fathered a child, let alone show up at her house demanding to see the boy.

Yet here she stood, allowing this stranger to hover over her child and look his fill. She couldn't explain her actions; she merely knew that it would break her heart to know she had a child and not be permitted to see him or her. And it said something about the man that he'd broken out of prison only to come straight to the place where he knew Matthew was being kept.

Callie chose not to focus overlong on the broken-out-of-prison part. She much preferred to think that coming directly to Purgatory—no short distance from Huntsville, either, especially in chains—was a sign of the man's finer parental qualities.

And if I squeeze my eyes closed tightly enough, when I open them, he might be wearing a halo and wings, she thought facetiously.

He lifted his head then, and Callie could have sworn she saw tears glistening in his eyes. He turned away too soon for her to be sure, and moved out of the room just as silently as he'd entered.

Callie straightened the thin plaid blanket over Matthew's tiny body and gave his back a gentle pat before following the stranger into the hall.

They returned downstairs, neither of them making a sound until they'd reached the pantry.

Callie stopped in the doorway, watching the man move farther into the room and stop just before the tub. With legs spread slightly apart, he put his hands on his hips as far as the chain of the shackles would allow.

"He's beautiful," he said quietly, sounding almost reverent.

Callie wholeheartedly agreed. "He is." And then, thinking to lighten the mood, added, "But he can be a dickens when he wants to be, too. Wait until he wakes up from his nap, and you'll see what I mean. He screams the roof off whenever he's hungry or needs a changing."

The man chuckled as he turned to face her. "I'll look forward to that. But I think maybe I should clean up first." He hitched his head in the direction of the bath. "Do you mind?"

Since she had no intention of finishing her own bath with a stranger in the house, she shook her head. "The water might need to be heated again," she told him.

He'd already begun to unbutton his blue, prison-issue shirt. "It'll be fine. Believe me, after where I've been the past eighteen months, even an ice bath would be heaven."

She didn't doubt that. Given the condition of his hair and clothes, it didn't look like he'd been allowed to bathe even once in the last year and a half.

"Dammit," he said with a growl.

Callie lowered her gaze and noticed that the shirt was caught around the back of his waist and at his wrists, impossible to remove with his arms still in shackles. "I'll be right back," she muttered, and headed for the living room.

In her sewing basket, right beside her shears, was her brother's revolver. Callie considered the weapon, considered using it against Wade. She could make him leave at gunpoint, even shoot him if necessary. Callie shook her head in silent dismissal. She could never shoot a man. And she felt certain Wade would have no problem overpowering her—even with his shackles—and taking the gun. Then he would be armed . . . and doubly as dangerous. It would make it that much easier for him to steal away with Matthew. No, Callie would humor Wade for the moment, do whatever it took to protect her child. For now that meant keeping Wade happy in her home, because having Wade and Matthew under the same roof was a lot better than having neither. Her decision made, Callie ignored the pistol and returned to the pantry armed only with the scissors.

"You don't have any particular fondness for this shirt, do you?" she inquired, positioning the shears in the *V* of one open cuff.

"Cut the damn thing off," he ordered in that low, gravelly voice. "And then burn it, for all I care."

Thinking that was likely the only thing one *could* do with a shirt in its condition, Callie cut a line in the fabric all the way up the arm, then moved to do the same on the other side. The material fell to the floor, leaving the man in front of her naked from the waist up.

Dirt or no dirt, it was an impressive sight. All smooth lines and hard bulges, with just a sprinkling of hair covering his upper torso and leading down to his abdomen. He smelled none too fresh, but her lilac water would fix that, she thought with silent amusement.

His hands moved to the buttons at the front of his trousers, and Callie quickly turned away. "You'll have to deal with the pants on your own," she told him, and held the scissors out behind her, waiting for him to take them.

"Are you hungry?" she asked, already moving toward the doorway that led to the kitchen.

"Starving," he answered, and she heard the shears rending the thick material of his trousers in two. "But don't feel like you have to fix anything on my account. I've intruded enough for one night."

She had a feeling he'd intrude a lot more than he already had by the time this was over. "Are you planning to stay here long?" she asked, even though she already knew the answer.

When next he spoke, his tone held a determined edge. "Until I can clear my name and make a proper home for my son," he clipped out bitterly. "Provided the posse doesn't track me down first."

Callie didn't respond, merely put a loaf of bread, freshly baked this morning—and with only a few blackened edges—into the warmer and began to unwrap a few handy hunks of cheese and salted pork. By the time she'd fixed a plate for him and carried it into the pantry, he was already immersed in the tub, his head back, his elbows propped on the sides, and his hands clasped at his chest because that was about the only position the shackles would allow.

As curious as she was, as hard as it was to keep her gaze averted, she managed not to glance beneath the water that came to just below his nipples. She hadn't had a chance to soap up enough to create suds before his untimely intrusion, and the lilac scent she added to her baths did nothing to cloud the crystal-clear water surrounding his naked body.

Still refusing to make eye contact with his nude form, she set the plate on the seat of the nearby chair. "I'm afraid I tend to add fragrance to my bathwater. You may come out of there smelling like a flower garden."

He snorted. "I'm thinking flowers would be a

hell of a lot better than what I smell like now."
Reaching to the bottom of the tub, he found the
block of soap she'd dropped and forgotten, and
began lathering it between his two large, work-
roughened hands. Hands that thankfully covered
a rather critical portion of his anatomy.

"Since you won't be able to wear your own
clothes again, I'll go upstairs and see if my
brother left anything you'll fit into," she offered,
unused to being in the same room with a man
while he bathed and anxious to get away for a
few minutes.

He started scrubbing, giving her no more than
a faint nod, and she hurried out of the room before her curiosity got the better of her. Although
she *did* peek at the area his cupped hands were
no longer hiding.

It occurred to Wade that Callie Quinn was tech-
nically his hostage. He shouldn't be letting her
just wander around on her own without him
keeping an eye on her. Then again, she hadn't
tried to run when he'd first broken into her
house, and she seemed pretty determined to stay
with Matthew. He hadn't expected her to feed
him, or find an extra set of clothes for him to
wear, or—Lord have mercy—help him get free
of his grimy garments so he could bathe.

That last action had surprised him most of all,
and he'd been damn glad she'd turned around

before he'd gone to work at removing his pants. No sense scaring her any more than he already had, but it had been a hell of a long time since he'd been with a woman, and if the sight of her initial nakedness hadn't stirred something in him, the way she'd looked at his bare-but-dirt-covered chest sure as blue blazes would have.

Even the now tepid water swirling around his lower body didn't help to extinguish the heat pooling in his groin. He hoped whatever trousers she managed to round up were a couple of sizes too big, or he'd send her screaming by dawn.

Wade dragged the bar of soap over his skin until his flesh felt almost raw and turned what he considered a healthy shade of pink. Incarceration offered little opportunity to practice proper hygiene, and he'd damn well missed it. He dunked his head and took to scouring his scalp just as roughly.

By the time he finished . . . and he wasn't sure he'd ever be truly finished . . . Callie's previously clear and fragrant bathwater was a disgusting shade of brown and smelled like a pig trough. But at least *he* no longer looked or smelled that bad. He hoped.

Grabbing the single towel from the floor where he'd spread it earlier for Callie, he stood and began drying his body as best he could. Then he threw the towel back to the floor and stepped out, careful not to let the damn shackles clasped painfully to his ankles trip him up. Of course, now that he'd made sure to protect Callie's nice, clean hardwood floor, he had no idea how he was supposed to cover himself.

From around the corner, Callie's bright, sing-song voice reached his ears before the sound of her footsteps did. "I brought you an extra towel, and I don't think you'll have a problem fitting into Nathan's things. He's fairly big, and you're . . ."

Her words trailed off as she stepped into the pantry, raised her head, and saw him standing bare-ass naked in the middle of the room.

But at least he wasn't dripping on her hardwood floor.

Mouth falling open, her wide-eyed stare went directly to that part of him that hadn't been subdued by the coolness of the bathwater or any other remedy Wade had tried.

"You're . . . you're . . ."

"Freezing my balls off," he said brusquely, in hopes of breaking the tension and keeping his mind off the fact that she was looking at him *there*. Or worse yet, that he liked it. He'd been in prison too damn long, and his choice of language in front of a lady wasn't the only proof of that fact.

"Mind handing me that towel so I can finish drying off?" he prompted.

She staggered the two steps forward that

brought her close enough for him to grab the towel himself. He shook it out and wrapped it around his waist, then happened to notice the object on top of the neatly folded shirt and jeans lying across her upturned palms. It made him just the teeniest bit nervous.

He glanced at her face, noticing that her gaze was still slanted downward at the most sensitive—and prized—part of his anatomy. His eyes returned to the menacing tool she held. Then again to the direction of her stare. Clearing his throat, he tried not to sound worried.

"Just what were you planning to do with that hacksaw, sweetheart?"

Chapter Three

Callie dragged her eyes from the towel slung low on Wade's hips to the saw she'd retrieved from the barn. She almost laughed at the wary look on his face.

Chopping him into pieces—or even just threatening to do damage to his private male parts—might not have been a bad idea when he'd first broken into her house and scared ten years off her life. That moment seemed to have passed, however, and now she lacked the blood-thirstiness or fear to do damage to anything more than the lining of his stomach with her cooking.

She inclined her head toward the metal cuffs and links binding his arms together. "I thought we might be able to use this to get those shackles off. They can't be very comfortable." She also had a chisel and hammer tucked under her arm.

Brows the same color as his now-clean hair and beard knit. "You left the house? Why didn't I hear you leave the house?"

Since he seemed so concerned about keeping abreast of her whereabouts, she considered telling him about the pistol in her sewing basket that she *hadn't* shot him with earlier. But then, a woman should be allowed some secrets. And she didn't actually know that the gun wouldn't come in handy down the road, so she kept her mouth shut.

"I went out the front," she told him instead. "It didn't take me long, and I didn't think you'd want to leave the house to get it yourself."

Tension radiated from every well-defined muscle of his still uncovered body. "Did you see anyone while you were out there?"

"You mean a dozen or so lawmen, armed to the teeth?" she teased, and then thought better of it when a muscle ticked in his jaw and his fists clenched around the towel at his waist. "No, no one. I didn't see anyone."

He nodded almost imperceptibly. "Good. But don't go out there again, all right? It's too dangerous, and I don't want anyone getting suspicious."

"We're quite a ways from town or any other houses, so I doubt there will be anyone to see, but even if there were, I would still have to go out to tend to my daily chores. The chickens aren't going to feed themselves, I'm sorry to say."

Wade didn't offer any further remarks, but his teeth continued to grind, and Callie thought it might be best to distract him from the direction his thoughts were taking. She set the change of clothes aside and took the plate of cheese and pork from the chair where she'd set it earlier and handed it to him.

"Sit," she ordered, waving a finger at the now empty seat. *And keep that towel tight,* she begged silently.

Wade sat, tearing into the food on the plate as if he hadn't eaten in a week. And for all she knew, he hadn't.

He was a big man, covered with glorious muscles that ran through his chest and upper arms, his abdomen and thighs. . . . She'd gotten more than just a glimpse at all those parts and didn't fool herself for a minute thinking he couldn't back up any threat he made with sheer sinewy strength. But around the musculature, his cheeks were thin, his legs lax, his stomach almost concave.

Without a word, she went to the kitchen and returned with the remaining chunks of bread, pork, and cheese. She would fry up some eggs or put a hank of beef in the oven for him later. And if he could chew through either, she'd have him fattened up in no time.

He accepted the extra portions gratefully and continued taking large bites from the chunk of meat in his hand.

Sinking to her knees, she set the hammer and chisel on the floor beside her and turned one of the manacles about his ankle so that she could work on it at a better angle. A heavy chain linked the two cuffs, but each shackle was actually held closed with a separate padlock. If she could just cut through the thick iron of these bolts, the rest of the hideous contraption would fall away. It sounded simple, but Callie knew she had her work cut out for her—four times over.

Taking a deep breath, she positioned the hacksaw against the metal fastener and began the repetitive back and forth motion that would hopefully gain Wade a bit more freedom.

Sweat began to bead on her forehead and upper lip. Her arm was so tired, she doubted she'd be able to lift it in the morning. And still she sawed.

When it looked like she might be making progress, she wedged the chisel between the two ends of the manacle and tried to pry it loose even more. Having finished off every crumb of food she'd given him, Wade set his plate aside and took over holding the chisel in place. He probably would have offered to take over with the hacksaw, as well, but at such an awkward angle, he never would have been able to manage it.

"Hand me the hammer," he said after another minute.

Callie leaned back, wiping her brow with the back of her arm. She set aside the saw and handed him the hammer, letting him pry and bang. She only hoped the racket wouldn't wake Matthew. With three more shackles to go, she didn't have time to heat a bottle and change his diaper, too.

"Stand back," Wade warned, and Callie scuttled a few steps away.

He gave the chisel one more hard hit with the hammer and the metal cuff snapped open, just missing taking off a toe with the sharp tip of the lever.

He pulled his leg away from the offending piece of metal as though it burned . . . and then Callie saw why, and let out a gasp of despair.

"My God," she uttered.

"Not a pretty sight, is it?" His words were tense and biting as he examined the damage himself.

The portion of his ankle where the manacle had rested was raw and bleeding. Callie thought every bit of skin might have been rubbed away . . . or if it hadn't, the area was too damaged and covered with blood to notice. He would be lucky if the wound wasn't already infected; if it was, he could very well lose his leg.

And to think that he suffered from three more marks exactly like this one.

"I can't believe anyone would treat a fellow human being this way. Why do they lock you in shackles if they know it causes this kind of injury?"

He snorted, an angry, derisive sound. "Do you think they care? They work prisoners until they drop, and even if they lose one from exhaustion or infection, there are plenty more to take his place."

"How did you ever get away?" Callie asked. If his wrists and ankles had already been in this bad a shape, how had he managed to make his way from Hunstville to Purgatory?

"It wasn't easy, I can tell you that. The guards watch us like hawks, and don't hesitate to shoot if it looks like we're trying to escape."

"Then how . . . ?"

"It took a few months to plan, and to find the perfect moment, but I snuck away when they took a group of us out to clear a field of stones. That's why I'm in shackles; they don't keep them on us when we're in our cells or the prison yard, but they do when they move us anywhere else. I don't think the guards noticed I was missing for a while, thank God, or they'd have shot me in the back. They know by now, though, and probably suspect that I would come back to Purgatory—at least briefly—to see old friends and collect money to stay on the run. They wouldn't know the real reason."

He shook his head, not meeting her eyes. "It may not be safe for me here much longer."

"You came back just to see your son?" she guessed.

He lifted his brown gaze to her own then, and gave a firm nod. "I didn't kill Neville Young, no matter what his son and Sheriff Graves said. They sent me to prison so they could steal my land, but I'm going to prove my innocence and get my ranch back. Then I'll have a place to raise my son the way he deserves."

Wade Mason. Of course, now she remembered the rest. A couple of years ago, the gruesome murder of prominent rancher Neville Young had been all the people of Purgatory talked about. And Neville's son, Brady, had never wasted an opportunity to rage about the bastard who'd shot his father in the back.

But from everything her brother said, Wade had been a fairly successful rancher. He'd have had no call to hassle with Neville Young, let alone kill him. And Nathan didn't think he had.

Maybe she couldn't believe completely in his innocence—it was hard for her to imagine a man spending eighteen months in prison for a crime he hadn't really committed—but he seemed brutally determined to clear his name.

Normally, she might have applauded his cour-

Heidi Betts

age and conviction. But if he did everything he
said he would—proving his innocence and regaining his land—then he would take Matthew
away from her. She wasn't sure she could live
with that possibility.

Somehow it didn't seem prudent to confront
a convicted felon about how far his parental
rights extended, regardless of the fact that Lily
had entrusted her child's welfare to Callie, with
no mention of how large a part Matthew's father
should play in his life.

Deciding to leave that topic for a later date—
perhaps after the authorities had recaptured
Wade and returned him to jail—she retrieved the
hacksaw and went to work on the second leg
iron.

"Let's get the rest of these off of you so I can
bandage your wrists and ankles. They're going to
hurt for a while before they start to heal."

Wade laughed and leaned back in the seat to
let her get partway through the other lock. "I've
lived with the pain this long, a couple more days
can't hurt any worse."

That's what he thought. But then, he'd never
been treated with her mother's special ointment
before. The balm was repulsive, smelling worse
than horse liniment and burning like brimstone
whenever it hit a patch of open skin. With the
amount of skin open on Wade's arms and legs,

48

he'd be lucky if he didn't shoot straight through the ceiling.

"Jesus, Mary, and Joseph!" Wade bellowed, clutching the underside of the chair in both hands to keep from lurching to his feet. "Christ on a cracker, woman, what the hell is that stuff?"

"Mama's homemade, all-purpose ointment," Callie answered, continuing to slather the wretched salve all around his left ankle. When she was satisfied with the amount of pain she'd caused him, she began wrapping the area with a clean length of fabric that would act as a bandage.

"Your mama must be one hell of a hard-hearted woman," he muttered. The damn stuff still stung and put him in none too good a mood.

"My mama's been dead for nearly ten years," she told him, "but she left me her recipe. And you'll be glad in the morning, when your wrists and ankles aren't nearly as sore as they are now."

"*Hmph.*"

She ignored his grumbling and went on to cover his other ankle and both wrists with the odious salve, then wrap them to keep out infection. Just as she was finishing, a high-pitched shriek rent the house and caused Wade to jump as though a snake had bitten him.

"What the hell was that?" he demanded, looking ready to bolt, if necessary.

49

"That," Callie said, climbing to her feet and winding the leftover bandages about her hand, "is your son. Up from his nap and demanding immediate attention, as usual."

Wade rose gingerly to his feet, testing just how much and in which directions he could move without causing undue pain, while Callie put away the ointment and rags, then brushed her hands down the sides of her robe and headed upstairs.

Having taken the time to discard the towel and change into the shirt and trousers Callie had provided, Wade was only halfway up the stairs when she appeared, Matthew in her arms.

The air froze in Wade's lungs as he got his first decent look at his son. The boy was beautiful. Wearing only the white square of a diaper on his bottom, his pudgy arms and legs flailed and his little potbelly stuck out. It took every ounce of restraint Wade possessed not to lean forward and press a kiss to the soft flesh above the baby's belly button.

Tears no bigger than raindrops balanced on the edges of tiny eyelashes from where the child had worked himself into a fit, crying for Callie, and a thin layer of baby-fine hair covered his round, oversize head.

Wade had never seen anything so breathtaking in his life. Unless, of course, it was the sight of Callie holding his son to her breast.

She wasn't the boy's mother, so he didn't know why the picture of her cradling the infant hit him so low in the gut, but it was enough to stop his breath and send his heart pounding at twice its normal rhythm.

She looked like she had been born to take care of babies. Tend injured men and nurse innocent babies. The thought almost sent Wade to his knees.

He needed to sit down. Fast.

Using his raw ankles as an excuse, he backed carefully down the stairs and returned to the chair he'd vacated earlier. Callie laid the baby on the flat surface of a wide cupboard that reached nearly to the ceiling and unpinned the sides of his diaper. From somewhere—Wade couldn't even begin to guess where—she produced a fresh, clean square of cloth and changed the child in less time than it took for Wade to figure out what she was doing.

Matthew kicked his little legs the whole while, and looked to be attempting to fit one entire fist into his mouth. When she'd finished pinning the corners of the material, she lifted the boy under the arms and perched him up near her shoulder.

Then she turned and headed straight for Wade. He knew by the expression on her face that he was in trouble. She stopped in front of him and held the squirming, gurgling, *breakable* child out to him.

He was already shaking his head and leaning as far back as the rungs of the chair would allow. "Uh-uh. I can't hold him."

"He'll want a bottle soon, which I need both hands free to fill and heat. Besides, as you so often reminded me when you first arrived, he is *your* son," Callie stated primly.

"But I'll break him. Or drop him. Or squeeze him too hard." When she didn't move away but waited patiently for him to take the baby, he leapt up and dodged behind the ladder-back chair, all in one graceless but effectively speedy motion. "No. I don't want to."

For a moment, when she shifted the child to her hip, he thought he'd been granted a reprieve. Instead, she'd merely changed her hold while she stalked around the chair in his direction.

"Of course you do."

He moved backward, she moved forward, and before he knew it, she'd put a hand to his chest and pushed him back into a sitting position.

Talking the whole time she positioned the baby, she said, "You'll be fine. Sit just like that and let him rest on your chest." She brought his arms up to wrap around the child, one to support his head and one under his bottom. "There, how does that feel?"

"Terrifying."

She chuckled, a low, knowing sound working

its way up her throat. "You'll get used to it. Just don't let him topple over."

"Oh, God."

This time, she laughed outright at his groan of despair. "I'll only be a few steps away in the kitchen. You'll be *fine.*"

Oh God, oh God, oh God, he thought. *Please don't let me drop him. Or break him. Or squeeze him too hard.*

The baby let out an ear-splitting screech and Wade jerked, clutching the baby tight to his chest. "What's he doing?" he yelled anxiously to Callie.

Sticking her head around the corner of the open doorway that separated kitchen from pantry, she smiled. "He's just talking. That's his happy squeal. If his lower lip starts to tremble, then cover your ears because we're in trouble."

She went back to moving around the kitchen but called out, "You can talk back, if you'd like, though he won't understand a word."

"What the hell am I supposed to say to a three-month-old baby?" Wade muttered to himself. And then he grinned wryly. "Well, for starters, I probably shouldn't say *hell,* huh? Damn, I said it again."

He probably shouldn't say *damn,* either, he realized ruefully.

"All right, let me start over." Taking a deep breath, he considered his options and decided introductions were probably in order. With Matthew's bulk feeling pretty well balanced on his stomach and lower chest, he risked moving an arm away from the child's back and taking one of the tiny, smooth baby hands in his own. He did his best to shake it the way he would any man's he met on the street.

"I'm Wade," he said softly. "Your father. Your pa. Your daddy." He liked the sound of *daddy* best of all, he thought. Less rigid than his own father, though both of his parents had been wonderful people. He was sorry they hadn't lived long enough to see their first grandchild. It might have been nice to have family around for support during his trial, too, but a part of him was glad they hadn't had to see their only son convicted of murder.

And having no family left was simply one more reason he wanted to be a good father to Matthew. He just hoped he'd have the chance to prove himself in that regard.

Raising his voice so Callie would hear, he called, "You said his name was Matthew, right?"

"Yes," she answered.

"Matthew Mason." Wade frowned. He wasn't sure that sounded quite right. A few too many *m*s for his taste.

"Who named him?" he asked. "Lily?"

Callie returned to the doorway, drying a glass bottle with what looked to be a new, clean dish towel. "I did, actually." Her mouth turned down slightly as she looked away. "Lily wasn't much up to naming him, I'm afraid. She was very sick after the birth."

Wade nodded. From Lily's letter, he was aware that she'd contracted childbed fever and died within days of Matthew's birth. Even if she hadn't fallen ill, however, Wade couldn't help but wonder how much contact she'd have had with the boy.

Lily's lifestyle hadn't been particularly conducive to caring for a baby, and worse than that, she'd been furious as she stormed away from the prison—already pregnant, but neither of them had known that at the time. He couldn't know whether she'd been happy or furious at the prospect of having a child. And the fact that it was *his* child might only have made an already bad situation even more dire.

"Is there a problem?" Callie asked, and he didn't miss the slightly annoyed tone that edged the question.

He shook his head. "I was just thinking that Matthew Mason is quite a mouthful."

"Well, that's no problem, then, since his name is Matthew *Quinn.*"

Chapter Four

Wade's eyes narrowed and he fought to refrain from lurching to his feet in a fighting stance. Only the child on his lap blowing spit bubbles and yanking on his beard kept him from doing just that. "You care to explain that?" he all but growled. "And make it real slow so I don't miss anything."

If he'd expected his words or tone to intimidate his hostess, he was sorely disappointed. She stood calm as an oak in a storm and held his gaze.

"His name is Matthew Quinn. You weren't around when he was born, Lily didn't know if you'd ever be around, and she turned him over to my care, legally. Which makes his last name Quinn."

The tugs on his beard made Wade wince, so

he carefully pried the baby's hand away. Not bothered in the least, Matthew became immediately entranced by the buttons running down the front of his father's shirt.

"We're going to have to talk about that issue," Wade said calmly. "He's my son; he should carry my name."

"Then you should have married his mother," Callie retorted with a snap, and flounced her way back into the kitchen.

Wade stared after her for a moment, wondering why she didn't seem more afraid of him. She should have been, considering where he'd come from and why he was here. Maybe he hadn't done a good enough job of intimidating her when he'd first confronted her. But he'd purposely tried not to scare her. He hadn't wanted to scare anyone; he'd merely wanted to see his son.

Then again, even if he did try intimidation, if he made a move Callie didn't like, he imagined she could flay him like a fish with her tongue alone. Besides, Callie was his link to his son. She knew how to care for Matthew, and now Wade had seen his son, held him, he realized how difficult—and impractical—it would be for him to try to travel on the run with an infant he knew less than nothing about caring for.

"Kid," he said, staring down at his son, "you've got yourself one hell of a guardian there."

Matthew raised his head, popped a spit-covered fist out of his mouth, and looked at him. Then, before Wade had a chance to recognize the telltale sign of a quivering bottom lip, Matthew's eyes puckered, his mouth opened, and a screech loud enough to peel the paper off the walls reverberated against Wade's eardrums.

Wade was about to yell for Callie to come rescue him when she miraculously appeared, bottle in hand. She took the baby, fixed him in the crook of one arm, and tipped the bottle to his lips. Matthew's mouth closed greedily on the nipple and began a steady sucking motion, both chubby baby hands coming up to close around the glass.

"I told you it wouldn't be long before he made his wishes known."

Wade blinked, both hands settled on his knees as he watched the pair. "I'll say one thing: that kid has got a world-class set of lungs. And he ain't shy about using them."

He got to his feet and stood back. "Would you like to sit down to do that?"

"Thank you." Callie took his seat and they both watched as the level of milk in the bottle went down with each hard pull of Matthew's mouth.

Then she looked at Wade, and he could feel her studying his beard. He lifted a hand to his chin and found it damp, covered with baby spittle. His grimace must have conveyed his feelings, because Callie chuckled.

"Unless you enjoy having your hair pulled and sucked on, you may want to think about shaving and cutting your hair." She flicked her own long tresses back over her shoulders. "I usually wind mine up to keep him from yanking it clean out of my head."

Wade scratched the itchy facial hair. "I think I'd like to shave, anyway. Growing a beard and mustache wasn't my idea to begin with. You wouldn't happen to have a straight razor around here, would you?"

"There might be an extra one in my brother's room. Upstairs, second door on the right."

"Thanks." Cautious of the bandages around his ankles rubbing against the bottom cuffs of his trousers, Wade started up the stairs toward Callie's brother's bedroom.

He remembered Nathan from before he'd been sent to prison. Nice man. Young and full of dreams, as Wade recalled, but a decent sort.

Stepping into the young man's room, he never would have known it went unoccupied. Not a speck of dust covered the numerous dark mahogany surfaces, the bed was made, and a few personal articles littered the dresser top. Callie, it seemed, kept the place spotless whether her brother was home or not.

On top of caring for a three-month-old and running the small farm single-handedly, he didn't know how she did it.

Guilt began to niggle at his conscience for adding even more to her workload just by being here. And it wasn't like he could be a huge help to her, because the law was already breathing down his neck. He couldn't go outside during the day in case someone spotted him, and that meant he couldn't do any of the outside chores as he would have liked.

Checking shelves and drawers, Wade finally found the straight razor he'd been looking for, and a strop to sharpen the blade, hanging inside the closet door. It would do. And he'd be grateful to finally be rid of this damn straggly beard.

Returning to the pantry, he found Matthew contentedly full and Callie struggling to arrange a quilt on the floor one-handed.

"Here, let me help you," he said, taking the blanket from her and spreading it out on a free section of the floor.

"Thank you." Callie crouched down to settle Matthew on his back in the center of the blanket, and his son immediately set to cooing and trying to catch his toes.

Wade chuckled. "Doesn't take much to keep him occupied, does it?"

"Not when his belly's full. I have some toys laid out for him in the other room, but he'll be fine there for a while. Did you find the razor?"

Wade held it up for her to see. "I couldn't find a brush or soap, though."

"I'm sure I can find something that will do. Sit down."

He watched her sashay into the kitchen before complying with her soft demand.

"You sure are bossy," he observed, loud enough for her to hear. "Do you tell your brother what to do, too?"

Small kitchen towel draped over her arm, she came back into view. "My brother wouldn't listen to me even if I tried. If he did, he wouldn't be off in California right now, wasting his time and leaving me at the mercy of an escaped convict."

Wade felt properly castigated. He lowered his eyes and tried to keep the heat he felt climbing his neck from settling in his cheeks. "I'm sorry about this," he said with all sincerity. "I told you I won't hurt you or the boy."

None too gently, she tucked the towel around his neck and into the collar of his shirt. "That and a handshake will get me exactly nothing." With the same pair of scissors they'd used earlier to cut away his prison garb, she began paring the longer hairs of his beard and mustache.

"You don't believe me?" he asked, a little affronted but careful not to move his lips into the path of the clacking blades. Sure, he'd escaped from Huntsville and come straight to her, but not to scare her, and not to cause her any harm. He just wanted his son. And now that she'd made

61

him realize he couldn't take Matthew with him as long as he was still deemed a criminal, he just wanted to spend a little time with the boy before he had to go on the run again.

Setting the scissors aside, Callie took the razor from him and opened it, causing the sharp silver blade to glint in the pale lamplight. "You haven't tried to hurt either one of us yet, which I count as a blessing, so it's possible you mean what you say. But how am I to know you won't change your mind if the posse tracks you here? Or if I say or do the wrong thing?"

Gritting his teeth, he said, "I would never harm my son. And I've got no cause to hurt you, either."

"For now. I guess it's just lucky I'm the one holding the straight razor."

Wade huffed. He didn't like this at all. Before he'd been falsely convicted of a crime and sent away to prison, no one had ever had the gall to doubt his word. A man's word was his bond. Only a lily-livered bounder like Brady Young went back on a promise.

But then, Callie didn't know that. She didn't know him at all, except for what she'd seen so far, and he had to admit breaking into her house probably hadn't been the wisest way to gain her trust.

He'd meant what he said about not harming her or Matthew, though. He'd cut off his own arm before he hurt a hair on his child's head.

But maybe she didn't need to know that. Maybe having her be a bit wary of him wasn't such a bad idea. He didn't know what the next few days—let alone the next few hours—would bring, and he might just need her fear as leverage. Be it against the posse from Huntsville, or even just to keep her safe when she didn't want to take his warnings to heart.

As she picked up the bar of soap he'd used to scrub earlier and dipped it into the now cold water of the bath to lather it into suds, he decided not to pursue the conversation. He could work at convincing her of his integrity later. For now, he'd let her believe what she liked.

Heedless of the chill temperature of the soap in her hands, she slapped one palm on either side of his face and began lathering what was left of his beard. Cripes, he thought. This woman could be one step down from a saint—like when she'd brought him those chunks of pork and cheese to fill his ravenously empty stomach—or a hairbreadth from being a harridan—like now, when she was shaving him with ice-cold water. And he didn't even want to think about what she might do with that blade, if she were so inclined.

She tilted his head back and to the side, so that he could see the razor slowly approaching his temple, and he swallowed hard.

"You don't have to do this, you know. All I

need is a mirror and I can shave myself."

"Hold still," she commanded in that soft, devil-or-angel voice. "I've shaved Nathan plenty of times; I don't mind. Besides, if you try anything funny, at least I'll be the one armed with a weapon."

His teeth snapped together as he fought the urge to tell her *again* that he wasn't going to hurt her, dammit.

If it made her feel more secure to be the one holding the razor, then he'd let her shave him. As long as she didn't cut him. One tiny slip and he'd wrestle the blade away from her.

Unaware of the track his thoughts were taking, she scraped the blade down his left cheek, then his right, then over the shelf of his lip and up over his neck and chin. The time she spent near his jugular unnerved him the most, but her strokes never faltered as she shaved away a strip of stubble, wiped the blade clean on the towel at his shoulder, then took another sweep.

Tipping up one corner of the towel, she wiped his face clean of soap, then stood back.

He ran a hand over his jaw, surprised to find it almost baby-bottom smooth. He hadn't thought she'd be so skilled. "Good job," he said.

"Thank you."

She closed the razor and set it across the room, he noticed, then picked up the scissors and moved around his back.

"Would you like me to cut your hair next?" she asked pleasantly.

Although he hadn't looked in a mirror yet, it felt like she'd done a good enough job on his face. He might as well let her have a go at his hair. It would be nice to have it short again, not full of grub and vermin and brushing his shoulders all the damn time.

"Why not?" he said, and sat back to enjoy the feel of her slim fingers feathering across his scalp.

Dear God! What was she thinking of, shaving the man while he sat in the middle of her pantry? Wasn't it bad enough that she'd thought him attractive with his long hair and matted beard and mustache? How could she not have realized he would be a hundred times more handsome without his face covered in bristles?

What was wrong with her? Was she losing her mind? Had too many days of working around the farm and too many nights of staying up with Matthew pickled her brain? Had she lost every single shred of common sense she'd ever possessed?

The man was a felon, for God's sake. A criminal convicted and sent to prison. Escaped from prison, she corrected. Which only made it that much worse.

And not only had she not run screaming, not hit him over the head with the nearest heavy object or retrieved her pistol while she'd had the chance, but she'd fed him. Let him scrub in her bath filled with lilac water. Given him a fresh change of clothes and let him hold his son. And now she was *grooming* him.

For the love of all things holy, she might as well turn the house and property over to him and forget about ever retaining so much as a semblance of her independence or dignity.

She wished Nathan was here, due home at any minute to discover this man's presence and rescue her . . . from herself, if nothing else.

She wished Lily hadn't told him who was keeping his son. *When* had Lily done that? Callie wondered. Hadn't she been too sick after Matthew's birth to do or say much of anything?

Most of all, she wished Wade was ugly. Fat, deformed, possibly even cruel or threatening. Then she would have no qualms about slicing his throat with the razor blade. Or fetching the revolver from her sewing basket and blowing him to kingdom come.

But he *wasn't* ugly or cruel, and she'd already done everything but make up a bed for him to spend the night. Which reminded her that she did, indeed, need to decide where he would sleep.

Because he was staying. Until he cleared his name, he said, or the posse caught up with him. If what he'd said about Brady Young framing him for Neville Young's murder was true, she couldn't quite bring herself to wish the law would arrive. But she wasn't sure she wanted him living under her roof for much longer, either.

Despite his promises not to hurt her or Matthew, she wasn't entirely sure they were safe in his presence.

And she was most vulnerable of all, for she couldn't help wondering how those full lips, now devoid of scratchy hair, would feel pressed tight against her own.

Chapter Five

Wade awoke the next morning in Nathan's bed, with a face not covered in itchy, wiry, dirty hair. He much preferred Callie's close shave over the beard he'd sported these past eighteen months.

With his feet hanging over the edge of the bed, his naked torso barely covered by the corner of the coverlet, he inhaled deeply. His first breath of morning air away from the penitentiary in longer than he cared to remember. It smelled delicious. Like freedom and choices and . . . burning bacon?

His mouth turned down as he sniffed again, then began to wonder how long it would take for the grease of that burning bacon to catch the house on fire.

Wasting no time, he shrugged into his dungarees and started downstairs before his shirt was completely buttoned or tucked in. The kitchen was empty when he arrived, a skillet of snapping, sizzling, charring bacon on one side of the blazing stove, a pan of blackened eggs on the other.

Grabbing a nearby towel, he wrapped it around the hot handle and carried the pan to the cast-iron sink. Then he repeated the action with the eggs and stood back to consider how salvageable any of it was for breakfast.

He was shaking his head, thinking they might have to start over, when his hostage—or maybe at this point hostess was the better term—came in through a back door that led directly outside. Matthew was hitched high on one hip, while Callie brushed her damp brow with the back of one arm.

"Oh," she exclaimed, and stopped in her tracks as soon as she saw him. "I didn't know you were awake yet."

"I just got up. Thought I'd better rescue breakfast before it was burned beyond recognition."

"Oh, no, not again." She hurried to the sink and stared down at the ruined food. With a sigh, she stepped back, her shoulders seeming to slump. "I always do that," she groused. "I think it will save so much time if I start breakfast before going out to work on morning chores, but by the time I get back, everything is burnt to a crisp."

She lifted her gaze and gave him an almost accusatory glare. "Why do you think I eat warm bread or porridge for breakfast most days, instead of fixing a big meal like I did when Nathan was here? I only put on eggs and bacon for you."

"And I appreciate it, but you don't have to do anything extra for me. I'm capable of fixing my own meals, and I don't want to make more work than you've already got to handle. Besides . . ." He used his index finger and thumb to lift a strip of blackened bacon from the cooling pan. "This still looks pretty good. It's only a little black around the edges."

And straight through, on both sides. But he'd be damned if he'd cause her to start breakfast over from scratch when she'd already been outside milking cows and feeding chickens, or whatever else she had to do in the barn.

To show her how edible her meal really was, he took a large bite off one end of the bacon strip and smiled, chomping away until she seemed reassured enough to turn aside. He made a face then and all but spit the bits of cinder into the washbasin, but forced himself to swallow what was in his mouth before returning the rest of the slice to the pan. For later. If he ever got hungry enough to finish it off. Which he doubted. Even after eighteen months of prison slop, he didn't think he'd ever be hungry enough to finish off Callie's good-hearted attempt at cooking.

He wondered if he should be worried about his son's stomach. Matthew was on a bottle now, but how soon before he started eating real food? Babies' constitutions weren't strong enough to digest coal and ash, were they?

"Do you need any help out at the barn?" he asked, thinking that would be a good way of getting her mind off the disaster of breakfast.

She shook her head. "No, everything is done. There's a pail of fresh milk on the back step for Matthew that needs to be put into jars and stored in the icebox down cellar. At any rate, you probably shouldn't risk going outside any more than you have to."

Wade nodded in agreement, her words backing up his earlier thoughts. "You're right. You may be a good ways from town, but you never know who might be passing by. If the posse is in town already, they may even be running patrols all through the area, looking for anything out of the ordinary."

He cocked his head and glanced at Matthew, then at the sprig of straw dangling from his diapered bottom. "How do you handle Matthew while you're doing barn chores?" He couldn't picture her mucking out stalls or milking a cow with a baby attached to her side.

"He plays in the straw while I work. Don't you,

sweetheart?" She turned a beatific smile on Matthew. "We have a blanket out there that we spread on the loose pile of straw and he wiggles and coos while I take care of Marmalade. That's the milk cow," she explained. "And gather eggs, and rake out a few stalls. He's a very good boy."

"I'll bet he is." Wade stepped forward and held his hands out toward Matthew. "May I?"

Callie hesitated for only a moment. Maybe because yesterday when she'd let him hold his son, she had been the one making the offer. This time, Wade was asking. But she lifted Matthew slightly and saw that he was properly tucked into the crook of his father's arm.

This would free her up to take care of a few other things, she thought. It was just that she was so used to managing everything one-handed, with Matthew firmly settled on her hip and reaching up for her hair, that it would feel somewhat odd to move around unhindered.

"Would you like me to put on another pan of bacon and eggs?" she asked. "I don't mind, truly, and it's my own fault the first batch burned."

Wade shook his head. And was it her imagination, or did he look slightly panicked that she might have to make another attempt at cooking?

"That's all right. I'm not very hungry, anyway."

"I'm not *that* bad a cook," she defended herself, hands on hips. "I admit I burn the occasional pot or pan of something. I have a tendency to walk away and forget what I'm doing. But if I'm right there, keeping an eye on the stove, I can fry an egg without too many problems."

"Only if you're sure," he finally acquiesced. "Otherwise, I'd be just as happy with a bowl of porridge or a slice of bread, like you were talking about. Better yet"—he came forward and dumped Matthew back in her arms—"maybe I ought to cook for you. It seems only fair, considering the trouble I've put you to already."

He moved toward the small table against the far wall and pulled out one of the two chairs. "You have a seat and relax. All you need to do is point me in the direction of what I'll need."

Callie sat, arranging Matthew in a similar position on her lap, too awed to do much more than follow his directive. *He* was going to cook for *her*? Could men even cook?

She'd never seen proof, that was for sure. Her brother could barely boil water and would have starved long ago if she hadn't been around. Of course, he'd learned early on to stick close to her while she was fixing his meals, as he wasn't particularly fond of burned food.

"Do you still want eggs and bacon, or would you rather have something else?"

"Do you know how to *fix* anything else?"

He turned away from the sink, where he was

retrieving the earlier scorched pans, and sent her a wide, toothsome grin.

If she'd thought him handsome last night, with that year's worth of beard shaved away and his hair trimmed short, he was absolutely devastating now.

Her heart flipped over so hard in her breast, she thought she might cease breathing. Her grip on Matthew tightened until he gave a low whimper, and her senses returned. She smoothed the finger marks away from Matthew's fleshy thighs and bounced her legs up and down until he settled.

Wade's grin remained locked on her, raising her temperature and sending her belly into little spasms of she didn't know what.

"I lived alone a lot of years before they sent me away," he told her. "I had a couple of hands to help around the ranch, but no one to cook or clean for me, so I took care of that myself. I fry up a mighty mean beefsteak, and my mashed potatoes aren't half bad, either." His smile spread. "Now do you want bacon and eggs or something else?"

"Is steak and potatoes on the menu?" she asked, suddenly curious to put his claims to the test.

"You got a steer we can slaughter?" he asked. "Or a slab of smoked beef somewhere?"

She frowned. "Afraid not. I guess bacon and eggs will have to do."

With that dangerously charming grin still on his face, he turned back to the stove to stoke the embers and clean out one of the skillets to reuse. "For the moment," he clarified. "But as soon as I'm able, I'd be happy to fry up one of my famous steaks for you. Straight from Mason beef, if I can swing it."

"Mason beef?"

"Got some more bacon?" he asked, seeming to ignore her question.

She pointed to a rolled-up dish towel on the counter, where she'd rewrapped the salted portion of pork but not had a chance to return it to its place in the cellar.

He unfolded the towel and found a knife, then proceeded to cut long, thin strips from the hunk of meat.

"I raise cattle," he said, finally getting around to answering her earlier inquiry. "Mason beef. My ranch is the Circle M. I move part of the herd east every summer to sell off but always keep enough head on hand to restock."

He turned slightly in her direction, barely taking his attention from his task long enough to meet her eyes. "Nathan never mentioned that? He came out a couple of times to talk cattle. I think he had in mind to buy a steer or two, maybe start his own herd."

Callie nodded. "Nathan might have said something. But then, Nathan is always running on about one great plan or another. Don't get me wrong; he's a good man," she added quickly, "but his head is too full of dreams for his feet to ever be firmly on the ground."

She left her seat long enough to retrieve half a loaf of bread from the warmer, then returned and began breaking off small pieces for Matthew. His pudgy fingers curled around the chunks as he gummed them and actually managed to swallow about a third of each bite. The rest covered his mouth, fingers, and shirt.

"When we settled here and started this farm, I thought it would be enough. I was certainly content with a simple life, as long as we had enough livestock to provide for ourselves. But before long, Nathan started talking about expanding, raising cattle or sheep. And then he heard there was a fortune to be made out in California by panning for gold, so he packed his things and moved out there."

"And left you alone."

The words were softly spoken but brought her head up to meet his gaze.

"Yes, but I don't mind. This place isn't so large that I can't run it myself. And as I said, I have everything I need. Granted, things have been a bit more difficult since Matthew came, simply because it's harder to see to livestock and the upkeep of the house all by myself with a baby to look after, too, but I'm managing."

"Quite well, from what I've seen."

Callie's spine straightened with pride. "Thank you. I appreciate that."

He shot her another heart-stopping smile, then drawled, "Sure thing," before turning to lay the fresh-cut strips of bacon in the bottom of the skillet she'd nearly set afire not twenty minutes before.

"So if Nathan strikes it rich, you'll be set for life," he observed. "You must be excited about that."

Her mouth turned down in a moue of disappointment. "If Nathan strikes it rich, I'll eat my best Sunday bonnet."

Wade let out a sharp, deep chortle of laughter, wiping his hands on his pants as he turned away from the stove. "Why do you say that?"

"Did I forget to mention that all of Nathan's grand plans have never resulted in more than trial and heartache? He probably hasn't found so much as a speck of gold dust yet, and he's been there going on six months. I only pray he remains safe and healthy until he comes to his senses and returns to Purgatory."

"A man's got to have dreams, Callie. Without that, every day is the same as the last, with nothing to work toward. No hope of bettering himself or his circumstances. Nathan just wants to discover a bit of gold so he can come home and provide more for you than he's been able to so far."

Put like that, Callie felt like weeping. Her eyes burned as she thought of her brother, so animated in the telling of his latest scheme. Always describing the things he would buy for her just as soon as he made it big.

She sighed. "I would be happier if he stayed home and helped with the farm. I don't need a fancy cookstove or a closet full of silk gowns. I need help with the pigs and vegetable patch."

Wade lifted his head and fixed her with serious, coffee brown eyes. "He's young yet. He'll settle down soon. And for the next little while, you've got me to help out around here. As best I can while hiding out, anyway."

As much as she appreciated his offer of assistance, she feared that the longer this man remained under her roof, the more danger she was in. Oh, maybe not in danger of him hurting her, but physical danger all the same. Healthy or not, a woman her age shouldn't be struggling to breathe, or having heart palpitations just because she was in the vicinity of a tall, broad-shouldered man, with eyes that made her swallow hard and a smile that nearly knocked her out of her seat.

Even more scary, the fact that he was an escaped convict did little to douse her attraction.

No, for her own safety Wade Mason needed to leave. The sooner the better.

"You said you'd go as soon as you were able," she blurted out, ignoring the pressure of Matthew gumming the back of her hand. "That you wanted to prove your innocence. How, exactly, do you plan to do that?"

He finished cracking eggs over the second sizzling skillet, then turned once again to face her.

She wished he'd stop that. She much preferred staring at his back than his expressive eyes and mouth and jaw and brow. His wide back with its rippling muscles was impressive, yes. His tight buttocks covered in equally tight denim impossible to ignore. But it was his eyes that caused gooseflesh to break out over every inch of her skin. His eyes that seemed to caress her without a single touch and beg her to believe in him.

"I do want to clear my name. And I've been thinking on how to go about that," he said finally, holding her gaze, his tone gentle, his calm manner one he might use to soothe a frightened calf. "The problem is, I may need your help."

Chapter Six

"My help? *My* help?" Callie lurched to her feet, remembering at the last minute to hold tight to Matthew lest he slide right off her lap and onto the floor.

The sudden movement jolted him and sent him into caterwauls of frightened displeasure.

"Shh, shh, shh, shh, shh." Callie turned him over and lifted him to her shoulder, patting his back and bouncing him in a soothing motion.

When Matthew's cries had diminished to a less than ear-splitting level, she turned her attention back to Wade. He stood leaning one hip against the counter, arms crossed over his chest.

"What do you mean *my help?*" she demanded, in a much subdued tone of voice. "Isn't it enough that I've let you stay here when I should have found a way to turn you in to the authorities? I've fed you, clothed you, helped you get out of your shackles . . . What more could you possibly want from me?"

Wade shoved his hands into the front pockets of his trousers and rocked back on his heels, an almost apologetic expression on his face. "I have no right to ask, I know. You've already helped me more than I deserve."

That apologetic look turned earnest, his dark eyes pleading with her to understand. "But I'm a wanted man, Callie," he continued. "I can't show myself in town without being shot in the back by some trigger-happy bounty hunter, or captured by the law and thrown back in prison. And if I go back there, Callie, I won't get out again. Ever. They'll make sure of that.

"If I could stay here forever, I would. But hiding out isn't going to prove my innocence, or get my land back." A crooked smile lifted one corner of his mouth. "And I have a feeling you wouldn't appreciate me hanging around that long. The point is, the more you help me, the sooner I can be out of your hair."

"And take Matthew with you." She held her breath, waiting for him to answer . . . and knowing she wouldn't like it when he did.

He glanced at the child cushioned against her shoulder, and then directly back at her. "Yes."

Her own eyes narrowed and she could feel her

mouth pulling down in a frown. "You can't honestly imagine that I'd be willing to help you at anything that might take Matthew away from me."

"No, I don't suppose I should. But I do."

His gaze took on a hard edge, and Callie could see why a judge would believe him capable of murder. He certainly looked capable of it at the moment.

His hands slipped out of the pants pockets and locked around his upper arms as he linked them across his chest. "I'd think you'd do just about anything to get me out of your house."

Callie swallowed and told herself not to be afraid. At least not to let it show. He already knew one of her weaknesses: Matthew. He didn't need to also know his intense gaze and broad shoulders intimidated her.

"Not if it means you'll take my child with you when you go."

His jaw tightened even more, his eyes all but shooting sparks. "He's *my* child."

Now more than ever, Callie wished she'd adopted Matthew through Father Ignacio over at the church. The priest ran the local orphanage and worked hard to find homes for the great number of parentless children who found their way to his doorstep. But because Callie and Lily had been friends, because Lily had asked her specifically to take Matthew, the baby had never spent so much as a night at the Purgatory Home for Adoptive Children. It also meant she'd never legally adopted Matthew.

Wade didn't have to know that, however. And since he'd said himself that he couldn't simply waltz into town, it was quite unlikely he'd ever make it to the orphanage to check.

"Not according to the adoption papers I signed at the Purgatory Home for Adoptive Children," she told him bravely, firming her shoulders and daring him to contradict her. "Besides, I'm the only mother Matthew has ever known. You wouldn't just be hurting me if you took him away."

Her voice nearly broke at the last, but she clamped her teeth together and blinked to dispel any signs of moisture that might be welling in the corners of her eyes.

For several long minutes, they stood there. Wade studied her from head to toe, taking in the child in her arms and her almost militant stance. Silence folded around them until Callie wanted to scream.

And then Wade let out a long sigh. Dropping his arms from his middle, he turned back to the stove and took up a worn spatula to work the eggs loose from the bottom of the skillet.

"We're not getting very far, are we?" he asked, a note of resignation tingeing his words. "We both want Matthew, and we're both willing to fight to keep him. Doesn't bode well for a compromise, does it?"

Still wary and ready for battle, Callie rigidly replied, "I won't compromise where Matthew's safety is concerned."

"And you don't think he would be safe with me."

It wasn't a question, but a statement. She answered anyway. "I don't know if he would or not. I suppose that depends on whether you were still wanted by the law. Regardless of what the future might hold, I do know that if Matthew were with you, he wouldn't be with me, and then I would have no idea how he was faring." Her brows rose in a challenging manner as she added, "And I've managed to keep him quite safe thus far, thank you very much. You, however, don't seem to live a very safe life at all."

Wade threw her a glance over his shoulder as he flipped several strips of bacon, sending hot grease sizzling on the stovetop. Mouth turned down with displeasure, he said, "Not by choice, believe me, sweetheart. Not by choice."

When the eggs and bacon were ready, he dished them up onto two blue- and white-speckled tin plates and brought them to the table. Callie was still standing, watching him cautiously.

"Sit," he told her, holding out a fork. "Eat."

She doubted the argument was over but assumed the food was a temporary peace offering. Accepting the fork, she returned to her seat and slowly began cutting into her eggs.

Cooked through, they were golden fried to perfection, as was the bacon, and Callie tamped down on a sliver of annoyance that this unmarried escaped convict was able to prepare a better breakfast than she'd managed.

She shifted Matthew back around to rest on one knee and tried to keep him from winding his chubby little fingers around the hot bacon on her plate. As she delicately nibbled a bite of egg Wade chomped down a few strips of bacon, all the while watching her, making her distinctly uncomfortable.

"What?" she asked finally, letting her fork drop with a clank to the metal plate and casting him a disparaging look.

He slowly lowered his own fork and sat back in his chair, crossing his arms negligently over his formidable chest. It took him another long minute to answer her.

"I was just wondering if you might be amenable to striking a deal of sorts."

"A deal?"

"I'd call it a compromise, but I already know your feelings on that subject." He grinned, letting her know he was teasing. "I was thinking more along the lines of an agreement. A way you'd be willing to help me without getting your petticoats in a twist."

Callie raised one brow, her only warning that he was treading on precarious ground. "If you hope to gain my support, you might want to refrain from insulting me."

His smile grew even wider and he winked—actually winked!—at her. "Yes, ma'am."

She wasn't certain if he was mocking her, or merely found her obstinacy amusing. Either way, she didn't like it.

Before she aimed a utensil at his forehead, she thought it best to get on with the business at hand. "What sort of agreement did you have in mind?"

His humor faded, and he shifted in his chair, carefully considering his next words. "We both want Matthew; there's no getting around that. And I doubt we'll ever come to an understanding on that score without resorting to a King Solomon-like solution."

Her arm instinctively tightened about the baby on her lap, and Wade shook his head. "He doesn't look like he'd much enjoy being split down the middle, so I say that option is out."

Callie chose not to answer, afraid of what might come out if she dared to open her mouth. King Solomon, indeed!

"But I think you may have in mind that I intend to snatch him away from you at any moment," Wade continued.

This time, she squeezed Matthew so hard that he began to whimper, and she told herself to relax before she bruised him in her desire to keep him safe—and with her.

Swallowing hard, she forced herself to speak past a tongue gone dry. "And do you?" she asked, more than a little fearful of his answer.

Instead of assuring her that he didn't plan to sneak off with Matthew in the middle of the night, he merely shrugged a loose shoulder. "That's not my immediate intention, no, but my future isn't exactly well mapped out at the moment. I don't know what's going to happen. If the sheriff shows up at your front door tomorrow, I may have no choice but to grab Matthew and head for the hills."

The chair rattled backward and crashed to the floor as Callie leapt to her feet. "You are *not* taking him on the run with you. I'll take Matthew into the hills myself and turn you in to the law before I allow that to happen."

Startled by the sudden commotion and her agitation, Matthew began to wail. She hadn't meant to frighten him, but given his father's most recent threat, perhaps the child should be upset.

Wade stayed where he was, letting her take a moment or two to calm the baby. "I'm not saying I want it to come to that, I'm just saying I may not have any choice in the matter."

"You could leave," she suggested desperately.

Matthew was turned to her shoulder as she swayed and patted his back consolingly. "You could leave now, leave Matthew here, and . . . maybe come back for him someday, when you're no longer a wanted man."

Before she'd even finished the thought, he was shaking his head. "I don't want to be on the run all my life, Callie. That's no way for a man to live. A boy shouldn't grow up without a father, or with a father who only shows up every few years when he isn't being hunted down like a dog. And they're not going to stop looking for me. Unless I can prove I didn't murder Neville Young, there will always be a price on my head."

"So you would take Matthew from me? Take him on the run with you, let him be tracked the same way the law is tracking you? What kind of upbringing is that for a child?" she demanded, angry as well as frightened now.

"That's just what I'm saying, Callie. I don't want either of those things for my son. I want him to grow up here, in Purgatory. With a permanent house to come home to, knowing his father. A father who lives free and doesn't have to keep looking over his shoulder. Which is why I'm asking for your help."

"Help that will take him away from me. I don't think you realize how much he means to me."

"I do. Because he means just as much to me."

He smiled wryly and let his hands fall to the

tops of his denim-clad thighs, pushing to his feet. "We're right back where we started, Callie, with neither of us wanting to give up our claim to Matthew."

"And just what do you suggest?" she asked suspiciously.

"You won't love it. It's not a proposal that's going to give either of us exactly what we want. But we both stand to gain, so I'll ask you to at least hear me out before you refuse. Can you do that, Callie?"

She remained silent for a moment, considering. She didn't miss the way he kept using her name in that soft, cajoling voice of his. It was meant to soften her, to win her over to his way of thinking. It wouldn't work, of course, but he didn't need to know that.

And he was right about the fact that they weren't likely to settle on an agreement that would fully satisfy them both. So she would listen. She would mull over his offer. Then, if necessary, she would bundle up Matthew in the middle of the night and hie off to wherever she thought they could seek sanctuary until the authorities took Wade back to Huntsville.

"All right," she said carefully. "I'm listening."

He gave a subtle nod of his head. "What if I promised not to take Matthew away any time soon? What if, in exchange for your help finding a way to prove my innocence, I concede that you're the best guardian for my son and leave him with you until I've cleared my name and once again established a safe, stable home for him at my ranch?"

"You still intend to take him."

"He's my *son,* Callie. I want him with me. If I told you differently, you'd know I was lying. And I won't lie to you, Callie."

His strong, long fingers flexed into his hips where his hands rested. "I can't tell you I won't take him with me eventually, but I'm promising not to sneak off with him, not to take him from you in *any* way without your full and clear knowledge. I'm promising to let you care for him, raise him, until such a time as my life is in order enough to give him a good home. And even when that does finally happen, you can see him whenever you like, I swear to you. You can come by every day, help him with his schoolwork, cut his hair, see he's eating properly. I won't ever turn you away."

His dark eyes were earnest, pleading. "I mean it, Callie. No matter what happens, I'll always see to it that you're in his life. As much as you want. I don't want to tear him from you. I just want to bring up my son the way a father is meant to."

Callie was listening, digesting his every word. And rejecting each one. She refused to contemplate *ever* being separated from Matthew, and no amount of arguing from Wade would change her mind.

But he didn't need to know that. She'd agreed to hear him out, and that was exactly what she was doing.

And maybe she'd actually go along with his plan. In the back of her mind, a niggling voice told her that agreeing to Wade's deal would put him at ease, make him think she was on his side. Which might give her time to get to the Purgatory Home for Adoptive Children and have Father Ignacio work up the papers for Matthew's official and legal adoption by her. Then, father or no father, Wade Mason would have an even harder time taking Matthew away from her. She would have the law on her side.

Callie was almost giddy at the prospect. She could tell Wade she would assist him, even do what she could to help him prove his innocence. But in the end, if she could get legal adoption papers from Father Ignacio, she would have just as much claim to Matthew as Wade.

"What, exactly, would you expect of me in exchange for these assurances?" she inquired, so calmly she surprised even herself.

"Lily was there the night Neville Young died. She saw everything. But with her being gone, she can't go to the authorities and tell them what she knows. And I doubt her letter will do me any good, since they could say I forged it myself . . . or had someone else do it."

He looked at her meaningfully, as though the

law might suspect she'd written the note for him.

"What I need is another witness to come forward."

"Was there another witness?" she asked.

"Well, Brady Young, for one. He shot his own father in the back, but something tells me he wouldn't be willing to say so. After all, my being in prison is the only thing keeping him from paying for his own sick crimes."

Wade paused. "There was one other person there that night. Someone who knows exactly what happened."

"So why didn't he come forward? Why didn't he testify on your behalf?"

"Because he's just as crooked as the rest of them," he said with a sneer. "But now, more than a year after the fact, we may be able to convince him to help me."

Callie swallowed. She doubted they would have much luck convincing another less-than-honorable man to help Wade clear his name, but given his situation, she wasn't sure they had any other choice.

"All right. Who is this man?"

Wade met her gaze and held it with those intensely dark eyes. "Sheriff Graves. He and Neville were old friends. They were working together to attempt to steal my land. Graves was there that night, was part of the beating they gave me to try to make me tell them . . ." Shaking his head, he left off with that train of thought and said, "He was in on Neville's plans to steal my land, and he was there to see Brady shoot his father in the back. If we can just get to him, sweeten the pot enough to have him turn against Brady, then there's a good chance he'll come forward to tell what he saw."

Callie's heart crumbled, her eyes growing damp as Wade's gestures became more animated, his hope obvious as he plotted how to regain his freedom.

"Oh, Wade," she breathed almost to herself, and for the first time realized what a truly terrible mess he was in.

Hearing her soft plea, Wade's mouth began to thin and a measure of tension moved into his tall frame. "What? What's wrong? Don't you think it will work?" he hurried on. "Don't worry, Callie, I've got something Graves is really going to want. No matter what Brady is paying him to keep his mouth shut, this is better; this will convince him to tell a judge what really happened."

"Oh, Wade," she whispered again, her heart twisting even more in her breast. "I can't believe you don't know. Of course, you've been away for so long, it's no wonder." She took a step forward and reached out to touch his arm with one hand. His muscles flexed angrily beneath her fingertips.

"Wade," she said as gently as she could, "Sheriff Graves is dead."

Chapter Seven

All of the strength seemed to go out of Wade's legs, and he began to crumble. If it hadn't been for Callie's swift move to slip a chair behind him, he'd have fallen flat on the floor. He blinked several times, swallowed even harder, trying to absorb the news she'd just delivered.

Sheriff Graves was dead. Jensen Graves, Purgatory's fat, lazy, dirty-as-a-coal-miner sheriff. The man who hadn't seen a thing wrong with Neville's harassment and abuse of Wade, as long as there was something in it for him.

He had stood by and watched Wade being beaten to within an inch of his life—punched, kicked, pistol-whipped into near unconsciousness. Then with cool detachment he'd witnessed Brady Young shoot his supposed best friend in the back. And the bastard had still had the nerve to testify against Wade. He had spun a tale about Wade being furious over a bar fight with Brady earlier in the week, describing how Wade had sneaked up on Neville and murdered the man in cold blood.

Never mind that—even though Wade *had* been the one to set foot on Young's ranch—he'd immediately been accosted from behind, his six-shooters taken away. Never mind that Wade's wounds had been so fresh when Graves dragged him off to jail that they'd still been oozing blood.

Brady had paid off Jensen—with money or promises, he didn't even know—and Wade doubted if the sheriff had lost so much as one night's sleep over putting an innocent man away for life.

The rotten bastard. He hoped Graves was even now roasting over a nice, hot spit in the deepest bowels of hell.

Pulling himself away from the slick precipice of despair, Wade lifted his head to where Callie was crouched beside his leg. She'd settled Matthew in a high wooden chair on the other side of the table with a piece of bread that he was mouthing to mush.

He looked down and found Callie's fingers twined with his own, stroking the top of his hand with her thumb. He must have given her quite a scare there for a minute, for her to be touching him like this voluntarily.

But he didn't pull away, didn't make any sudden movements that would cause *her* to pull away. He merely sat there, letting her stroke his hand and stare up at him in concern.

"How? W-when did he die?" he asked shakily, finally finding his voice.

"It was . . . a little over a year ago. He was killed at the Updike house. Did you know them?"

He nodded.

"They don't live in Purgatory anymore. Nolan fell down the stairs and broke his neck. After his death, Veronica took the children to live with her mother." She shook her head in sympathy. "But it turns out Nolan didn't just fall. They say he was pushed."

Callie took a deep breath before going on. "You mentioned that Sheriff Graves was crooked, and I guess you would be right. No one ever suspected a thing, but it turns out Nolan Updike and Sheriff Graves were in on some kind of deal together to steal money from the bank. I don't know what went on or how it happened, but rumor has it that Graves ended up pushing Thomas down those stairs and killing him. And then when Purgatory's new sheriff—Sheriff Walker, who was a Texas Ranger at the time—figured out what was going on and confronted

Graves, Graves ended up shot. It was in the paper and all over town for the longest time. Not that you'd have been getting news from Purgatory all the way up in Huntsville."

Wade shook his head. He hadn't heard a thing. In fact, all the time he'd been locked up in that dank, dark cell, he'd done little more than think of different ways to get Graves over on his side; he'd imagined all sorts of enticements he could use to bribe the old tub of lard.

And now all those possibilities, all his dreams of being free, had disappeared with four simple words: Sheriff Graves is dead.

He'd been shot, and Wade could only pray it had been in the back . . . with numerous bullets . . . and hadn't killed him right away. It made him happier to imagine Graves writhing on the ground, howling in pain. For hours, maybe even days.

"He got what he deserved, no doubt about that," he told her. "I just wish he'd lingered long enough to tell the truth about the night Neville Young was killed."

Callie straightened but didn't let go of his hand. She merely leaned back against the edge of the table, her skirts brushing his knees and making him wish he had the right to pull her forward, onto his lap, and kiss her the way he wanted to. Maybe then he could forget that all

Heidi Betts

his plans for the future, for regaining his freedom, had just gone up in smoke.

With a slight squeeze to his fingers, she asked, "What will you do now?"

He laughed, actually laughed, but the sound was loud and hollow and furious. "I have no idea. Graves was my one chance of bringing forth a witness to tell the truth and clear my name."

"There has to be something else we can do," she offered softly.

"Like what?"

"I don't know, but we'll think of something." She sounded ruthless, suddenly, like a she-wolf protecting her pup.

Not for the first time, Wade thought of what a good choice she was to care for Matthew. Lily might have made mistakes in her life, but turning her child over to Callie to raise hadn't been one of them.

"Maybe I can go into town and talk to the new sheriff," she went on. "He seems really nice, and he had no patience for Sheriff Graves or the backhanded things he was up to. Maybe he'd be willing to hear me out, and help if he can."

Wade was already shaking his head. "No."

"Why not?"

"For one thing, he'd wonder why you were so interested in clearing my name. He's got to know by now that I escaped from prison and would probably put two and two together to figure out

98

where I'm hiding. For another, I don't want you risking your reputation. We'll think of something, like you said, but going to the sheriff isn't it."

"But I could show him Lily's letter, tell him I believe her, and that he should look into your conviction."

"No, Callie. At least not yet." His fingers flexed on hers. "That letter isn't enough to convince anyone of my innocence, not without Lily to back it up. We may be able to use it later, but for now, I need more evidence to plead my case. To convince the law—or this new sheriff, if you really think we can trust him—not to take me straight back to the penitentiary. Can you understand that?"

She nodded, though not very convincingly. "I suppose so. But if we don't get Sheriff Walker to help, what else are we going to do?"

He didn't miss the way she said "we," as though his fight had suddenly become her fight, too. It warmed his heart, and brought to life feelings he hadn't experienced in far too long. And if he thought it had been hard not to draw her close and kiss her before, it was damned near impossible not to do that now.

Not damned near, it was impossible. He tugged gently on her hand, urging her forward. One step, then two. He parted his knees and let her settle into the *V* of his legs. She came willingly enough, her eyes still locked on his. She looked . . . mesmerized, and it was the one clear sign that she felt even a fraction of the stirrings he did at that moment.

"Callie," he whispered, drawing her near, drawing her down, even as he stretched upward to reach her. His mouth brushed across her own, light as butterfly wings. Her lips were warm and soft, and she smelled of lilac water.

He brushed her mouth again, lingering longer this time, sighing in pure pleasure.

"Callie," he breathed again. "You are so beautiful." Their hands fell apart, and his moved to her waist, around her back, down to her buttocks beneath the thick layers of her skirt.

Too far, too fast. He knew it the minute her body tensed beneath his touch. She stepped away, lifting her shoulders primly. He expected her to slap his face, scream at him for making inappropriate advances toward her.

Instead, she calmly smoothed the folds of her clothes and leaned back against the tabletop. "That was rather improper of me," she said, a bit breathless. "I do hope you'll accept my apology."

Her apology? He was lucky she didn't race to the door and start hollering for the posse right then and there. He almost told her as much but didn't want to put ideas in her head.

Pushing back his chair, he stood, careful to keep a good distance between them. "I should be the one to apologize, Callie. It's been so long since anyone showed me any tenderness, I got a little carried away there for a second."

It had been a long time for a lot of things, one of which was kissing and bedding a beautiful woman. But he didn't dare tell her that or she'd definitely get scared off.

And he didn't want that. In fact, he wanted to kiss her again. That and more.

He didn't have the faintest notion of how to go about romancing Callie but he wasn't going to do anything to spook her before he figured it out.

Yep, he decided, coaxing more kisses from Callie would go on his to–do list, right below proving his innocence. It was a good addition. Number one: Clear my name. Number two: Seduce Callie Quinn.

Chapter Eight

He kissed her. Wade Mason kissed her.

That had been two days ago, and her lips were still numb and tingling. She couldn't feel her heart at all . . . that organ had pumped so hard, she was afraid it had jumped clean out of her body and was somewhere down Mexico way by now.

After the kiss, she'd pulled herself together enough to change Matthew, give him another bottle, and then put him down for a nap. They'd mostly been avoiding each other ever since.

Wade was doing his best to be kind and solicitous, and to basically stay out of her way. Likely because he feared she'd club him if he got too close again.

He needn't have worried. Chances were better

that Callie would grab him by the collar and wrap his body around hers rather than flattening him with a rolling pin.

My, was it getting hot in here?

She glanced at the stove, only to see that the embers had been left to burn themselves out. And it wasn't any hotter outside than usual. She shouldn't be all flushed like this without barn work to make her sweat.

Which left only one possible explanation for the way her blood was bubbling in her veins and her stomach was fluttering like she'd eaten a pound of uncooked jumping beans.

Wade.

Wade, and that amazing, momentous kiss, were sending her all into a tizzy. Two whole days later.

She'd known the man less than a week.

He was a prisoner on the run.

He meant to take Matthew away from her.

All of these things—or any one of them alone—should have been cause enough to throw him out of her house.

So why, instead, did she want to call him into the room and ask him to kiss her again? Longer this time. And firmer. Until their bodies pressed tight together and her feet didn't brush the floor.

Because she was a harlot, that's why. A shameless, brazen hussy who deserved to be dragged into the street and stoned. My lord, she was actually standing here, sending silent messages into the air in hopes of Wade hearing them and bursting into the room to ravish her.

Callie groaned and let her head fall to her chest. She was hopeless. And so wicked, it was lucky God hadn't sent a lightning bolt from heaven to strike her dead.

She rolled her eyes skyward.

It was early yet. He might have been busy at the moment. She should be careful, just in case.

Drawing in a deep breath, she slapped the towel in her hand down on the countertop. This was getting her nowhere. She'd remained in the kitchen most of the afternoon, avoiding Wade, avoiding the tingle of awareness that rocked through her body every time they were in the same room together.

But there were only so many things she could dust or wash or fold or put away before the room sparkled and it became obvious she was hiding. And realizing she was doing just that—hiding—bothered her even more than Wade's kiss had.

Callie Quinn was not a coward. She would not let one little kiss make her quiver like a frightened rabbit. She would put her shoulders back, march into the other room, and confront Wade Mason head-on.

Well, maybe not confront, but she would certainly go in there, act as though nothing was wrong, and go on with her life.

And if Wade tried to kiss her again, she would simply . . . simply . . . melt into a puddle of spineless human flesh, damn his eyes.

Callie lifted her head in determination. She would just have to make sure he didn't try anything, then. She could do that. She could be in the same room with him and still be on the alert. And if all else failed . . . she would run.

Ignoring the brittle voice in her brain that wanted to know if she would actually be running from the man's advances or from her own growing weakness where Wade was concerned, she pushed through the kitchen door and made her way to the sitting room.

Wade was standing with his back to her, hunched over the long, high table between two west-facing windows, using the bright midday light to illuminate his task. He looked intent, almost desperate, as he scribbled and scratched at the piece of paper in front of him.

"What are you working on?" she couldn't help but ask.

At the sound of her voice, he started. Turning in her direction, he shook his head and ran an agitated hand through his now clean and closely clipped chestnut hair. His equally brown eyes were wild with frustration.

"I keep trying to picture what happened that night. Where everyone was standing, who saw what—something, anything that will help me prove my innocence." He shook his head again and clawed the paper off the tabletop, crumpling it in fury.

"Somebody besides Lily has to be willing to tell the truth." His mouth curled in a scathing sneer. "Of course, at the rate the witnesses are dying there won't be anyone left to recount the events at all."

"That isn't true," she told him, moving toward him with a sense of purpose and prying the wrinkled-up paper from his tightly clenched fingers. "Let me see."

She took a seat on the edge of the nearest armchair and smoothed the paper out on her lap. It was a roughly sketched diagram of what had taken place the night Wade supposedly killed Neville Young. Everything was clearly labeled, the barn, the house, and each person's position.

It looked as though Wade and Neville were facing each other, likely in the confrontation Wade had mentioned. Jensen Graves stood to Neville's left.

"Where's Brady?" she asked, raising her head to glance at Wade, who had come to stand above her. "You said he was there, that he shot his father in the back."

"He came up behind me right after I arrived. Took my guns from me," he said, sticking his hands in the front pockets of his trousers and hunching his shoulders.

"All right," Callie instructed. "Hand me the pencil and a fresh sheet of paper."

"Why?"

"Just do it," she told him, wiggling her open fingers and waiting as she continued to study the drawing in front of her.

Wade passed her the writing materials, and she patted a corner of the sofa nearest her. "Sit down. Let's go over this again."

He hesitated for a moment, then dropped to the blue brocade settee, slouching against the medallion-shaped back. Callie quickly re-sketched the basics of Wade's original diagram on the new square of paper.

Lifting her gaze, she said, "Now tell me what happened."

"I already did," he told her with a frown that looked suspiciously like the beginnings of a pout.

"Tell me again. I want to know exactly what happened, who you saw, what everyone said, where everyone was standing. Every detail; don't skip anything, no matter how insignificant it might seem."

With a despondent sigh, he slid even farther down the back of the sofa. "Neville had been try-ing to buy my land from me for months, I told you that."

"Why was he so interested in your property?"

He hesitated and looked away.

She studied his profile, silently waiting for an answer.

Wade turned back to her, meeting and holding her gaze for so long, she almost squirmed.

"He thought there was a gold mine somewhere on my property, and he wanted it."

"Was there?"

"I suppose it doesn't much matter if there was or not," he answered vaguely. "Neville got it in his head that I had gold on my land, and he wanted to mine it and make a fortune." Wade took his hands out of his pockets and sat up a bit. "First, he started coming around as a friendly neighbor interested in talking about cattle and ranching. Soon after that he tried to buy my property, saying he wanted to expand his own business. When I turned down his initial offer he upped his bid."

"And then you turned him down again."

"Yep. His next offer was quite a bit higher than the other two, but it came with the underlying threat that I'd sell if I knew what was good for me. If I didn't, he said, bad things would start happening around the Circle M."

"Did they?"

"Oh, yeah. Within a week of sending Neville packing, I started finding fences cut, cattle missing—one of the watering holes was even poisoned. I lost a number of good steers headed for market before I figured out what was going on."

"What did you do?" Callie asked, incensed and horrified by the lengths Neville Young had gone to just for a strip of land that might or might not have harbored a gold mine.

"I rode over to Young's and warned him not to mess with my cattle again. That if he or any of his men were caught on my land, I'd send them home hanging over their saddles. Then I hired a dozen new hands to keep watch and ride guard along the fences. A couple of them were shot at, their horses spooked, but no one was hurt, and we never caught Young or his men on my property."

"And the destructive incidents stopped? No more cattle showed up missing or poisoned?"

Wade shook his head, one corner of his mouth lifting wryly. "There was no need. Somehow, Neville—or his whelp of a son, or one of his men—got into my house and stole the deed to my land."

Callie gasped.

"I didn't even know it until I received a letter from some St. Louis attorney Neville had hired to inform me that I was occupying privately owned property and had exactly forty-eight hours to pack up and get off or they'd send the law out to remove me."

"What did you do?"

"I went looking for my deed. I knew damn well I owned that land, fair and legal, and I wasn't giving it up without a fight. Not even to high-and-mighty Neville Young."

"But it was gone."

He nodded solemnly. "It was gone. I headed for the registrar's office to see if I could get a copy, since they keep all those sorts of records there. But the only thing they had on file concerning the Circle M was a deed in Young's name."

Wade swore, low and lethal. "The ink wasn't even dry on the cursed thing, and everyone acted like it had been there for a decade or more. I think Graves had something to do with switching the forged document for the original in my name."

"So it looked like Neville owned the land, and you were trespassing."

"That's right. Which is why I went over to Neville's house that night. I didn't think his underhanded ways would stand up in court, but I wanted my deed back." Wade gave a dry, humorless chuckle. "I wanted to hit him, give him a few belts to pay him back for what he'd done to me. But I had no intention of killing him. I'd have been happy to just get my papers back, and his forgery out of the county register."

"What happened once you got there? Did you go in the house at all?"

Shaking his head, he said, "Neville met me before I even got to the door. Brady and some hand

I'd never seen before came up behind me, stuck a pistol barrel against my spine, and took the Colts out of my gun belt."

Callie began to make notes.

"I didn't even get worked up over it because I spotted the sheriff standing beside Neville and figured he could help me get the whole mess straightened out. I started to tell him about the trouble I'd had at the ranch, my missing deed, and the one with Young's name on it replacing the original at the registrar's office."

Wade's tone lowered and turned flat. "I shouldn't have wasted my breath. Graves just wiped those pork sausage fingers under a couple of his flabby chins and told me that if Neville Young's name was on record at the county seat, then that was proof enough for him of who owned the land. Said if I wasn't off the Circle M in two days, he'd be over with a couple of deputies to drag me off, just like the lawyer's letter warned."

Sometime during the telling of the story, Callie had shifted farther off the edge of the chair. The hand holding the worn-down pencil stub moved to cover one of Wade's knees comfortingly.

He leaned forward now, too, agitated. His breath danced across Callie's cheeks, and his fingers gripped the wrist of her free hand.

"What happened next?" she prompted, indifferent to the closeness of their faces, the nearness of their bodies.

His eyes fluttered closed, as though to better recall the details of that night.

"I was furious. I wished Neville and Graves both to the devil. Instinctively I reached for one of my guns . . ." His fingers clenched, mimicking the motion he'd made that night. "But Brady had disarmed me. I was weaponless."

"And then . . ."

"And then Neville said something about being tired of talking to me. That all of this could have been avoided if I'd just accepted his offer to buy the land in the first place. He owned it all now, anyway, and had gotten what he wanted, the same as he always did."

Wade grimaced. "I remember the look on his face when he said that, like there had never been any doubt he'd control my land and the gold mine he thought was located there—it was only a matter of time and how far he'd have to go to get it."

Wade's eyes opened and he stared straight at Callie. "Neville turned to go back inside then, but Graves was still facing me. I heard a shot, so close it sounded like an explosion, and I thought I'd been hit. But Neville fell instead. There was a hole in his back the size of a silver dollar."

"Who shot him?"

"Brady. Brady shot his own father. Either that,

or the ranch hand, but the hand looked as shocked as Graves and I were.

"He stepped around me, gun still smoking in his hand, the bastard, and started yelling about how I'd killed his father. Before I could do more than blink, he cracked me on the skull with the butt of that still-hot revolver and started screaming for the sheriff to arrest me."

"But Graves had to have seen that Brady did it. He had to have known you were unarmed. Didn't he say anything, do anything?"

Wade shook his head miserably. "The only thing he did was check to make sure Neville was really dead, then stand there watching while Brady kicked the shit out of me. Oh, and he dragged me off to jail. Bleeding, slipping in and out of consciousness, with a couple of broken ribs, he hauled me into town and threw me in a cell to await trial. Nothing I said had any impact on him. Not even knowing the truth of what happened that night mattered to the son of a bitch."

"You think Brady bribed him, made it worth his while to keep quiet."

"I think Graves was a slimy jackal who didn't go out of his way very often to uphold the law. But, yes, I think Brady ended up bribing him somehow to keep him from telling the judge what he knew. Maybe they had the judge in their pocket, too, I don't know. I suppose it doesn't much matter at this point."

"But Lily was there, too. Upstairs, you said. Why didn't she come forward to tell what she'd witnessed?"

"Lily looked out for herself, and only for herself," he said as Callie made another notation on the paper in her lap. "I guess you'd have to, being in the type of business she was. I don't think she wanted to get involved at first, maybe for fear of what Brady Young would do to her—he had no qualms about shooting his own father in the back; God only knows what he'd have done to a two-bit whore who tried to cross him."

Callie flinched at his crass description of the mother of his child but said nothing.

"Then, when Lily thought of something she wanted and could use the information to get it, she decided to come forward."

"What did she want?" Callie asked.

A muscle in Wade's jaw ticked slightly and he looked away, fixing his gaze on something across the room.

"What?" she asked again. After all, it couldn't have been that terrible.

"She wanted me to marry her."

Callie blinked. Of all the things he might have said, she hadn't expected it to be anything even close to that.

"Marry you?" she repeated, embarrassed by the rasp of her voice around the words.

Wade seemed reluctant to say more, studiously

avoiding her gaze. "That's how Matthew . . . came about."

"Matthew? But didn't—" She'd been about to mention that babies usually came after the wedding vows, but in this case, she knew that to be untrue. And with a woman like Lily, things had never been very likely to be played out in proper order.

"She came to visit me in prison," Wade said by way of explanation. "We . . . spent a little time together before she told me why she was actually there."

"And why . . . um," she cleared her throat, "was that, exactly?"

"She wanted to stop working, I guess, leave the Painted Lady. And she thought the best way to do that would be to marry me and set up a home of her own."

"And you didn't want to marry a prostitute, is that it?" Callie snapped. She wasn't sure why that idea made her so angry, especially when the thought of Wade *wanting* to marry Lily had bothered her so much to begin with, for reasons she couldn't have explained even to herself.

"It's not that," he answered automatically, and then tempered his response with a bit more honesty. "I don't know if that was a part of my refusal or not; I'd never considered marriage at all before. Lily announcing that she'd seen Neville's murder that night and would tell the authorities if I agreed to marry her came so out of the blue, I hardly had time to take it all in. And if I'd known she would get so mad and run off the way she did, without telling anyone the truth of what she'd seen, I probably would have gone along with her scheme just to get out of that hellhole at Huntsville. But I didn't want to hurt her. I didn't want her to end up miserable because she'd married me—and forced me to marry her— for all the wrong reasons."

Damn him. That sounded so bloody noble, when Callie had been fully prepared to rake him over the coals for his shabby treatment of Lily.

Instead, he'd actually had her best interests at heart and refused to marry her even though it could have been the key to his very freedom.

It was a hard fact to wrap her mind around.

Callie glanced down at the paper in her lap, at the small stick figures she'd drawn, with names written beneath each. So far, she'd arranged Wade, Neville, and Sheriff Graves, Lily high behind them in a bedroom of the house, and Brady and the unnamed ranch hand Wade claimed had been there, as well.

"You still have Lily's letter, telling what happened that night, right?" She waited for an affirmative gesture from Wade. Though he'd never shown her the letter, she knew how protective he was of its contents and assumed he was either carrying the missive on his person or had hidden it somewhere in her house for safekeeping. "But it won't do you much good unless you have someone else who can testify that what she wrote is the truth."

Again, he nodded.

"Then we have to find the only other person who was there that night. The only other person besides Brady and yourself who isn't already dead."

Wade looked at her askance.

She held up the paper for him to see. Only one stick figure had a question mark beside it instead of a name.

"The hired hand," he uttered almost beneath his breath.

"The hired hand. All we have to do is find him. Convince him to go to Sheriff Walker, and make it worthwhile for him to do so. If we can do that, we may just be able to clear your name."

Chapter Nine

Wade stared at the picture in his hand, his fingers so tight, one corner of the paper crinkled. The noise echoed through the room, breaking the almost deathly quiet that Callie's shocking pronouncement had produced.

He looked from the diagram to her, to the diagram, then back to her. Could she be right? Could the unnamed man Wade had seen only that once be the solution to his problems?

It seemed too easy to be true.

And then Wade realized it *was* too easy to be true. How in God's name were they supposed to find this stranger who had shown up only long enough to witness Neville Young's murder and Wade's beating and then—for all Wade knew—disappear again?

With a muffled curse, he shot to his feet and balled the brittle paper in his angry fist. "It's useless. No way in hell are we going to be able to track that fellow down. He could be all the way to Stockton or Philadelphia by now."

"But what if he's not? What if he's still in Purgatory?"

Wade spun around, only to find Callie's gaze following his quick, caged movements.

"What are the chances of that?" he demanded with a derisive snort.

"What are the chances of you breaking out of prison and keeping the law from finding you for this long?" Callie returned, a hint of annoyance coloring her words. "This may be your only chance to prove your innocence, Wade. It may be a long shot, I admit. But wouldn't you rather take the chance and consider the possibility of finding someone who can testify on your behalf than sit around here waiting for the posse to track you down?"

Wade ground his teeth together until his jaw ached. How could she sit there so primly and tell him to bet everything on such a lousy hand? She didn't know what it was like to be accused, tried, convicted, and thrown in a squalid pit like Huntsville for a crime she hadn't committed. She didn't know what it was like to be on the run, to look over her shoulder, to live in fear every minute of every day. To not even be able to take her son home and be a proper parent because she was still wanted by the law.

What did she know about risk, dammit?

But she was looking at him with such wide, guileless eyes. Out of a face that could make angels weep. And it occurred to him that somewhere along the way, she'd stopped weighing the possibility that he'd done what he was accused of and simply believed he'd been wrongly imprisoned. Even more, she was trying to help him clear his name.

God in heaven, she believed in him. And he couldn't recollect a single memory of the last time anyone had done that.

Taking a deep breath, he closed his eyes and willed himself to relax. His jaw loosened and his fingers flexed.

"I can't say that I think this has a chance in hell of working out, but if you think it's worth a try, I don't suppose I'm in much of a position to argue with you. So where do you think this man might be? Where should I start looking?"

"I think the most logical place to begin is the Triple Y. If he was working for Neville or Brady a year and a half ago, there's a fair to middling chance he's still on the payroll there. But *you're* not going to be the one to go looking for him. Besides the fact that you're on the run and would likely be shot the minute you stepped outside this house, you're *especially* unwelcome at the Young ranch."

She stood to face him, smoothing her skirts and linking her hands together at her waist. "I, however, have known the Youngs since Nathan and I moved here. Brady and Nathan are the same age, and Brady has always treated me as a bit of a sister. He would think nothing of my dropping by to say hello."

The ache in Wade's jaw returned full force, along with a pounding in his head and a roiling in his gut that he didn't think had anything to do with Callie's earlier attempt at fixing breakfast.

The very thought of her being anywhere near Brady Young sent his blood boiling. The idea of that bastard so much as looking at Callie, let alone laying a hand on her, made Wade see red.

He hadn't contemplated murder eighteen months ago when he'd faced Neville Young with a gun at his back, but he was damn well considering it now.

"No. Absolutely not." He took a menacing step forward and curled his fingers into his palms to keep from reaching out and shaking some sense into her. "They'll be throwing ice cream socials in hell before I'll allow you to walk into that pit of vipers."

"Would you rather have your likeness on a WANTED poster for the rest of your life? I'll be fine, Wade. Brady won't suspect a thing if I drop by with a plate of cookies or a pie."

"He's obviously never sampled your baking skills," he muttered, only half to himself.

Callie's lips thinned in annoyance, but she otherwise ignored his muffled remark. "In fact," she went on, "he'll probably bend over backwards to accommodate me."

"Why?" Wade demanded caustically. "Because he fancies himself in love with you?"

He didn't know how close that taunt came to the truth until he saw the expression on Callie's face.

"I wouldn't call it love but he's certainly never made a secret of his . . . interest in me."

Wade turned his head to one side and swore, low and foul. "All the more reason for you to stay the hell away from him," he said, turning back to her. "You don't want to give a man like that any reason to come calling, Callie. If he gets ideas in his head, you might not be able to discourage him later. You could get hurt."

"Just let me go over there. I'll pay a call early in the day, when the housekeeper is there and plenty of hands are working close by."

"Dammit, Callie, what do I have to do to convince you of how dangerous Brady Young is? He shot his own father in the back, for Christ's sake! There's no telling what he might do to you."

"He's not going to do anything to me. There's

no reason for him to. And, frankly, I don't see that you have much say in the matter. I can visit anyone I like."

At that, Wade's eyes narrowed to slits. "Are you so sure about that? You *are* my hostage, after all."

"Am I?" She raised a brow of her own, which only served to draw his attention to her cornflower-blue eyes and the heart shape of her soft, lovely face.

"That was the plan," he said in a low voice.

When Callie spoke again, her words were pitched as soft as his own, and he couldn't help but notice the slight hitch of her chest as she struggled to breathe normally.

"And I suppose you expect me to quake with fright," she said. "Well, I've got news for you, Wade Mason, I'm not afraid of you. I might have been at first, but I imagine if you were going to hurt me or Matthew, you'd have done it by now.

Wade's own heart was pounding like an Indian chant. He took a step forward and laid his hands lightly over her bare, delicate forearms. "How can you be so certain?" he rasped. "I might even now be making plans to ravish you."

Callie laughed, but the sound came out stilted and breathless. Her tongue darted across her dry, but ever so tempting lips. "I'm sure you are, but I doubt you intend to use force."

He stared at her, stunned. "You mean to tell

me you wouldn't object if I kissed you? Right here, right now?"

"You've already kissed me. In the kitchen, remember?"

"Oh, I remember. It's not something I'm ever likely to forget. But if I kissed you again, it wouldn't be gentle, or chaste, or nearly as innocent as the last time."

She swallowed, and he saw the cords of her throat ripple with the gesture. "What . . . would it be like?" she ventured, refusing to meet his eyes.

Sliding one hand up the length of her arm, across her shoulder and collarbone, and over the slim smoothness of her neck, he used the side of his thumb to tip her head back, forcing her to face him.

She blinked those fathomless blue eyes, looking pure and so damn beautiful, he ached with it. He wanted her more than he wanted his next breath, and yet he knew that to touch her was to taint her with the turmoil of his own past and present circumstances.

Still, he couldn't quite help himself from leaning forward and taking her mouth with his own.

There was no brush of butterfly wings this time, no light, subtle touching of only lips.

This time, their kiss was fiery hot and all consuming. His tongue delved deep, and Callie never made a move to stop him. Instead, she let her mouth fall open beneath his own, her fingertips digging into the flesh of his upper arms before traveling upward and clasping his neck.

Her hands feathered through the hair at his nape and sent a shiver down his spine, a slither of need that thickened as it descended, pooling in his groin.

Did Callie feel the same? Could she possibly be experiencing the same heat, the same headiness, the same want and throbbing desire that raced through his veins?

If there was a God in heaven, she did.

If there was a God in heaven, Wade would be a very, very lucky man, indeed.

Releasing her lips, coming up for air, he dug his hands into her hair, holding her head immobile while he gazed into her blue eyes clouded with what he hoped was desire.

"Tell me how you feel, Callie," he murmured softly, stroking the feather-soft flesh of her cheeks with the pads of his thumbs. "Tell me."

"Warm," she whispered, so softly, he had to lean closer to hear. "Tingly. I tingle all over, like little caterpillars are crawling beneath my skin. Especially my lips and . . . lower."

She looked down at the last, which only served to intrigue him more.

"How low? Tell me where."

His fingers continued to knead the back of her head beneath the silky strands of her dark chestnut hair, his thumbs drawing circles just beneath the high lines of her cheekbones.

"Tell me, Callie. I want to know."

She drew in a shaky breath, fidgeted a bit, then said, "My . . . breasts. They feel . . . heavy and tight."

"Like you might want me to touch them?" He moved a hand from the nape of her neck to the slope of one breast, cupping its weight in his palm. "Stroke them . . . maybe tease the tips?" Through the thin material of her gown, he did just that.

She sucked in a startled breath and tried to pull away, but Wade wouldn't allow it. He wrapped one well-muscled arm around her waist and pulled her close, holding her against the hard line of his body. Making sure she felt just how much he craved her, in every way a man can crave a woman.

"Do you like that, Callie? Does it make you want to be kissed again?"

Hesitating only a fraction of a second, her head bobbed once, slowly.

He grinned and swooped in for another pulse-lashing kiss. His fingers continued to fondle her firm, now beaded nipple beneath her bodice, eliciting moans of pleasure as his tongue dipped and stroked. He traced the line of her teeth, sucking gently, and urging Callie to do the same.

Shy and modest, she remained passive at first,

letting him do what he would while her fingers curled like talons into his back. But after several long, sensual moments, curiosity won out and she began to experiment.

She moved her own tongue, running it along his tentatively, then with more confidence when her actions made him groan. Instead of staying bunched in his shirt, her hands began to wander lower, past the waistband of his trousers, and she pressed as close as she could get along the front of his body. Her breasts flattened against his chest, the hand that was doing such wicked, wonderful things to her nipple trapped between them. And lower, the hard bulge of his manhood ground into the very spot that was burning and throbbing most.

Changing the pattern of their kiss from firm and demanding to softer, lighter pecks, Wade's scratchy, passion-laden voice broke through her muddled thoughts.

"Let me take you to bed, Callie. Let me carry you upstairs and make love to you."

Licking her raw, trembling lips, she considered all the repercussions of what he was suggesting. Could she go to bed with him? Let him touch her the way only a husband should touch his wife?

His gentle brown eyes gazed down at her, and she didn't think she would ever feel about another man the way she felt about Wade Mason at this very moment.

She opened her mouth to tell him just that, to ask him to please do what he'd offered—to carry her upstairs and make love to her. In Wade's arms she felt like a beautiful, sensual woman, and she longed to revel in this new and heady sensation.

But just as she would have capitulated and sent her wanton soul straight to the devil, her ears rang with the high-pitched squall of baby Matthew waking from his nap and demanding both a new diaper and a warm bottle to fill his empty tummy.

Wade's eyes drifted closed, his lips moving in what she thought might have been a curse. Callie felt her own heart dip with disappointment . . . and to be perfectly honest, a touch of relief. No matter how much she might want it, the idea of being with Wade *that way* made her supremely nervous.

"If this is a prime example of the trials of fatherhood, I'm thinking I should reconsider," he grumbled, resting his forehead against hers.

"Too late. Babies really do make the best chaperones, don't they?" She forced herself to smile bravely, and stepped away from him. "Besides, it's better that we were interrupted before things . . . went too far."

As she turned for the stairs, Wade snagged her

elbow and whirled her back to face him. "I hope you don't think this is over," he warned. "We may have been interrupted, but that doesn't mean we can't pick up later where we left off. And we will, Callie girl. Believe me. There's no way in hell we won't be playing this out to its logical conclusion. Eventually."

She swallowed hard. *Eventually* was exactly what she was afraid of. That, and falling in love with a wanted man.

Chapter Ten

Early the next morning, Callie dressed in one of her better everyday gowns—a light blue calico print with tiny yellow flowers—and adjusted a wide-brimmed straw hat over the loose twist of her upswept hair.

Matthew had already been fed and changed and was lying on a blanket on the parlor floor, trying to work his toes free of the long dressing gown he was wearing.

She'd just finished dropping a few extra coins to the bottom of her drawstring reticule when Wade came into the room. He wore another of her brother's snug shirts, this one a solid shade of butternut that added color to skin that had gone too pale after all those months in prison.

"Going somewhere?" he asked, taking in her

hat, the satchel at her wrist, and the worn tips of walking boots sticking out from beneath her skirts.

She'd known this moment would come, that Wade would be unhappy to realize she was going through with her plan despite his disapproval, and had rehearsed what she would say to him.

"Yes, actually, I'm going into town, just as we discussed."

"Discussed and decided against, you mean," he retorted with a scowl.

"You decided against. I still think it's a good idea. The best chance we have of finding the ranch hand who was there the night Neville Young was killed. Speaking of which," she rushed on before he could try once again to dissuade her, "you need to tell me what this man looks like, so I can ask Brady about him—subtly, of course—and maybe watch for him while I'm at the Triple Y."

"You're more stubborn than a two-headed mule, aren't you?" His brow was still wrinkled with displeasure, his arms crossed mutinously over his broad chest.

"I think this is a rather generous favor I'm willing to do for you. You should be thanking me."

"Thanking you? Brady Young is a conscienceless sidewinder. I won't rest easy for one minute knowing you're anywhere near him."

His obvious concern softened something deep

in her heart and she smiled wistfully. Taking a few steps toward him, she raised a hand to his cheek and stroked his firm, rough jaw.

"I'll be fine, Wade, I promise. And I won't be gone any longer than necessary, so you won't have to worry for more than a few hours. Now tell me what you can remember about this stranger."

She felt a muscle in his jaw tick as his teeth ground together in indecision. Then he closed his eyes, trying to recall details from a dark night eighteen months earlier.

"He was about Brady's height, maybe a little taller. Dark hair; brown or black, I'm not sure which. I don't know what color his eyes were, but he had a mustache at the time."

Wade's eyes flashed open. "And a scar on his right cheek. I remember it flashing kind of silver in the moonlight and thinking he probably got it in a knife fight. He looked like a rough sort, used to busting his way out of saloons and brawling over women."

"Dark hair, possibly a mustache, scar on his right cheek." With a brief nod, she moved across the room, away from Wade, to scoop Matthew up off the floor.

Her parasol rested in a tall, porcelain, vaselike receptacle near the door, and she retrieved it while struggling to keep Matthew from yanking the fabric roses free of her hatband.

"We won't be long. It's only a mile or so into town, and then another quarter of a mile to the Young place. Is there anything you need from town, as long as we'll be passing through?"

"You're taking Matthew?"

She wedged the handle of the fringed umbrella under one arm and pried Matthew's tiny fingers from the flowers before he ruined them. "Of course I'm taking him. He always comes with me when I go into town."

Wade studied her for a moment, his eyes narrowing. Then he moved purposely forward and snatched the baby out of her arms. "Not this time."

"What are you doing?" she exclaimed, keeping one hand clutched in the long hem of Matthew's gown as Wade took a wide step back.

"Matthew stays with me," he told her shortly.

"What?" She couldn't believe what she was hearing. Couldn't believe Wade would snatch Matthew from her that way.

"If you're determined to pay Brady Young a visit, then you can go, but my son stays with me."

"I'm not leaving him here." He'd never been away from her a day in his life.

"Good. Then you won't be going to the Triple Y, after all."

Callie frowned, wondering if that had been his plan all along. "I am going to town, and Matthew is coming with me."

"He's my son, and I say he's not. Besides, you're my prisoner, remember? How can I be sure you won't tell someone about me while you're gone, or that you'll even come back, unless I have a bit of leverage to ensure your co-operation?"

"You're using a three-month-old infant to blackmail me?"

His mouth tightened in obvious distaste, but he nodded his head affirmatively. "I guess I am."

"You're despicable," Callie whispered.

"I'm desperate."

The minutes ticked by as she stood there, contemplating her options.

She could stay home, of course, but then when would she be able to meet with Father Ignacio and begin the process of Matthew's adoption? And she might still be wary of Wade and confused about this entire situation, but she couldn't help beginning to believe in his innocence. She didn't want Matthew's father to be regarded as a murderer, and they might never get another opportunity to locate this mysterious ranch hand or succeed in finding even a scrap of evidence in Wade's favor.

Despite how safe he might feel at the moment, locked up here in her house, that bubble would burst eventually. It had to, because she doubted the posse would give up until they had Wade in custody once more.

She could argue vehemently with Wade over whether or not she should be allowed to take Matthew with her to town. After all, she always took him with her. In fact, people's curiosity would likely be piqued if she showed up in town *without* him.

But from the locked square of Wade's jaw and the unbudging glint in his eyes, she suspected she would have more luck convincing him to put up a bright, multicolored flag alerting the posse to his whereabouts.

Which left the third and final option: leave Matthew home with Wade and pay a call on Brady Young just as she'd planned.

His threat to hold Matthew "hostage" held no weight whatsoever now that she knew him better. No man would risk his life and freedom to escape prison and find his son only to harm the child. And he'd been nothing but concerned and solicitous every time she'd watched him interact with the boy. She would just have to trust him to uphold his end of their deal and not run off with Matthew.

Her tightly clenched fingers loosened from Matthew's dressing gown and she retreated a step. "Fine. You watch him while I'm away, then. He last ate about an hour ago, and I just changed him. You'll likely have to feed and change him again, though, and see him down for his nap."

135

She fixed him with a doubtful glance. "Is that something you think you can manage?"

The expression he cast back at her was scathing. "I think I can handle caring for a young child, Callie. I know where everything is."

Oh, yes, but he'd never been alone with a three-month-old, rather demanding baby boy before. If Matthew took it into his head to throw one of his famed tantrums, Wade would be climbing the walls.

Then again, maybe being alone with Matthew was just what Wade needed. He wanted to be a real father, take Matthew away from her to raise on his own. . . . Perhaps getting a true taste of what it took to care for a child by one's self would actually work in her favor.

She couldn't say she was completely confident with the idea of leaving the two of them alone, but it seemed like her only plan of action at the moment.

"All right," she said, trying not to sound reluctant. "I won't be long."

Walking away from Wade, standing there cradling a happily gurgling Matthew, was one of the hardest things she'd ever done in her life.

She wasn't even quite sure why, except that it reminded her a little too vividly of Wade's grand scheme of clearing his name and taking Matthew away to live with him. Permanently. When that happened—*if* that happened—images like the one behind her, still burned into her brain like a brand, would be commonplace. And Callie would be visible nowhere in that picture.

That thought caused her fingers to tighten on the brass knob in her hand and her breathing to shorten painfully.

Without looking back, too much of a coward to face the tender father-son tableau again, she opened the front door and stepped out onto the wide, whitewashed porch.

The morning sun was bright overhead, and Callie knew she had a hot day ahead of her. As she made her way down the steps and across the yard, she popped open the parasol and lifted it over her head to shade her from the powerful rays, and then started off toward town at a brisk pace.

The sooner she got there, the sooner she could get back.

Her next thought—*and the less time Wade and Matthew would be alone together*—flashed through her mind before she could stop it.

She planned to go to the Triple Y and talk to Brady Young, but first a quick stop at the Purgatory Home for Adoptive Children was in order.

Chapter Eleven

"Señorita Quinn, what a lovely surprise." Father Ignacio crossed the wide yard where dozens of children ran and played, reaching for Callie's hands. He squeezed them lightly and gifted her with a bright smile. "Where is our little *niño* Mateo this morning, eh?"

Of course Father Ignacio would notice that Matthew wasn't with her. She shouldn't be surprised. She'd be lucky if everyone she met today didn't ask, considering she never came into town without him.

"He's . . . staying with a friend while I run a few errands." She created the lie quickly, and prayed God wouldn't strike her dead for telling a falsehood to a priest on holy ground.

"Ah, I see. It is good that you have some time

138

for yourself. You take such excellent care of that boy. A better *madre* he could not ask for."

Callie couldn't help but be warmed by his effusive compliment. "Thank you. He's a very easy child to love."

Her gaze moved to the full yard behind him. "How are the children today?"

Glancing back over his shoulder, his pleased expression remained as he said, "Oh, *bien*. Very well indeed. This is a much happier place now that many of Purgatory's fine citizens come by to visit so often. To bring new clothes and gifts and sweets for the children. And many little ones have found wonderful homes, with Señora and Señor Walker working so hard to place them."

"I'm glad," Callie responded, and meant it.

She had always felt sorry for the children consigned to the orphanage, and though many times she'd considered offering her assistance, she never had for fear it would hurt too much to see all of those parentless and homeless children in one place. Or worse, that Nathan's oft-spoken fear would become a reality, and she would end up dragging them all home with her.

But she slipped a few dollars into the church's poor box whenever she was able, and had been pleased when Regan Doyle—now Mrs. Clayton Walker, the new sheriff's wife—had begun to show such an interest in the home and gotten the other townspeople interested, as well.

Callie herself had even begun to get involved—until Lily asked her to become Matthew's guardian and she'd suddenly been immersed in caring for the newborn baby all on her own.

Nathan had already been in California by then, though she would have dearly appreciated his help in those first few hair-raising weeks of unexpected motherhood. As it was, she'd cursed his absence many a time in those days.

Drawing her attention away from the playing children, Father Ignacio asked, "You look troubled, my child. Is there anything I can do to help?"

Her mind shifted immediately to her reason for being there. "As a matter of fact, Father Ignacio, there is. Is there somewhere we could speak privately?"

"*Sí*. Of course, of course. Come with me, my dear."

Turning, he led her through a nearby door of the orphanage and down a short hall leading to the vestibule of the church. They moved to a small room at the back of the church where the priest changed his vestments before mass and spoke with parishioners who required counsel, but not necessarily confession.

Callie fell into the latter grouping.

When Father Ignacio waved her toward a chair, she smoothed her skirts and lowered herself carefully to the hard seat. Her closed parasol leaned against one leg as she removed her bonnet and laid it safely on her lap.

"Now, Callie, dear, tell me what it is that puts such a shadow in your eyes."

"There's nothing wrong, Father," she said carefully, as she considered how to go about making this request. "I guess I'm feeling a bit insecure about Matthew. With him growing so fast, and me not being his real mother, you know."

At least she hadn't been forced to concoct another lie. She cast her gaze toward the floor, afraid those very real words would cause equally real tears to pool in her eyes.

Shifting closer, the priest gave her hand a comforting pat. "There is no need to fear, my dear. Mateo adores you. You are the only mother he knows, and you will always be the only mother he loves."

At that, Callie's eyes did begin to prickle painfully, and she blinked several times to keep from embarrassing herself.

"I'm sure you're right, Father Ignacio, but . . . I know that you deal with this sort of thing quite often and was wondering if you might help me adopt Matthew legally. I'd like to be his true mother, have him carry my name. When he gets older, I want to have papers to show him that I became his mother officially and by choice, not just because he was forced on me by his birth mother's death."

She was so focused on getting the priest to agree with her that she'd forgotten to take a breath. Now that she'd reached the end of her plea, she stopped, stared desperately at Father Ignacio, and inhaled deeply.

"You want to adopt him," the father repeated. "As though you had come here looking for a child and taken him from the orphanage into your own home."

"Yes, exactly." Relief that he understood her request washed over her. "Can you help me do that, Father?"

For a long moment, the priest merely watched her, and the air hitched in her lungs.

And then a peaceful smile spread across the older man's dark-skinned face. "I do not see why we cannot do this for you, my child. It is a small thing, and if it calms your worries to have a certificate saying such, then I will be happy to comply. When would you like to complete the paperwork?" he asked.

She sat back, somewhat stunned at Father Ignacio's swift acquiescence and almost blissfully relieved that she would soon have a legal document to hold against Wade's threats to take Matthew away from her.

"Right away," she answered promptly. "Now, if it's possible."

The father stood and began shuffling through the drawers of the small secretary behind his backwards-turned chair. "I do not see why that should be a problem. We try to keep things simple here at the home, the better to place more children more easily. Ah, here it is."

He returned to his seat, pulling the chair around so that he sat facing the desk. Finding his fountain pen, he tapped the end to his chin, thinking.

"Señora and Señor Walker are kind enough to keep me supplied with the documents we use for adoptions, since each has to be written out by hand. Then I need only fill in a few names and have the new parents sign, and another child has a home."

Father Ignacio beamed with obvious pride at the efficiency of the system. Callie didn't blame him. Every child should have a proper, loving home, and a rather large number had gotten just that, thanks to the efforts of the priest.

"Now, this should not take long at all. We know the child's name, of course. . . ." He slowly sounded out Matthew's name as he wrote the letters, complete with flourishes on the capital *M* and lowercase *t*s.

"We do not know the father's name, so shall we use Señorita Lily's last name for the *niño,* or would you prefer to leave it simply Mateo?"

Callie knew the father's name. In fact, she

143

knew the father. But the entire purpose of having these papers drawn up was to keep Wade Mason from taking Matthew away from her.

"Matthew White would be fine," she answered, tamping down her guilt.

As Father Ignacio continued to write, he spoke almost to himself. "And we know your name . . . Señorita Callie Quinn. Would you like your brother's name on the document as well?"

Since Nathan hadn't been in Purgatory when she'd taken Matthew in, and she hadn't discussed any of this with him, she didn't think it would be wise to unwittingly make him one of Matthew's legal guardians.

She shook her head.

"Well, then, I will just sign here at the bottom . . ." He scrawled his name in large, looping letters.

"And you will sign here . . ." He slid the papers across the desk toward her, tapping the spot where she was to place her signature.

She did so, and then sat back with an almost audible sigh of relief. That relief lasted for all of three seconds, until even more niggling doubts began to intrude upon her conscience.

The priest handed her the adoption certificate, a wide smile creasing his face.

She took it, letting her fingers run over the thick, yellowish vellum. "This is all I need, then? Matthew is mine?"

The priest smiled gently and patted the back of her hand. "Mateo has always been yours, my dear Callie. But, *sí,* he is yours now, in the eyes of both the law and the church."

"What about . . ." Her voice caught, and she had to take a moment to settle herself. "What about Matthew's father? What if he should come back someday, looking for his child?"

An image of Wade, standing in the middle of her parlor cradling Matthew, flashed through her mind, followed quickly by a spurt of fear.

"We do not know who Mateo's father is," Father Ignacio said kindly. "Señorita Lily did not tell us that."

But Callie knew. And he was her biggest concern at the moment. She couldn't tell Father Ignacio the truth, however, so she needed to find another way to extract an answer.

Carefully folding the adoption papers, she placed them in her reticule and retied the strings. "But what if Lily did tell someone? What if the father, or even one of the father's relatives, should come to Purgatory looking to claim Matthew? To take him away from me?"

"No one is going to take him away from you, my dear." The hand covering hers tightened reassuringly. "If someone were to come to town looking to claim little Mateo, they would have to prove they are truly blood relatives of the *niño.* But you are the one who raised him. You are his mother. Even when he is older, Mateo will not leave you, no matter who comes for him. And now these papers say that the orphanage and church both see you as Mateo's sole guardian."

That wasn't the answer Callie had come here for. She'd wanted the priest to say that with the adoption certificate in her possession, Lily herself couldn't take Matthew away from her, even if she rose from her grave.

But Wade didn't need to know that Father Ignacio's response to her question had been less than satisfying. Callie could still use the documents to convince Wade he could never take the child away from her. And unless he succeeded at clearing his name in the very near future and began asking around—or hired a lawyer to ask the proper questions for him—the papers might be enough to save her.

They would have to be. Callie didn't see any other options open to her, and it was too frightening to consider that Wade might actually be able to take Matthew from her.

She would take the documents home and hide them somewhere safe until she needed them—if she needed them. They would be her ace in the hole, her trump card, should Wade try to remove Matthew from her care.

And if all else failed, she would simply scream bloody murder.

Chapter Twelve

Where the hell was that woman?

And why wouldn't the kid stop screaming?!

Wade clamped his hands over his ears and prayed for Matthew to cease his caterwauling. Or, barring that, for Wade himself to be struck stone cold deaf.

He'd fed his son—twice, and once when Matthew hadn't been too keen on keeping the teat in his mouth. Wade's shirt was already beginning to smell like spoiled milk.

He'd changed him three times—not a job he cared to repeat, thank you very much. The squares of cloth had only been wet two of those times; the third, it'd been brown and kind of runny. He shuddered at the repulsive—not to mention smelly—memory. And if the boy was

147

wet again, he could just sit there soaking in his own juices until Callie got home.

Where the hell was she?

The hands—and now two pillows from the sofa—on either side of his head did little to staunch the high-pitched cries that threatened to shatter his eardrums.

With a less than mild curse, he threw down the tapestry squares and strode to where Matthew lay on his back, squalling like a cat with its tail caught in a meat grinder.

"All right, kid, that's enough." He raised his voice until he thought Matthew could hear him over his own wailing. "Dammit, this is your father speaking, and I said that's enough."

Bending down, he swooped the baby into his arms and lifted him to one shoulder. "Why are you doing this? Callie's going to be back any time now—" She'd *better* be back soon, or Wade would say to hell with who might be watching and head out after her. There was only so much a man could take.

"Callie . . . I guess you consider her your mama . . . she doesn't think I can take care of you properly, and if she hears you screeching like this when she gets home, she'll figure she was right all along."

Amazingly, the child seemed to be calming down a bit—just a bit though. He was still sobbing, his little chest hitching, his bottom lip quivering, and tiny tears trailing down from his red and swollen eyes.

Damn, but Matthew looked downright pathetic, and if Callie got a gander at him, she was going to tan Wade's hide.

Wade began to bounce, mimicking a motion he'd witnessed Callie use on more than one occasion to hush Matthew when he'd begun to get worked up. Swaying up and down and from side to side made Wade feel like an idiot, but if he thought it would work, he'd hop on one foot singing "Sweet Betsy from Pike."

The idea of singing hadn't entered his mind before, but now . . . well, he couldn't look more ridiculous than he already did, could he?

Wracking his brain for a decent tune, he began to hum. Then, when he realized he'd begun to sing a song meant to lull cattle to sleep on the trail, he figured it might work just as well on an ornery infant.

As Callie climbed the porch steps and approached the front door, she thought she heard singing. A lullaby of some sort, it sounded like.

Unless someone had dropped by while she'd been gone, which was highly doubtful, it could only be Wade humming the soft tune. But even though her logical mind processed that information, she still hesitated to believe it. Wade hadn't struck her as the lullaby sort. Frankly—

and perhaps a bit cynically of her—she'd expected him to keep Matthew alive, and that was all.

Sleepy winks of light along the far skyline, Time for millin' cattle to be still, drifted to her as her hand turned on the knob and she stepped into the house.

Yah-ho, a mol-la holiday, So settle down, ye cattle, till the morning.

The sight that greeted her stole her breath. Wade was slouched in a corner of the settee, one of his long, tapered legs crossed over the opposite knee, a peacefully dozing Matthew snuggled belly-down on his chest. Matthew's face was turned toward her, the little mouth pink and slack, a narrow line of baby saliva dribbling down his chin to widen the already wet spot spreading on the breast of Wade's shirt.

When she finally found her voice, all she could think to say was, "You're singing to him about cows?"

Wade raised his head and glanced in her direction, then lifted a finger to his lips. "Shh," he mouthed. Then, so low she could barely hear him, he said, "It's not a song *about* cows, it's a song you sing *to* cows. To settle them on the trail."

Her nose crinkled as she studied the big man cradling the tiny baby. That image bothered her enough, but to think that Wade equated his son with lowing cattle on the way to market was almost too much to bear.

"You're not on the trail, and Matthew is not a cow," she insisted, marching forward with the intention of tearing the child out of his embrace.

Before she could reach him, however, Wade held out an arm—and stuck out a foot—to keep her back. "I just got him settled down," he told her calmly. "Don't you go waking him now."

Standing there somewhat stunned, she let her arms fall to her sides. Why was it that the more time Wade spent with Matthew, the less she felt like an adequate mother? He had such a way with the baby; the right touch, the right speech patterns . . . the right blood, directly linking them together.

Her fingers drifted down along the strings of the reticule hanging from her wrist and let them tighten around the pouch that held the only thing that brought her even a fraction of security—the adoption certificate.

He'd taken fine care of Matthew, and even gotten him to drift off to sleep. Fine. She should be grateful. She should thank him for giving her this much needed time to herself. She could catch up on . . . things. Cleaning, laundry, correspondence. Perhaps she'd even lock herself away in her room and read a book, something she hadn't done in the three months since she'd brought Matthew home with her.

Taking a deep breath, she stepped back from father and son and made herself go about the mundane tasks of hanging up her hat and putting away her parasol.

Once that was accomplished, she turned to face Wade once again and smoothed the bodice of her dress. "Well, then, if you don't need me, I guess I'll go about my business."

The words came out just as angry and resentful as she felt, but she hated that her voice conveyed those feelings to Wade. He didn't need to know how threatened she felt by his presence, his ability to care for his son.

Looking like he wanted to say something, he glanced down at the baby sound asleep against his chest, glanced at her, then nodded.

As though she needed his permission, she thought waspishly, letting her heels click a staccato rhythm as she crossed the hardwood floor and headed for the second story of the house.

Once in her room, she changed out of her town gown and walking boots into a dress and shoes more suitable for working around the house. She had laundry to do, livestock to feed, and supper to start. Not to mention that tonight was Matthew's bath night.

She could let that pass, of course, but after leaving him in Wade's care all afternoon, Callie *wanted* to bathe the child, if only to establish that she really was Matthew's prime parental figure.

She fed him, changed him, bathed him, put him to bed each evening, and just because Wade had survived a single day of caring for the three-month-old did not mean he was going to make a decent father . . . or take her place as Matthew's mother.

With that thought to shore her resolve, she made her way back downstairs, through the sitting room where Matthew continued to nap in Wade's arms, and into the kitchen.

In one corner sat a basket of dirty clothes and linens that had been piling up for a week. Not to mention several soiled diapers that were in great need of a good scrubbing.

Starting a fire in the cookstove, she put on several pots of water to boil. With the basket clutched beneath one arm against her hip and a bar of strong lye soap, she headed outside. Setting up the tub and washboard, she began separating out the items that needed immediate attention. Just in case she didn't get around to washing all of the laundry, which was quite likely when it came to finishing chores and caring for Matthew at the same time.

Of course, she might not have to care for Matthew this evening, now might she? After all, he was sound asleep in his father's arms, showing no signs of needing her at all.

And she *wasn't* bitter, Callie insisted when she

stopped to consider the direction of her thoughts. Merely . . . annoyed.

Returning to the kitchen, she carried one pot after another of boiling water out to the washtub and rolled up her sleeves.

An hour later, she had a dozen clean diapering cloths hanging on the line. When the back door opened and Wade appeared in the shadows, she was on her knees, sweat dripping from her face and dampening the front of her gown between her breasts.

The minute she spotted him standing there, just inside the doorway, carefully hidden from prying eyes, holding Matthew, who greedily sucked on a new bottle, the hands she had wrapped around a bedsheet slipped and her knuckles rapped all the way down the hard metal washboard.

She swore beneath her breath. *Merciful heavens, but that hurt.* And she hated the effect this man had on her, causing her lungs to hitch and every rational thought in her head to turn as murky as the used water in the tub before her.

"You should have told me you planned to wash," he said, keeping his voice soft enough that it wouldn't travel farther than her own ears. "I'd have helped you carry water and such."

Callie wiped the back of one hand across her damp, heated forehead, wishing for probably the first time in her life that she looked more presentable.

All for a man who was wanted by the law and trying to steal her child away from her.

She looked at the chunk of soap in her palm and decided it must be the lye. The eye-watering pungency and earlier malodor of Matthew's dirty, day-old diapers had curdled her brain.

Her apparent loss of common sensibilities, added to the still smarting memory of Wade snuggling baby Matthew, easily combined to further darken her already dire mood.

"I'm certainly capable of washing dresses and linens by myself," she snapped.

Her remark seemed to catch him off guard. "Of course you are," he said carefully. "I just meant that I'd have been more than happy to help you once Matthew woke up." He shifted the baby a bit but didn't let the nipple of the bottle slip even a fraction from Matthew's eagerly slurping mouth.

He sounded so amenable and sincere, Callie felt a twinge of guilt. More than a twinge, and she didn't like it.

"I'm fine," she said, tempering her next response. "Thank you, though." When he continued to stand there, watching her, she made herself turn back to the washing. "I won't be much longer."

A few drawn-out seconds ticked by; then he

gave a silent nod, stepped back, and closed the door behind him.

Callie sat back on her heels and blew out a breath, which fanned the straggling pieces of hair about her face. She considered submerging her head in the bucket before her just to cool down. And considering the wash water was still hot enough to give off spirals of steam, that was really saying something.

Why was it that one look, one smile, one nod from that man sent her into palpitations? She didn't even particularly like him, given his desire to steal Matthew away from her.

But her mind and her body were at odds over whether to kick him out of her house . . . or drag him into her bed.

And she was ever so afraid her body was winning.

Chapter Thirteen

As soon as the door closed behind him, Wade leaned back against the heavy wood and squeezed his eyes closed. "Jesus, Mary, and Joseph," he muttered, trying to get a handle on his labored breathing.

"Did you see that, kid? Your mother was washing your diapers. With water. A lot of water."

His eyes popped open as the image behind them grew too intense. Too erotic.

"A lot of water," he said again. "And not all of it stayed in the basin."

He left off there, not wanting to get into a discussion with his three-month-old son about how water tended to soak through clothing and highlight—on women, especially—certain parts of the anatomy. Certain parts—on women—that beaded and became hard, poking against that wet fabric to drive men like Wade mad.

No, Matthew didn't need to hear any of that about the woman who wiped his bottom.

Damn, but this was hard. *He* was hard. And he didn't know how much longer he could take being in the same house with Callie Quinn without some sort of relief.

Which wasn't exactly the type of thought he should be having with an innocent babe in his arms.

"Come on, kid. Let's finish this bottle and get some dinner started so Callie doesn't have to do that, too, when she comes in."

The next couple of hours were filled with the banging and clanging of pots and the smells of cooking food as Wade gathered up what he could find to make a meal; a number of glances in Matthew's direction and frequent breaks to play with or settle him; and the occasional glimpse of Callie as she hung clothes on the line outside or made her way to and from the barn for what Wade assumed were her evening chores.

He wished he could help her more. At this point, he'd enjoy a bit of heavy, honest labor. Shoveling out a few horse stalls might be just the thing to burn off all this extra energy and pent-up sexual longing.

No, the only real thing that would put a

damper on his growing needs was a few hours spent in blissful passion with the lovely Callie Quinn. But sweating off a few pounds performing back-breaking chores would be good, too.

Unfortunately, while there was plenty of work to be done inside—most of it centered around a certain baby—none of it was the hard manual labor he craved. And he couldn't go outside for fear someone, whether posse member or simple passerby, might see him.

He'd eagerly fixed breakfast and dinner over the last few days, sometimes even lunch, depending on whether or not Callie got to it first, not only to avoid Callie's cooking, but to keep himself occupied—and if he was honest with himself, to try to lighten Callie's work.

It shouldn't surprise him that Callie sometimes acted so defensive toward him. After all, he was the six-foot, two-hundred-pound reason for most—if not all—of her current troubles.

But he didn't want to be a problem for her. He didn't want to scare her or make her nervous by his presence. And he hadn't wanted her to go to town this afternoon, at all.

He'd been on edge every minute she'd been gone. The only thing that kept him sane—in a manner of speaking—was Matthew's squalling. If the baby's constant needs and upset hadn't kept him busy all those hours, Wade wasn't sure he wouldn't have gone after Callie, regardless of the danger to himself.

Her trip to town—which she had yet to speak two words about—was the only reason he'd opened the back door earlier. Otherwise, he'd have stayed far away from any windows or openings for fear of being spotted.

But he was dying to know how her conversation with Brady Young had gone. The very thought of her paying the man a social call set his teeth on edge, but since she'd gone ahead with the visit despite his protests, he longed to find out what had been said.

If it hadn't been for Matthew finally sleeping peacefully and Wade's fear of waking him, he'd have started questioning Callie the minute she walked in the door. Now, his skin prickled like fire with the need to know what had happened this afternoon while he'd been trapped inside, hiding like a wounded doe.

He was just stirring the meat-and-vegetable stew he'd thrown together with the ingredients he could find among the supplies stored in the cellar when the back door opened and a tired, dirt-streaked Callie walked in.

Her feet seemed to root in place when she took in the scene in the kitchen. Matthew in his special high chair, beating the edge of the table with a wilted-looking, more-brown-than-orange carrot Wade had given him to play with. Wade standing near the stove in one of her aprons, a long wooden spoon in his hand.

He did look rather ridiculous, he supposed. Nowhere near masculine enough that he'd ever want any of his male friends to see him this way. But the clothes he was wearing weren't his own, and Callie worked hard enough without having to scrub his dungarees, too. So he wore the bright yellow, neck-to-knee apron any woman might, and prepared a dinner that he hoped would make Callie's mouth water.

"What are you doing?" she asked, brushing a sweat-slick strand of chestnut hair away from her eyes.

"Fixing supper," he said cheerily, refusing to let her dour expression intrude upon his fairly decent mood and his desire to question her—in the most friendly and civil manner—about her trip to the Triple Y. "It's almost ready. Why don't you have a seat, and I'll set the table?"

He moved to collect some bowls and spoons, then halted when he noticed Callie looking down at herself.

"I shouldn't . . . I'm a mess," she began.

Before she could get any further, Wade set the dishes in his hands on the table as he passed, then moved to stand so close to Callie, she shied back a step. With the tip of his index finger, he reached out to gently stroke one cheek pinkened with heat, exertion, and exhaustion.

161

"You look beautiful, as always, but if you want to take a few minutes to freshen up, Matthew and I will wait."

She held his gaze for what seemed like an eternity. Not for the first time, he wished he could tell what she was thinking. More, he wished he could be confident that she wouldn't pull away if he leaned forward and kissed her.

With a quick intake of breath and a swipe of her tongue over dry lips, she inclined her head and darted past him.

Wade let his head fall forward and waited for his pulse to stop pounding. It never did, of course, but after a few seconds, his heart seemed to slow enough for him to function.

He turned to look at Matthew, who simply smiled his toothless grin and returned to banging his disintegrating carrot on anything he could reach.

"I'm not going to make it, kid. If your mother and I don't get down to some serious business soon, I'm going to go up in flames."

Matthew giggled, a trickle of drool dribbling off the end of his chin, and smacked his carrot— *bang, bang, bang.*

Wade scowled. "Just you wait, little man. Wait until you grow up and find a woman who sets your insides on fire . . . not to mention other body parts," he grumbled. "You won't be laughing then."

With the sounds of Callie bustling about on the floor above them, Wade returned to the cookstove and filled two bowls with the bubbling mixture. Then he moved the pot of stew away from the heat and sat down to await Callie.

When she walked back into the room, the tipped-back feet of Wade's chair hit the floor with a sharp *thunk*. His eyes widened and his breathing all but stopped.

She had to be the prettiest thing he'd ever seen. If not, then his mind was playing tricks on his eyes, 'cause he sure as hell couldn't remember a more attractive woman ever crossing his path.

She'd washed her face and hands, combed her hair and twisted it into an artful coil at the nape of her neck. The dress she wore was new and clean, too, a deep lavender that reminded him of wildflowers, and the lilac water she used in her baths, and ripe, kissable lips.

Callie's lips. Which always looked infinitely kissable and drove him a fraction closer to the edge of the precipice on which he'd been teetering half the day.

His gaze sliced to Matthew before settling back on the vision before him.

Grabbing her up and making love to her in the middle of the kitchen floor probably wasn't such a smart thing to do in front of a child. But after Matthew went to bed . . . well, they would have plenty of privacy then.

Heidi Betts

Wade began to wish he hadn't worked so hard at getting the baby to sleep earlier. If he'd just put up with the crying, Matthew would even now be drifting off, and Wade would be that much closer to seducing Callie.

Step two. That hadn't been far from his mind since he'd added it to his list.

He saw her breasts rise as she inhaled deeply, and felt a clutch in his groin.

"It smells wonderful," she said, and didn't seem nearly as testy as she had earlier. Which wasn't surprising, considering how weary and hot she must have been after working so hard most of the day. Getting a chance to clean up and cool off had undoubtedly made her feel much better.

"Sit down," he offered, waving her to the chair opposite his.

She did, giving Matthew a loving pat on the head as she passed. Spreading a linen napkin on her lap, she lifted her spoon . . . and halted, meeting his gaze across the table.

"Aren't you going to eat, too?" she asked, studying him.

Dumbly, he nodded, wondering when his tongue had turned to a block of wood in his mouth.

He grabbed his spoon and dug it into his bowl of stew. They each took a mouthful and chewed,

164

Matthew's nonsensical chatter the only sound in the otherwise quiet room.

"This is very good," Callie said finally, breaking the uncomfortable silence. "You told me you cooked for yourself quite often, but I didn't realize you were so . . . versatile."

One side of his mouth quirked up with amusement. "By that you mean you thought I only knew how to make two things: bacon and steak."

"And eggs," she added.

Wade threw back his head and laughed. "And eggs, right. Three things, then."

"But I underestimated you, I see."

She took another prim bite of stew and savored it while Wade watched the slow, sensual motions of her mouth. When she moaned in pleasure at the rich taste, he almost shot through the ceiling.

"You're much more talented than you let on," she added.

A great roar started in his head, like a riverbed full to overflowing or a barn roof threatening to cave in on his head. And all he could think was, *You have no idea. You may very soon find out, but you have no idea.*

Aloud, he couldn't help but say, in a low, seductive tone, "At more than just cooking."

When she raised a startled gaze to his own, he met her stare straight on. It was time Callie realized this was a game of cat and mouse. He was the cat, she the mouse, and before this night was through, he fully intended to catch his prey.

His hot-as-coals scrutiny must have made her uncomfortable because she squirmed in her seat and seemed to discover something terribly interesting in her stew all of a sudden.

He let her go, deciding not to press either his suit or his luck. Soon enough, he would be given an opening. A moment when he could kiss her, when they were alone and he could do even more than that.

The promise of soft lips, supple skin, and feminine moans of pleasure sent a jolt of desire to the tips of his extremities. *All* of his extremities.

Wade figured it was a good thing he was sitting down. Otherwise she might see his blatant arousal and get skittish. And the last thing he wanted tonight was for Callie to shy away from him.

No. He intended to do everything in his power to lure her straight into his arms.

Matthew, ever the diligent chaperone, squealed loudly and launched his carrot drumstick across the room. The thing missed Wade's head by an inch, hitting the wall behind him and plopping to the floor.

Wade slanted his head to look at where the battered and beaten carrot had fallen. "That kid's got quite an arm," he said, turning back around. "As soon as he's old enough, I say we put him to work digging fence posts or chopping wood."

He'd expected Callie to laugh at his jest. Instead, her bright blue eyes met his for the briefest fraction of a second before darting away once again. And he didn't know why. He'd purposely tried to lighten the mood of the room, to put her at ease so she wouldn't worry herself into losing her appetite thinking he planned to leap across the table and ravish her. Though he would have dearly loved to do just that.

If he didn't stop picturing those enticing images, he might not be able to help himself. But there was a small child in the room, and he was that child's father. Therefore he should probably strive to maintain some semblance of adult maturity.

Wade mentally scowled. This fatherhood business wasn't as idyllic as he'd expected it to be. In fact, it was damn frustrating when his manhood was pounding like a sledgehammer in his pants, the woman he wanted was sitting not three feet away, and he couldn't do an everloving thing about it because his son was in the room.

He fixed a concentrated glare on Matthew and willed him to grow sleepy. He was a baby. He hadn't napped in nearly five hours. How much longer could he stay awake?

Bolstered by that small speck of hope, Wade turned his attention back to Callie. She was chopping and mashing portions of potato and carrot and catching them on the end of the spoon, feeding them to an eager Matthew.

"I didn't realize he was old enough for real food." When she'd left that morning, she'd only told him to see that Matthew got a bottle.

She nodded. "It has to be soft enough for him to chew and bland enough that it doesn't upset his stomach."

"He seems to like it."

Offering a tentative smile, she said, "He's probably glad to get someone else's cooking for a change. I'm afraid he's only been subjected to my limited kitchen skills before now."

Wade couldn't think of a response to that, but Callie seemed to be less tense and speaking to him now, so he thought this might be the perfect opportunity to bring up the topic of her trip to town.

"So, Callie . . . I know we haven't discussed it, but I've been awfully curious about what happened at the Triple Y." He tried not to get angry but couldn't seem to help the immediate, gut-clenching reaction that overtook him at the very thought of Callie being within breathing distance of that bastard Brady Young.

She held another bite of stew to Matthew's mouth and waited as he slurped the thick broth.

"Nothing happened," she answered, without pulling her attention away from her task.

He bit back a rude retort at her short and less than informative response. "Even if you don't think all of the details would be of interest," he told her, "I'd still like to hear." There, that sounded diplomatic enough.

Her eyes brushed over him as she dipped into the bowl and took a spoonful for herself. Then she got a bit more for Matthew and said, "I'm not keeping anything from you. Truly, nothing happened. Brady wasn't at home when I got there."

As much as he'd been hoping to learn of a witness to what happened the night he'd been arrested, he was almost relieved that she hadn't come in contact with Young. Hadn't been touched or contaminated by that Brady parasite.

"I went to the ranch," she continued, "but the housekeeper said Brady was gone for the day. He might have been in town, but I didn't go looking for him. I didn't think speaking with him away from the ranch would be the best way of broaching the subject of the hired hand. Besides, I've never had occasion to approach Brady before, and I was afraid doing so now would give him false ideas about my . . . interest in him."

"You mean that if you'd found him in town and begun asking questions, he'd have thought you were inviting his attentions," he gritted out.

She lifted her eyes to his. "Yes."

"And you don't particularly like him, so you

don't want to give him any reason to think he should come calling."

At that, her gaze darted away. "Yes."

He couldn't explain the relief he felt at her two very indisputable answers, but they raised a weight from his shoulders and loosened something even deeper inside him. He feared it might be . . . his heart.

Chapter Fourteen

He wasn't falling for this woman, certainly. She was beautiful, yes. More beautiful than a hundred hurdy-gurdy girls. More lovely than a cool breeze on a hot day, or a field of colorful bluebonnets in the distance.

She was sweet enough to turn apple vinegar, and he hungered for her the way a starving man hungers for a mere crust of bread.

But he wasn't falling for her.

It was simply the situation that made it seem that might be the case. The anxiety of being a wanted man, the close quarters of being trapped inside the house, the fact that he was a man and she was a woman and he hadn't been with a woman for quite some time. All of that blended together to make him think what he was feeling might be a stronger emotion than lust.

But lust it was, and he'd prove it just as soon as he got the chance to sample Callie's delectable charms.

"I'm sorry I didn't get any answers for you today. I looked around while I was there, but I didn't see any workers who fit your description of the unknown man."

Her apology broke into his thoughts, dragging him back to the present and away from the erotic image he'd conjured of Callie's dark, loose hair fanned across an ivory pillow as she waited for him to join her in bed.

He shook his head. "I'm glad you didn't have to deal with Young. And I appreciate you keeping an eye out, although I wish you hadn't felt the need to do something even that risky."

"But you're no better off than you were before. Now it will take even longer to find out who that man was and if he might be willing to come forward in your defense."

Her spoon clinked against the side of the bowl as she let go and began twisting her hands in her lap. He couldn't reach her across the expanse of the oaken table, but he stretched his arm out nonetheless, turning up his palm in an offer of comfort.

"It's all right, Callie. I don't blame you, and I'm not upset. We'll just have to think of something else." Wade let his lips curve. "I'd rather not bring you into this, anyway. You'll be safer that way."

His words didn't seem to overly reassure her, so he scraped the last of the stew from the bottom of the bowl and downed it. "Come on," he said, rolling a hand in her direction. "Let's finish up here and get Matthew ready for bed. It's getting late." *And there are things I want to do to you before morning.*

Startled, she began eating a bit faster but didn't rush to follow his lead. "Tonight is Matthew's bath night," she said. "He'll fall asleep soon after that, but he usually likes to play in the water for a while."

Bath night. Curses. It seemed his son was forever going to be a thorn in the side of his plans for seduction.

But instead of giving voice to those thoughts, he merely smiled and tried to give off an air of anticipation. "Great. How do we go about that?"

Finished with her dinner, Callie let Wade take her bowl away while she wiped Matthew's face with the napkin from her lap and lifted him out of his chair.

She wasn't quite sure what to make of Wade's behavior tonight. One moment, he was studying her as though she was a fluffy pastry he wanted to devour. The next, he was smiling and joking, doing his best to set her at ease.

Which was a ridiculous notion. As long as he

173

remained in her house, underfoot, and in her line of sight, she would never relax. The man made her blood all but boil. She could sense his presence in a room even before she saw him. It was as if his body sent out silent but deadly signals to her own. To those deep, secret places within her that began to hum and throb whenever he came near, making her want things no decent, God-fearing, virtuous woman had any business wanting.

Of course, it might no longer be appropriate for Callie to think of herself as virtuous. Not after the liberties she'd already allowed Wade to take. Kisses that still made her lips tingle. Kisses that had led to fantasies that kept her up at night . . . and once she did fall asleep, gifted her with the most wonderful dreams she'd ever experienced. But certainly none of those things could be considered virtuous. Wanton, maybe.

She didn't want to be wanton. It wasn't a quality her mother had raised her to aspire to.

Her mother was gone, however, and Wade was here. He was very, very close and creating responses in her unlike any another other human being had ever made her feel.

It was getting to the point where she didn't trust herself around him. He caused her to become too breathless too often. Just being in the same room with him, sensing those warm brown eyes upon her, sent her heart rate skittering.

Too many times, she found herself wondering what it would be like to lean close as he spoke, to feel his breath caress her skin the way his words caressed her mind. Have his hands on her arms and shoulders and back as he plunged his tongue deep into her mouth. Have his hands stroke other places, his lips kiss other places. And perhaps worst of all, she wondered what it would be like to give in to all those lascivious fantasies and let him do with her what he would.

Would he be gentle, or would he be forceful? Would he sweep her into his arms and carry her upstairs to one of the bedrooms, or would he drag her down to the floor with him and have his wicked way with her right there? Would she struggle out of modesty and an ingrained sense of morality, or would she end up whimpering like a child who wants another piece of candy, and beg him to make love to her before she expired?

Whatever course their relationship might take, she suspected tonight would reveal the beginning of that path. The air fairly sizzled with an underlying thread of sexual tension. Wade's movements were slow and deliberate, his eyes glittering like glass and warning of things to come.

Callie couldn't decide whether to skip Matthew's bath and put him directly to bed or to draw out the chore to avoid the temptation she sensed nipping at her heels.

Striving to postpone events as long as possible, she bustled about collecting things, all with Matthew nestled safely against her side. Once she had towels and soap and the other necessities laid out, she grabbed a bucket and headed for the water pump outside.

Wade caught her arm before she reached the door.

"Here," he said, holding out his hands. "I can't go outside, but let me take him while you do that."

She hesitated for a fraction of a second. Not because she didn't trust him with the child—certainly she now realized how good Wade was with Matthew—but simply because she still could not accustom herself to having help, to not needing to have Matthew with her every moment of every day.

With a nod, she passed Matthew to his father and continued on to the pump, filling the metal pail, which she then put on the stove to heat.

During all of this, Matthew sat on the countertop, Wade propping him up with one arm while he clapped and tickled with the other, making faces until the baby rolled with laughter. Every time she heard Matthew's excited squeals or caught a glimpse of his happy, expressive face, she couldn't help but laugh along.

It was the most fun she remembered having in quite some time. She often played with Matthew herself, of course; it was one of her favorite activities. But something about watching father and son together, hearing Matthew's burst of amusement and seeing Wade's animated features set on entertaining his child, warmed a place deep in her heart.

Callie wasn't sure she liked the sensation. It scared her too much, made her think about the day when Wade would want to take Matthew away from her. Or almost worse, in a way, about how easily Wade fit into her household and daily life.

If things had been different . . . If things had been different, Wade might not have gone to prison. She might have met him one day in the general store or at a town social, and the feelings she was having might have led to courting and romance. They might have married and settled into a home of their own. Matthew might be their child, born on the proper side of the bed linens and of their genuine love for each other.

But that was not something Callie wanted to contemplate for long. For one thing, it hurt too much to yearn for a future—or even a past—she knew was impossible. For another, Wade was a fugitive, taking refuge in her house. And unless they succeeded at proving his innocence, he would have no future at all.

Then there was the fact that she did *not* have feelings for this man. She might be having *sen-*

timents of a sort; small tugs at her heart because of the way he acted with Matthew, and a more noticeable throbbing in some of her more private, core areas. But that did not mean she had *feelings* for the man.

If anything, she was clearly aware of the difference between physical desire and emotional attachment. A blind man could see the attraction growing between Wade and herself, but even a university scholar would be hard-pressed to prove her heart was engaged in their current sensual skirmish.

And that single thought was what kept her sane, when a tiny part of her deep inside wanted to run away screaming.

That voice was making itself heard now, warning her that it was dangerous to remain in this house with Wade. Not that she had anywhere else to go.

Matthew let out another ear-splitting giggle, slapping his hands on the flat surface of the counter. Wade's answering chuckles drew lines of merriment at the corners of his eyes and dimples in his cheeks. A day's worth of stubble coated his cheeks and chin, making him look ruggedly handsome.

As though he needed anything to add to his attractiveness.

Pulling back sharply on the reins of her runaway captivation, Callie returned her attention to the stove to test the water. It was just a tad too hot, but she dumped the contents of the bucket into the stopped-up sink nonetheless, knowing the water would cool if allowed to sit a few minutes.

"Is there anything I can do to help?" Wade asked from over her shoulder.

She inclined her head only slightly as she said, "You can take his diaper off and bring him over here. But be prepared to get wet," she warned, rolling up her own sleeves.

"I think I can handle it," he teased.

With a cake of gentle soap in her hands, she waited for Wade to strip Matthew and carry him to the cast-iron basin. She noticed that he dipped his fingers into the water to check its temperature before depositing the baby in its shallow depths. A very fatherly thing to do.

The minute Matthew's toes touched the water, his arms began pumping up and down as he cried in delight.

Wade stepped back, eyes wide. "He sure likes his bath, doesn't he?"

"He *loves* his bath." She dipped the soap to get it wet, then began to lather Matthew's little potbelly.

While she washed him, Matthew wiggled in pleasure, splashing water on her clothes, into her face, onto Wade, who stood beside her, even on the walls and ceiling. "After I get him clean, I usually just let him play until he tires himself out. Then he falls right to sleep."

She felt the heat of Wade's body as he sidled closer and suddenly found it hard to think. His breath danced along her neck and sent a shiver down her spine. But even that couldn't prepare her for the bolt of pure awareness, of desirous longing that his next, softly uttered words brought.

"Good," he murmured in her ear. "That will give us more time to ourselves."

That statement alone nearly brought her to her knees. But when he reached up and tucked a strand of loose hair behind her ear, lingering to stroke the tip of one finger over the pulse in her neck, she realized just how much danger she was in.

Chapter Fifteen

It took over an hour to bathe the kid and let him play with the bubbles to his heart's content.

An hour during which Wade fought a raging erection and the urge to grab Callie and do all the things he'd been dreaming about right in the middle of the kitchen floor. Baby or no baby.

But finally Matthew's eyes began to droop, and Callie grabbed a soft, thick towel to wrap him in.

Already wet from Matthew's splashing and not concerned about growing wetter, Wade reached over and lifted the child from the basin, holding him up until Callie could enfold him in her arms.

He watched her carefully, almost diligently, as she ruffled the baby with the towel, drying him from head to toe, playfully tickling his more sensitive body parts.

The thin layer of dark brown, baby-fine hair on Matthew's head—the same shade as Wade's own, he thought with a small lurch of his heart—stuck out at all angles, and even though he yawned, he grinned up at Callie like she'd hung the moon.

Wade thought the kid had the right idea. He was pretty damn fond of the lady himself, and couldn't wait for the little one to fall asleep so he could get on with the business of Step Two.

Step One was as far from his mind at this point as the Canadian border was from Mexico.

"Now what?" he asked, in a hurry to move things along so he and Callie could be alone.

His question must have startled her, because she stopped teasing Matthew and turned a straight face toward him. "Now we get him dressed and ready for bed. Before he falls asleep right here on the table."

Matthew didn't look like he was anywhere near falling asleep on the hard, flat surface. If they could get him upstairs and tucked into his own crib, however, that possibility might not be far off.

"Let me," he said, moving forward to take Matthew when she would have lifted him to her own chest.

All right, so he had an ulterior motive. He wasn't simply being obliging. With as much water as Matthew had slapped out of the sink, along with what was absorbed just from trying to hold on to the child as he bounced around, the front of Callie's dress had gotten soaked through. The arms and skirt were wet, as well, but it was the bodice that most interested Wade. Like earlier this afternoon as she'd crouched over the wash-tub scrubbing dirty clothes, the top of her dress clung to her skin, outlining her perfect physique.

Even better, the light purple fabric of her current gown was less sturdy than the one from earlier in the day, so Callie's nipples appeared larger than before. Her breasts looked fuller, more pert, and he liked to believe he could see a hint of the darker area of the areolae that surrounded them.

He also wanted nothing more than to strip away the fine material. To see those beautiful breasts—not to mention the rest of Callie's mouthwatering form—without the barrier of her clothing.

Toward that end, he wasted no time carrying Matthew upstairs, standing by while Callie changed him, and then helping her tuck the child into his cradle.

He enjoyed putting Matthew to bed. Most of the nights he'd been here, he'd lingered over the task to watch every yawn, every wrinkling of Matthew's tiny nose, to hear every muffled sigh.

But tonight he had other things on his mind. Much more urgent things, if he ever wanted to walk a straight and painless line again.

He waited while Callie pulled a light blanket up to Matthew's ears and gave his back an affectionate pat. When she turned to leave the room, he took her elbow and walked with her.

When they reached the hall, Callie moved toward the stairs, but Wade pulled her up short. He spun her around, drew her flush with his chest, and kissed her, all in one smooth flash of motion.

His mouth moved against hers, his tongue teasing hers, until she sagged against him, until he felt a soft sigh ripple through her body. When he released her, it was only to let her suck in a much needed breath of air. He did the same, but quickly lowered his head and ran his lips over her cheeks, jaw, and earlobe, and down the slope of her beautiful neck.

"The bedroom," he rasped. "We should move to your bedroom." He would have taken her to his room, but he didn't think she would feel comfortable making love in what was, in actuality, her brother's bedchamber.

For a minute, he didn't think she would answer. And if she turned him away now, he truly expected to expire. He would draw one last breath and wither away to nothing more than a pair of worn dungarees and a red plaid shirt.

But then she nodded her head slowly, her eyes never wavering from his, her gaze filled with desire.

Wade covered her mouth with his own, bending slightly at the knees to swoop her into his arms. Relying on nothing but the vision from one corner of his eye, he stalked toward the promised land.

He lifted his foot to kick the door open rather than taking a single hand off Callie's delectable body, but remembered Matthew and knew if he woke the boy, any plans he had for the next several hours would be abruptly—and possibly indefinitely—called off.

Careful not to drop her, he reached out and twisted the knob, pushing the panel wide on noiseless hinges. He did kick it closed behind them, albeit quietly.

Every step across the room, Wade expected her to balk. To call out for him to put her down or stop. And if she did, he would. Or at least he would try. No matter how badly he wanted her, he wasn't going to force her.

But with each step, she only twined her fingers more firmly into his hair, stroked his cheek, met his tongue thrust for thrust.

My God, she was amazing. No wonder he desired her so strongly, had such an earth-shaking reaction whenever she walked into a room.

When he reached the bed, he laid her down on the soft mattress, stretching out with her atop the neatly tucked in coverlet. He raised his head to look down at her, to drink in every detail of her beautiful face. The smooth skin, expressive blue eyes, and heart-shaped mouth. Her lips were swollen now from his kisses, and a deeper rose color than usual.

Running his fingers through the hair at her temples, he framed her face with his rough palms. "You knew this would happen, that we've been moving toward it almost from the moment we met. But, Callie, I want you to be sure. I won't have you accusing me later of taking advantage of you, or forcing you into something against your will. Do you understand?"

With his hands still on the sides of her face, she nodded.

"So tell me, Callie. Do you want to make love with me?"

The seconds ticked by and he held his breath. If she said no, he didn't know how he would walk away. He didn't know if he *could* walk away. But he did know that he would never do anything to harm or frighten her, so if she asked him to leave, somehow he would manage the Herculean feat.

What seemed like hours later, Callie's delectable lips parted and a whisper of sound drifted out. It sounded like "yes," and his heart stopped beating.

But he had to be sure. "Did you say yes?" He pushed the question past a tightly closed throat, praying all the while that his ears weren't playing tricks on him.

A beatific smile curved her mouth and she lifted her arms to more fully encompass his neck. "Yes," she breathed again, loud enough for him to hear clearly this time.

He felt the muscles in his cheeks contract and knew his grin far surpassed her own. Pressing a light peck to her forehead and the bridge of her nose, he said, "In case I forget to tell you later, I'm the happiest man in the world right now."

"I'm glad," she said softly, and he couldn't help but kiss her.

How had he gotten so lucky? He might not be a murderer, but he'd never done anything extraordinary enough to deserve a woman like Callie. And yet she was here, in his arms, inviting him to make love with her.

Wade figured he could die this very minute—without doing anything more than they had already—and still not suffer a single regret.

But seeing as he didn't cock up his heels on the spot, he took that as God's blessing and a sign to keep right on going. Which he did, with great pleasure.

As his lips ran along her jaw and throat, his hands explored her shoulders and moved down to cup her breasts. The sensations that rocked through her as Wade ran his thumbs over the thin cotton of her dress, teasing her nipples, made Callie moan deep in the back of her throat.

How could he do such things to her? How did

he know just where to touch her, when, and how much? However he knew, she thanked heaven he did, and arched toward him like a feline leaning into its owner's stroking palm.

She felt the buttons down the front of her gown being undone and opened her eyes to see his nimble fingers spreading wide the lavender sides of her bodice.

Although the evening air was only a few degrees cooler than it had been that afternoon, it still raised goose bumps on her exposed flesh. With one arm behind her back, he lifted her slightly off the bed in order to slip off the sleeves of the gown. From the waist up, she was left in only her thin linen camisole, which did nothing to hide the effect he had on her body.

"Wade," she breathed, trying to get his attention as he rubbed her bare arms and kissed a line across her collarbone. "Wade."

He raised his head and looked down at her, his eyes the warm brown of hot cocoa and filled with an emotion she'd never witnessed before—desire. She'd especially never seen a man gazing at her that way.

"What?" he asked, his voice deep and gravelly. "Darling, what is it?"

Swallowing past the lump of anxiety in her throat, she attempted to form her earlier thoughts into words. "I've never . . . I don't want you to think . . ."

"That you do this with every man who breaks into your house?" he finished with a cocky slant to his mouth. "Don't worry, I didn't think that."

"But I've never . . . at all," she tried again, needing him to understand how special an experience this was for her, how much she trusted him.

A muscle ticked in his jaw and his eyes grew serious. "Good," he clipped out. "It wouldn't make a difference, I hope you know that, but still . . . good."

Their lips met, and any other thoughts she might have had flew right out of her head. From somewhere far away, she heard her shoes drop to the floor and realized he was divesting her of her skirts. And then she truly was exposed but for the paper-thin material of her drawers and camisole.

His hand ran from her ankle, over the curve of her calf, along the outside of her thigh, and beneath the hem of her drawers to cup a buttock.

That intimate contact caused her to gasp, not only from the boldness of it, but because of the lightning-like jolt it sent into her belly.

And suddenly having him caress her, disrobe her, wasn't enough. She wanted to touch him, as well, to see what lay beneath his clothing. She'd dreamed of his naked form, fantasized what it might be like to undress him. Now here was her chance.

A flutter of modesty made her hesitate, but she pushed it aside. She'd already decided to make love with him; they would be joined as man and woman in the most intimate way. With that prospect lying in her not so distant future, removing his clothing the way he'd removed hers was nothing, really. Not so scary that she shouldn't just go ahead and start.

Tentatively, she reached out to undo the top button of his plaid work shirt. Then another. And another. Encouraged by his continued attention to her mouth and the shifting of his body to give her better access, she yanked the tucked-in fabric from his trousers and pushed the shirt from his shoulders. He released her only long enough to shrug out of the offending garment and toss it to the floor; then his hands moved to the waistband of his jeans.

Covering his fingers with her own, she said, "Let me."

He gazed down at her and nodded. Holding his weight away from her, he watched as she slowly slipped the metal rivet at the front of his trousers through its hole.

The lower she went, the less give she found in the heavy fabric because of the press of his arousal. She had to work her fingers in beneath the material, flush against his heated manhood, to slide the last few buttons free.

Instead of letting her push his pants down over his hips the way he'd done with her gown, Wade rolled away for the briefest of seconds and shucked out of the dungarees himself.

Callie almost chuckled at the speed with which he stripped . . . until she caught a clear glimpse of his body.

He wore nothing beneath his trousers. She realized with a start that while she had loaned him Nathan's shirts she had never considered how he managed without undergarments. Now she knew. Perched above her, balanced on his hands, all that separated their bodies was a diaphanous layer of white linen over her breasts and torso.

She waited a long minute for some sense of fear or alarm to overtake her, to send her running from the room. But that feeling never came, and she found her gaze drifting downward, toward that part of him that she'd never seen before on any man. It stood out from the rest of him, seeming to strain in her direction.

Her body turned liquid, blood rising to the surface of her skin and heat pooling in her womanly core. Wade—so patient it threatened to bring tears to her eyes—merely stared down at her, waiting for some sign that he should continue.

She thought wrapping her legs around his waist and telling him to get on with it might be a bit too brazen, even for the wanton woman inside her who had unexpectedly made her presence known. But she did link her arms around his neck and draw his face down to hers. With her lips pressed whisper soft against his, she said, "What are you waiting for? Make love to me, Wade Mason."

Chapter Sixteen

Wade wondered if he'd died and gone to heaven.

Fast on the heels of that thought was the notion that if he'd known this would be what greeted him on the other side, he might not have been nearly so eager to escape the gallows at the time of his trial.

Either that, or Callie was an angel sent down to earth. Because no way was any mortal woman half as beautiful, giving, soft-spoken, or receptive as his Callie girl.

Uh-oh. Slip of the tongue. Or rather, a slip of the mind.

Callie girl was all right, but he hadn't really meant to call her *his.* He'd gotten swept up in the moment, carried away by the fact that this woman—mortal or angel, he wasn't sure which, and didn't particularly care—was lying beneath him, open and willing, asking him to make love with her.

He'd have to be crazy to stop now. Judging by the state of his arousal, he might not even have a choice in the matter. He was lucky she hadn't panicked and fled the moment she saw him without his trousers. He didn't think he'd ever been so hard in his life, and Callie was the reason.

Now if he could only keep from either devouring her or embarrassing himself. Both were distinct possibilities.

He smoothed the hair away from her face, tracing the lines of her delicate features. From where her soft brown hair met the pale porcelain of her skin to the slightly upturned corners of her half-closed, darkened-with-passion cornflower blue eyes. From the cute-as-a-button tip of her nose to the heart-shaped curve of her now swollen lips.

He didn't deserve her, didn't deserve this, and he knew it. But damned if he had the strength to hand her dress back and tell her to get while the getting was good.

Playing his tongue against her lips, he felt her open beneath him, felt her warmth wash over him. With her arms looped around his neck, the tips of her fingers sifted through his hair, causing a trickle of anticipation to dart down his spine.

Snagging the hem of her lacy white camisole,

he drew it up the narrow expanse of her abdomen to the outline of her breasts, and then over them. They were just as beautiful as he'd imagined in the dreams that kept him tossing and turning through the night. Pert and firm, with tight raspberry nipples begging to be kissed. Which he did, bussing first one and then the other.

But as much as he might have liked to, he didn't linger. He was too eager, too randy, and there was more of her yet to explore.

The drawstring of her drawers needed to be untied, which he did, sending a quick prayer of thanks skyward when the knot immediately came loose. Hooking his thumbs into the meager material, he pulled the drawers down the coltish length of her legs and tossed them aside.

They had quite a pile of discarded garments falling to the floor beside the bed. Wade figured it would be easier to find them later, when they wanted to dress.

If they ever got out of bed.

If he ever again let Callie wear clothes.

She shouldn't count on it.

The image of Callie, stark-naked and happy to be that way, played through his mind. Washing dishes, scrubbing laundry, fixing supper . . . No, not fixing supper. He'd be the one at the stove, watching while she set the table or played with Matthew.

Yep, that was just one more fantasy concerning Callie to add to his growing list. For now, though, he was going to focus on living out his number one fantasy: making love to Callie.

Wade's hands spanned her belly, stroking up and down the slight indentation on either side of her waist between chest and hips. His thumbs stroked the undersides of her breasts, then teased her navel. He brushed each of her pouting nipples, then the springy hair at the very top of her woman's mound.

Everywhere his hands touched, his mouth followed, wetting the sensitive pucker of her breasts, tasting the undersides of those cushiony globes. The tip of his tongue trailed along her rib cage, into the dip of her belly button, all the way to the slope of her inner thigh.

Moving back up her body, he brought that leg with him to hook over the ridge of his hip. Flesh against flesh, they lay there while he devoured her mouth, teased her with his fingers. His rigid length brushed the opening of her body, her enticing warmth urging him to lunge forward and make them one.

But he held back, wanting Callie to be as aroused as he was. With that in mind, his other hand slipped between the growing warmth of their bodies and into her silken folds.

Callie gasped as Wade touched her there. It was so unexpected, so unlike anything she'd ever experienced before, that her hips arched off the bed of their own volition.

His throaty chuckle made her blush, but the fierceness with which he took her mouth in the next instant washed away all her unease. As the strength seemed to go out of her limbs and her arms slid farther down his back, her head fell even deeper into the pillow and she turned herself over to the delicious sensations Wade was creating deep inside her.

His fingers tickled the outer rim of her womanhood, then delved deep, shocking another sharp intake of breath from her already overwrought system.

But she liked it, she really did. The rough pads of his fingers against her sensitized, never-before-breached folds. The rush of wet and warmth from her own body, brought forth by the exquisite slide of coarse against fine. The tantalizing rasp of his tongue tangled with her own as he kissed her.

He kissed the way she'd always dreamed a man would kiss her. Deep and long, until she was at risk of forgetting her own name.

It was at that moment she realized she hadn't been waiting for just any man to kiss her this way, she'd been waiting for *the* man.

The man little girls envisioned from the first time they saw a bride in white frills and lace walk down the aisle of the church toward a black-clad groom. The man her mama had always told her was out there, waiting for her. The man who would come along one day and sweep her off her feet, make her want marriage and children and forever.

Callie's stomach did a full flip and brought her heart up to her throat.

What if Wade was *the* man? He kissed the way she'd always expected *the* man to kiss. And though she'd never been brave enough to imagine how *the* man would touch her, he surely did that right, as well. If he didn't, her eyes wouldn't even now be rolling back in her head.

Wade smiled at her, and the world went away. She watched him with Matthew and she saw . . .

Oh, no. She saw *visions*. Terrible, awful, terrifying visions.

She saw good-morning pecks and good-night embraces. Bridal gowns and colorful ribbon curling over anniversary gifts. God help her, but she saw babies. More babies than just Matthew. *Her* babies, born of her womb and put there by none other than Wade Mason.

Lord have mercy, she was in trouble.

Wade Mason might be *the* man, she thought sourly, but that didn't mean she had to do anything about that fact. She certainly didn't intend to inform him of the ridiculous tangent her brain had just taken. The chances were low that he would stick around even if she did tell him.

And just because he was lying above her, doing increasingly wicked things to her senses, didn't mean this was leading anywhere even close to marriage and forever. It was just sex.

People didn't have to marry to make love. Lily and the other working girls at the Painted Lady were prime examples of that sweeping truth.

And though Callie had always been a good girl, she'd also been unaccountably curious about the more intimate goings-on between men and women.

Now was her chance, without jeopardizing her reputation with the town. After all, no one even knew Wade was here, so they never need know just how tempted she'd been or how many liberties she'd allowed him. She could use Wade's presence to answer all her scandalous questions and still . . .

Goodness.

Just then, driving all rational thought from her head, Wade's fingers dipped farther inside her, stretching her inner muscles and making her moan at the sheer pleasure of the burgeoning fullness he created.

Oh, yes, she would let him make love to her—beg him, if necessary. And it didn't matter what came after that, because she already had the best part of him right here in her bed.

Wade stared down into Callie's eyes, watching as she returned from wherever she'd gone just a moment before. He'd seen her fading off, letting her mind take her somewhere far away from where they should both be going together.

Which didn't say much for his seductive abilities, he thought wryly. But he'd increased his efforts and shocked her back to the here and now. It was the thrust of his two fingers that did it, the mimicry of what he would soon be doing with his body.

At his intimate touch, her eyes went wide, her hips shot a good inch off the mattress, and she once again focused totally on him. Just the way he wanted her to.

"Feel that?" he demanded, turning his fingers half a circle, making sure she knew exactly what he was talking about.

He waited until she nodded in acknowledgment, her front teeth biting down on her lower lip—to keep from screaming in ecstasy, he hoped.

"That's what it will feel like when I'm inside you, Callie girl. Since you've never been with a man before, there may also be some pain, though. When your maidenhead is broken. Understand, sweetheart?"

One chestnut brow winged upward and her nails dug into the hard sinew of his back. "I'm not completely ignorant, Wade. I do know the rudiments of the situation, if nothing else."

He grinned at the acid sharpness of her words.

If she was tearing a strip from his hide, then she was definitely awake and aware. No more drifting off to places unknown, when he wanted her right here in the same county—the same room—with him.

"Good. Then it won't surprise you if I do this." He let his fingers slide out of her narrow channel and replaced them with his throbbing length. Her mouth fell open as she gasped for air, and he smiled in triumph.

He didn't go all the way in, afraid of causing her pain. He would hurt her, of course; there was no help for that. But he would ease her into it, do his best to make everything else so enjoyable that she almost wouldn't notice the exact moment he stole her virginity.

"It's all right," he murmured gently, "that's as far as I'll go." For now, even though it was killing him.

He ran his hands over her hair, letting the fine strands sift through his fingers. "Does it hurt?"

She shook her head. "I feel . . . filled. Good."

He grunted in pure male satisfaction. "Pretty soon, you'll feel even better. Do you think you can take more of me?"

Callie shifted and wiggled beneath him, finding a better position. Her legs widened, and without trying, he slipped even farther inside.

His breath hissed out of his lungs, and this

time he was the one struggling to accommodate to her.

When he could again speak without sounding like a strangled cow, he pressed his forehead to hers and said, "Hey, who's in charge here?"

He didn't have to lift his head to see her expression; he could feel the corners of her mouth curling upward.

"I am," she responded without a hint of trepidation.

And then she flexed her inner muscles around his hardness and the top nearly shot off his head. "Jesus, Mary, and Joseph, woman! Are you trying to kill me?"

He didn't wait for an answer, instead rolling them across the bed until he was lying on his back and she was perched above him.

His sudden flip and the surprise of this new position rounded her mouth into a startled *O*. "What are you doing?"

"Putting you in charge." His grin was wicked and he knew it. But he wanted to see just how brave she was, what she would be willing to do to please both herself and him.

She shook her head, that glorious mane of mahogany hair spilling around her face and trickling down her back. "I can't. I don't know what to do."

"Do whatever you want, whatever feels right. You'll know."

Her straight white teeth gnawed on her lower lip, her nails curling into his chest in uncertainty.

"It's all right, sweetheart. There's nothing to be scared of or embarrassed about. It's just the two of us, and I think you're darn near perfect. There's nothing you can do that I would consider wrong."

After another minute of watching the skepticism play across her face, he began to run his hands up and down her waist, over her arms and thighs.

"What do you want, Callie girl? Do you want to kiss me? Run your hands over my chest? How about seating yourself a bit more firmly and letting me fill you again?"

Still biting her lip, she nodded.

He gave a strained chuckle. "Which is it?" he asked, trying to coax her into doing something, anything, before this desperate balancing of desire sent him over the edge.

Her lashes fluttered as she whispered, "All of it."

"Jesus," he muttered again. She really would be the death of him. "Go ahead, then," he rasped out. "Don't let me stop you."

Shifting from side to side, she found a better position straddling his hips. Wade had to grit down hard to keep from shouting out while she wiggled around, but it was well worth it once she settled and leaned forward to put her hands on his shoulders.

Her wet heat surrounded him, but still he wasn't inside her to the hilt. She held herself a little away from him, just beyond the point where he would puncture her hymen.

Her fingers traced eight narrow trails over his chest, stopping to explore the protrusion of his collarbone, the darker circles of his nipples with their budded centers. Over his rib cage and the sunken contours of his stomach as his diaphragm constricted with his indrawn breath.

Not to be the only one driven to the brink of madness, he reached up to cup her breasts. He weighed the heavy globes in his palms, thumbed the aroused peaks, then levered himself off the mattress to swipe at them with his tongue.

At that, Callie sat back, staring at him with wide eyes. "I didn't know we could do that," she said warily.

"I told you, you can do whatever you like. Touch me, taste me, ride me," he said, rotating his hips slightly in an imitation of what he desperately wanted her to do to him.

Her eyes darted away and that bottom lip disappeared between her teeth again. "I don't want it to hurt," she admitted.

"Oh, darlin'." He reached up to tuck a strand of long hair behind one ear. "It will hurt; I won't lie to you about that. There's no help for it. But it doesn't have to hurt for long. It can be fast, and I'll do everything I can to make it pass quickly."

Her head bobbed slowly up and down, but she still didn't look convinced.

"Tell you what," he went on. "Let's get this out of the way so we can get on to the real pleasure, all right? Close your eyes." He ran two fingers from her brows to her cheekbones, forcing her to comply. "Now relax, and don't think about anything but how wonderful you feel. How soft my fingers are on your skin. How warm you're getting. How much you want me to move inside you."

Gently, so as not to startle her or push any further inside her than he already was, he wrapped his arms around her waist and rolled them back to the other side of the mattress until he hovered over her once more.

Her fingers curled more firmly into his upper arms, but she kept her eyes closed as he'd asked.

Covering her mouth with his own, he proceeded to kiss her as his hand slipped down to that spot just above where their bodies were locked together. He found the bud of her desire and began to leisurely stroke.

At the first touch to that spot, Callie's mouth opened wider beneath his own. He kept them connected, kept her distracted, and continued a slow building of tension until she was bucking beneath him.

When he knew she was on the verge of her very first climax, he braced her hips with one hand, increased the pressure of his finger, and thrust forward as far as he could go.

Callie gasped, her head jerking back to break their kiss, her eyes snapping open.

"Shh, it's all right. It's over." He waited a moment, watching the disillusionment fade from her pain-shrouded eyes. "How does it feel? Does it still hurt?"

For the briefest of seconds, she didn't reply. Then she shook her head. "No. It doesn't. It did, but it doesn't anymore."

Wade smiled, unaccountably relieved. "Good."

He lowered his head until their brows met. "You're mine now, Callie girl. All mine."

Pressing a light kiss to the corner of her mouth, he asked, "Are you ready for the rest?"

Chapter Seventeen

Oh, yes, she was ready. Now that the painful and fearful parts were past, she was more than ready for Wade to show her what it meant for a man and woman to come together. All of it. There were times already when he'd made her feel so wonderful, she knew *the rest* must be truly spectacular.

He was spectacular. His smooth shoulders. The rippling muscles of his arms that held her so solicitously. The firm planes of his chest and abdomen pressed close to the softness of her own.

A thin sprinkling of dark hair covered his chest, leading in a line down to his belly and lower, all the way to where their bodies joined. Those same short, springy hairs tickled everywhere they touched, further stimulating her already highly sensitized nipples and making her want to rub against him, to build on the heightened energy vibrating through her body.

But there was more. She knew it not only from Wade's words, but from the swirling sensation in her belly, the increased pulsing in her veins, the urge to move beneath him and slide along that long, rigid part of him embedded so deeply inside her. She raised her hips a fraction in encouragement, and he wasted no time pulling out a little, then pushing back in.

"You're still in charge, sweetheart," he murmured close to her ear. "Do you want to stay like this, or do you want to be on top again?"

She worked her bottom lip, considering. She had liked towering over him for a change, bracing herself on his wide, muscular chest. But she liked it this way, too. "Let's just . . . keep going. We can try the other later, can't we?"

Wade made a sound that seemed to be half chuckle, half groan. "Oh, yeah. We sure can, Callie girl. We sure can."

And he began to move, wrapping her legs more firmly about his waist, sliding a hand around to caress the line of her spine. Instinctively, she linked her ankles behind his back and relinquished herself to the feel of having every inch of her naked body flush with every inch of his own.

Wade's motions increased until he was pounding into her, and Callie met each of his thrusts willingly, wanting harder, wanting faster, wanting more.

"Yes," she breathed. The word passed her lips without thought, but her whole body was humming it.

She felt glorious, as though she was flying. Sensations were building in her almost more rapidly than Wade was moving above her, and she wanted nothing more than for him to send her sailing, careening over the edge of this passion that, before tonight, she hadn't even known existed.

"God, Callie," Wade bit out, and lifted her just a fraction more, thrust into her just a mite faster.

And then everything froze. Her mouth opened in a great inhalation of breath that filled her lungs to overflowing, and Wade took the opportunity to kiss her as his tall frame rocked into her. A second later, he gave a great groan of pleasure and spasmed, sending a wave of liquid warmth all the way to her womb.

Their harsh breathing filled the room as he collapsed atop her. His weight felt wonderful, and she wrapped her arms around him to hold him near, even as the strength went out of her legs and she let them slip to the mattress on either side of his narrow hips.

Tucking her into his shoulder, he rolled to his back and cradled her against his long, sturdy body. "Have I told you lately that you're an extraordinary hostess? I'm enjoying your hospitality a whole hell of a lot."

Callie laughed. A flush climbed her neck and face, but she wasn't embarrassed enough by either his comment or their complete nudity to turn away or cover herself. Wade had done things to her, shown her things she'd never even imagined before. She was forever changed, and she rather liked it.

"Why, thank you, kind sir. Please don't hesitate to speak up if there's anything else I can do to make your stay more pleasurable."

That statement alone was bolder than she'd ever been in her life, but on top of that, she canted a leg until her knee rested barely a fraction below his now flaccid manhood. She didn't dare *look* at it, of course; she wasn't nearly that brave after only a single bout of intimacy.

His fingers dug into the soft flesh of her waist as he squeezed her tight. "Give me a couple of hours, darlin', and I might just take you up on that."

She nodded languidly and snuggled farther into the crook of his arm. While the rough pads of his fingers splayed over her left buttock, she drew lazy circles on his chest.

"Mmm," he moaned, eyes closed, breathing even.

"Wade?"

"Hmm?"

"What we just did . . ." she began tentatively.

The long lashes of one eye parted and he fixed her with a dark brown half-gaze. "Yes?"

"It was . . . nice. More than nice."

"Damn right it was," he muttered, sounding cocky and self-assured.

Taking a deep breath, she forced herself to ask what was on her mind. "Was it that nice with Lily?"

At that, his body jerked beneath hers and both coffee-colored eyes popped open. "What? Why would you ask something like that?" he growled.

"Because I want to know," she told him, sticking to her guns.

His arm around her now was tense, fingers digging rather than caressing her naked flesh. The fingers of his other hand raked roughly through his hair and he struggled to look anywhere but in her direction.

"Why?" he demanded harshly. "What does it matter?"

"It doesn't matter, except that . . . well, maybe it does. I want to know if a man experiences the same thing with every woman he takes to bed."

"Jesus," he muttered, sitting up and letting her fall back to the mattress alone.

She watched the stretch and pull of his muscles as he sat on the edge of the bed, leaning forward to scavenge for his clothes in the pile on the floor. She'd never seen him bare from this angle before; he had a broad, smooth back that led down to a very nice behind. Firm and well-rounded, and when he stood to pull on his jeans, she noticed two tiny, attractive indentations on either side.

Funny, he didn't have dimples on his other cheeks, she thought with a grin.

But when he turned back around, fastening the top button of his trousers, she wiped any sign of amusement from her expression.

With Wade now half-dressed, she felt suddenly exposed and pulled a corner of the quilted coverlet loose to drape over her hips and breasts.

"You don't have to get upset," she said. "I'm not jealous of your time with Lily. You were together even before Matthew was conceived; I understand that. It doesn't bother me." Well, perhaps a little, but he needn't know that. "I'm just curious about why it's all right for men to visit with any number of women at establishments like the Painted Lady, but women—decent women, at any rate—are expected to keep themselves chaste until marriage and then remain with that one man for the rest of their lives. Even though their husbands may still go into town upon occasion for the same thing they paid for before they wed."

Digging his hands deep into his pockets, Wade hunched his shoulders and rolled his eyes. "For

God's sake, Callie, you'll have to go all the way back to Adam and Eve if you want answers to questions like that."

"Then tell me why you do it." Her brow crinkled as she frowned. "Nathan has visited the Painted Lady a time or two himself, I'm aware. I can't say I approve, but then, that's the way of the world, I suppose. Which is what I want to know: *Why* is that the way of the world?"

"How the hell am I supposed to know?" he snapped. "It just is."

She shook her head, far from satisfied. "No, I think there must be a reason. Bread dough rises because you add yeast. Cows give milk because they're carrying a calf. Matthew cries because he's either wet or hungry. Men visit loose women because . . . why?"

"Because men have needs, Callie." He threw his hands up and set to pacing. "That's all I can tell you."

She considered that. "Needs of a sexual nature. All right," she agreed, "but don't women have needs, as well? I quite enjoyed what we did together, and I imagine if I was given the choice, I'd like to enjoy it again. Are you saying that men *need* that, but women don't? That you'll get the urge to . . . do what we did and not be able to control yourself, but that I'll merely find the act pleasurable once you've started?"

Wade's head dropped forward and he covered

his face with his hands. Then he let his arms fall and looked heavenward. "God, if you're listening, I'd appreciate a nice lightning bolt to strike me dead right about now. Or a tornado to rip the roof off and take me with it."

Callie's lips pursed as she struggled not to laugh. "That doesn't answer my question," she replied primly, refusing to let him off the hook. "Does that mean we'll only make love again if *you* get a hankering, and not if I do? Or is it assured that I won't get any inklings along those lines?"

Which couldn't be right, she thought with confusion. Wade stood a scant few feet away, in stocking feet and no shirt, and already she was beginning to feel tingles in her breasts and lower belly region.

He pinned her with a smoldering glance. "We can do it whenever you like, sweetheart. And I sure as hell hope you get some hankerings, same as me."

"So women do get urges. Why, then, do they have to be so virtuous? Why aren't there brothels with working men for women to buy?"

A cross between a squeak and a groan rolled up from Wade's throat. "Why is this so important?" he asked in return. "Why can't you just accept that things are the way they are? I feel like a damn fly having its wings pulled off, for Christ's sake."

"Just tell me why you spent time with Lily. Were you . . . acquainted with her—in that manner, I mean—before she started working there?"

Callie doubted that was possible, since she and Lily had arrived in Purgatory on the same wagon train, and Lily had gone to work at the Painted Lady almost immediately afterward.

"Did you pay for any other girls?" she wanted to know. "There or in other whorehouses?"

Wade scowled. "No, I didn't know Lily before she started working at the Painted Lady. And, yes, I'd slept with others, there and elsewhere. That's just the way it is, Callie. From the time things start stirring down there"—he waved an angry hand over the area of his crotch—"when we're boys, we know where to go for relief. Certain types of women spread their legs for money, and men take them up on the offer."

"But you still expect your future wives to be virginal," she commented.

His eyes narrowed in frustration. "Yeah, I reckon we do."

Callie held the blanket more firmly about her breasts. "That hardly seems fair. And I suppose that means I'm soiled goods, now that I've done what I've done with you."

In one long stride, he reached the bed and sat on its edge, cupping her cheek in the palm of his hand. "You're not a whore, Callie."

She blinked, then leaned back, her shoulders

ramrod straight. "I never said I was. I merely observed that I'm no longer a virgin; therefore, perhaps I'm no longer marriageable, either."

"You're plenty marriageable," he told her firmly. "Any man would be lucky to have you as his bride. And crazy if he thought the lack of a maidenhead would change that."

"Thank you, I guess," she replied. But inside she was thinking, *What about you? You took my maidenhead. Would you ever marry me?*

Which was probably the silliest thing ever to cross her mind. Wade didn't love her; he'd simply been attracted to her enough to take her to bed, and she'd been attracted enough to him to let him. He was running from the law, at great risk of being sent back to prison, and even if he wasn't, she didn't delude herself into believing the idea of marriage would ever cross his mind. At least not marriage to her.

"So you were intimate with Lily because . . ."

"She was selling and I was buying," he answered, his mouth twisting at both the ugly truth and the bluntness of that answer.

"But at the prison, when Matthew was conceived . . . you didn't pay her then, did you?"

"No, that was all Lily. On the house."

"And you went through with it—"

He cut her off. "Because I had a crowbar in my pants. I'd gone without for a hell of a long time. I wasn't going to turn any woman away."

She nodded, not the least affected by his candid statement. "I can't say that I understand everything about this. Why men seem to have all these urges they find impossible to deny, while women apparently don't experience very many urges at all—or none they're permitted to fulfill. But I suppose I'm beginning to see why so many women turn to that sort of lifestyle. Pleasuring men for money, that is."

"You do, huh?" His voice turned low and grating, and he leaned closer to hear her answer, looking pointedly at the spot where her fingers held the quilt in place.

"Yes. The sex act is quite gratifying, from my limited experience," she replied matter-of-factly. "I rather think I could do it more than once a night. And if I were to earn a few dollars from a task I enjoyed . . ."

A dark brow winged upward in alarm. "I hope you're not thinking of taking up at the Painted Lady. 'Cause that's something I won't allow. You're too good for that place, Callie girl. Too sweet and too damn pretty to grow old before your time the way those girls do. No," he said with a determined shake of his head. "You get that notion out of your head right this minute."

"Oh, I wasn't considering becoming a working girl; I was only saying that I understand why some women do. I've always thought lying with a man would be a painful, unpleasant business, but it isn't. And some women—like Lily—need the money awfully bad."

The room fell into silence, and then she cast him a sly, sideways glance. "Wade."

"Uh-oh." He eyed her warily. "What?"

"How much do you think men would be willing to pay for me?"

His brows lifted, but he resolutely answered, "There isn't enough money in the world, sweetheart. You're priceless."

She grinned, flattered right down to her toes. "I guess no one would hire me at one of those places, then. Being too expensive and all."

"That's right." He seemed to stalk her, crawling even nearer from his spot on the edge of the mattress. "You're all mine, Callie girl. Every precious inch of you."

"But you don't have a penny to your name," she teased. "I know because I burned the clothes you arrived in and the pockets were empty."

"Are you saying that if I were to hand over a couple of greenbacks, you'd be more of a mind to let me make love to you again?" he tossed back.

She looped her arms around his neck, letting him ease her into the pillows until she was lying full length beneath him, only the thin quilt and his denim trousers between them.

"Oh, no," she whispered. "You don't need money with me, Wade Mason. For you, it's always free."

Chapter Eighteen

Early the next morning, Callie heard a loud and persistent knocking, and wanted nothing more than to cover her head with a pillow and ignore it.

Matthew had awakened only once during the night, thank goodness. Wade, as generous a partner as a lover, had whispered for Callie to stay put, then proceeded to change the baby, give him a bottle, and wait for him to drift off again before climbing back into bed with her.

Sleeping next to Wade made her feel drowsily sensual, their bodies pressed close and naked beneath the soft, fresh-smelling sheets. Lying in his arms, even waking up beside him was a delightful luxury she'd never thought to experience.

But she didn't enjoy waking up beside him in

this manner, being jolted out of a deep and pleasant dream world by the sound of pounding at the door downstairs.

When the knocking didn't stop, Callie sat up. Wade was already on his feet, hurriedly tugging on his trousers and shirt, gathering up every hint of his presence from her room.

"Are you expecting anyone this morning?" he wanted to know.

"No." With Nathan being gone, she rarely got visitors. Living as far from town as she did, people rarely stopped by just for a casual visit.

"Get dressed."

He tossed her discarded lavender gown across the bed, and she quickly stepped into the wrinkled folds of material, buttoning the bodice without bothering with underthings.

"You're going to have to answer," Wade said, still rushing about the room. "Whoever it is may get suspicious if you don't. But be prepared; it could be the law, someone from the posse out looking for me."

Callie swallowed. Except when Wade had first appeared in the center of her pantry, she'd never considered the authorities showing up on her doorstep. She didn't know what to tell them or how to protect Wade from being discovered and dragged back to prison. "Where will you be?"

"Right behind you," he said, tucking his shirt the rest of the way into his pants and brushing at the skirt of her gown to help her look more presentable. "I'll hide in the stairwell so I can hear what's going on."

With her hand clasped tightly in his own, he led her into the hall and toward the front of the house. "What do I say if it is someone from the posse?"

At the top of the stairs, he paused and turned to face her, slowing his breathing for the first time since they'd both jumped out of bed.

"I don't know, sweetheart, I really don't." His mouth twisted wryly. "This may be a prime opportunity to turn me in, if that's what you've been waiting for."

Her fingers tightened reflexively. "Don't say that. I would never tell them where you are."

"Then you'd better think of something else right quick. And if they want to search the house, put them off. Tell them to start in the barn or root cellar so they won't wake the baby. That'll give me time to . . . I don't know. Think, or hide, or get away."

The pounding came again, rattling the glass in the door below.

"Go," Wade whispered.

She started down the steps and he followed, stopping where the wall ended and opened into the sitting room. Callie continued on, checking the row of buttons trailing down her dress and running a hand through her mangled hair.

Her heart was pounding like a drum, fear causing cold sweat to break out along her upper lip and between her breasts. She took a deep breath, put her hand on the cool brass knob, and turned.

When the door swung open, she saw Clayton Walker—*Sheriff* Clayton Walker—standing on her porch in the early morning sun, a silver star pinned to his tanned leather vest.

"Mornin', Miss Quinn," he greeted her, removing his dusty Stetson.

"Good morning, Sheriff Walker." She remained inside the house, letting the heavy portal support her weight, since her legs were none too steady at the moment.

"I hope I'm not disturbing you," he said, taking in her slight dishevelment.

"No, it's just that I was . . . still sleeping. Matthew had a rough time of it last night," she lied. "I ended up walking him for hours and never had a chance to change out of my clothes before falling straight into bed."

The sheriff chuckled. "I know what that's like. All too well. Regan and I used to take turns staying up with Olivia when she was your boy's age. Regan says raising that baby is the only thing that ever really straightened her hair."

A grin stretched across Clay's handsome features, and Callie couldn't help smiling with him. Along with her extremely generous nature where the orphans at the Purgatory Home for Adoptive

221

Children were concerned, Regan Walker was best known for her very long, very curly, very red hair. For any child to straighten those kinks, she must have been a true horror.

"How is your little girl?"

"Oh, real good, real good. Getting into one bit of trouble after another, and sprouting out of her clothes faster than we can buy them."

"I'm glad to hear it. And the rest of your family?"

"The same. Regan's got her hands full with Livvy being a rambunctious two-year-old and a boy eighteen going on thirty. But we are both really happy we adopted David. He's turning out to be a nice young man. I'm real proud of him. And even though Regan will tell you different if you ask, she loves being a mother. Still brings orphans home with her now and again, until I think I can't tell which tykes are my own."

A hint of red began to seep up from his collar and he suddenly found something interesting about the toes of his boots. "Don't know if you've heard yet, but we're expecting again."

"No, I hadn't," Callie replied with surprise. "Congratulations. I'll have to pay Regan a visit and wish her well."

"She'd like that."

After that, the conversation seemed to fizzle, and Callie stood there nervously, wondering why the sheriff was on her doorstep to begin with.

Finally, she asked. "What brings you by this morning, Sheriff Walker?"

"I'm not sure if you're aware of this or not, Miss Callie, but there was a jailbreak up at Huntsville. A felon by the name of Wade Mason got away from a group of prisoners they had out clearing fields. He used to live around these parts, and it's suspected that he may have headed back this way. I'm making the rounds, checking to see if anyone's seen a stranger lurking about."

Reaching into the pocket of his blue chambray shirt beneath his vest, he pulled out a piece of paper and unfolded it to reveal a WANTED poster. Wade's bearded countenance stared back at her from a crudely drawn sketch, with the words $500 REWARD printed in large block letters below.

She swallowed down a lump of panic working its way up her throat.

"This is what he looked like while he was locked up, but he may be clean-shaven by now."

She shook her head. "No, I'm sorry. I haven't seen anyone at all, let alone that man."

"All right, then. You'll let me know, though, if you do?"

It was almost more of a statement than a question, but she nodded all the same. "Is he . . . dangerous?" she made herself ask.

Wade was standing less than five yards behind her, hidden by the wall of the stairwell. But it was a question she thought any woman living alone would ask, and could only hope he'd understand.

"Could be," Clay responded.

His answer surprised her. She'd expected him to immediately claim Wade was a highly menacing convicted murderer, and that she should be careful.

"He was sent to Huntsville for murdering Neville Young. Neville's son, Brady, is hopping mad about Mason's escape. He's the one offering the reward." Clay tapped the parchment in his hand before folding it up and slipping it back into his breast pocket.

"I don't think you need to be too worried. Rumor has it he doesn't make a habit of killing people, just of wanting to get his ranch back. That's why we think he may have hightailed it back to Purgatory. I'd say keep an eye out, stay away from strangers, and let me know if you see anything suspicious. It wouldn't hurt for your brother to be here, just in case," he added with a frown. "That is, if you have any way of contacting him and asking him to come home. Or if you're worried, you can always come stay at the house with us. I'm sure Regan would enjoy the company, and she'd probably be more than happy to walk that boy of yours for a night or two if you'd be willing to chase little Livvy around."

Callie laughed to keep herself from slamming the door in the sheriff's face and rushing to Wade's side to see what he thought of this newest turn of events. "That won't be necessary, Sheriff. I appreciate the offer, but I'll be fine where I am."

Dipping his chin in acquiescence, he replaced his hat and fit it snugly on his head. "Well, I just wanted to check up and see that everything was all right. You let me know if you need anything, you hear?"

"I will, Sheriff Walker. Thank you."

The sheriff started down the porch steps and crossed the yard to where his piebald mount was tethered and waiting.

As soon as he was out of earshot, she shut the door, turning and leaning against the wooden frame in relief. The tightness in her lungs eased and her diaphragm expanded as she took her first truly deep breath of the day.

"He's gone," she said, moving forward as Wade stepped around the wallpapered barrier and into the parlor.

"That was Sheriff Walker," she told him, not sure how much he'd heard, or how clearly. "He was asking about you but didn't seem as . . . bloodthirsty as I'd have expected. He's looking for you, but not above all else."

"I didn't hear him say anything about a posse," Wade commented, rubbing the knuckles of one hand with the palm of the other in an apprehensive manner.

"No, and I didn't ask." Toying with the lace bordering her sleeves, she said, "But Brady Young put up a five-hundred-dollar reward for your capture."

He gave a rude snort. "Figures. He shoots his own father, and now he wants to give every bounty hunter, lawman, and dirt-poor farmhand five hundred reasons to hunt me down."

"Wade," she said softly, waiting until his wild eyes calmed and he turned his full attention to her. "The poster, the one Sheriff Walker showed me. It said you were wanted . . . dead or alive."

A cold, sinking feeling washed over Wade's body. He'd known he was in trouble, that any number of lawmen were looking for him, but he hadn't known he had a target attached to his back. With a bounty on his head, things were even more dire than before.

"Maybe I'd better go."

A flash of confusion passed over Callie's delicate features. "What do you mean? Go where?"

"Anywhere. Away from here. Every minute I stay, I put you and Matthew in danger."

He turned on his heel, stalking toward the stairwell. Before he'd even reached out to touch the newel post, Callie's hand grabbed hold of his elbow.

"You can't leave. You'll be killed if you do."

He set his jaw, refusing to succumb to the shiver of fear her words produced. "Not necessarily. I could be hauled back to prison and left to rot," he bit out, thinking he'd almost rather be shot in the back by some overeager plowboy.

Her fingers fell from his arm, but her voice when she spoke was razor sharp. "And where do you think you'll go? Back to your ranch? It doesn't belong to you anymore. Do you think you'll simply run anywhere you can, scavenging for food and shelter, forever looking over your shoulder? That's no kind of life, Wade."

"What the hell do you want from me, Callie?"

Furious, he whipped around to confront her. The woman he'd made love to just last night. The woman who might as well be the true mother of his child. The woman he was beginning to think would make a nice addition to his life—if he could ever find a way to rebuild it.

"I won't put you and Matthew in jeopardy just because I've been safe here so far. Better for me to leave the two of you alone, at least until the law has forgotten about me."

"Do you really think that's going to happen?" she demanded, but never gave him a chance to answer. "I wouldn't wager on it, not anytime soon. You're an escaped convict, sent to that penitentiary for killing a man. As far as they're concerned, you're capable of murdering again. They won't stop until they find you, especially if

Brady Young continues to encourage them with his inflammatory lies and cash rewards."

"Then what am I supposed to do, hide out here for the next ten years?"

For an idea he'd have found oddly appealing mere hours before, it now made him feel like a coward. He shared a roof with his son and his woman—for last night, Callie had become his woman—but he could do nothing to provide for them, help them, or even protect them if the need arose. He might as well be trapped in a dank prison cell, with no chance of ever again escaping.

"No," she replied solemnly. "I think you have to fight. Prove your innocence and get your land back."

"Considering that's been my plan all along—though it hasn't worked too well up to now, has it?—just how do you suggest I go about that?"

"Find the deed to your ranch."

Chapter Nineteen

What happened to his prim and proper, almost demure Callie? Had all her cautions and common sense flown out the window last night, along with her maidenhood?

"I'd like nothing more," he said bluntly, "but I told you, either Neville Young or Jensen Graves took the copy from the registrar's office and replaced it with one of his own."

"I've been thinking about that." With her tone returned to normal, even thoughtful, she walked to the sofa in the middle of the room and sat down.

She looked lovely, in the same bright lavender gown as yesterday, the very same one he'd had the distinct pleasure of stripping from her twelve hours earlier. He wished they could forget about his being on the run, and the sheriff's visit, and go back to bed. They wouldn't sleep, of course, but they'd have a damn good time playing at it.

Callie's mind, however, seemed to be on anything but physical intimacies. "Even though Neville had one of the copies removed from the registrar's office, I wouldn't be surprised if he kept it. Maybe even kept the deed he stole from you, as well."

Wade's brow crinkled as he rounded the mahogany-framed settee and took a seat adjacent to Callie on the edge of a matching armchair. "What do you mean?"

"I mean, I think there may still be proof that you originally owned the Circle M. And possibly a way to show it was wrongfully taken from you."

He knew doubt was written all over his face but said nothing. Just sat back and let Callie go on with her little plan, which he didn't see as going much of anywhere.

"Brady Young is nothing if not arrogant. But he comes by it honestly; his father was smug and self-important while he was alive, too. Neville prided himself on being wealthier and more intelligent than anyone else in Purgatory. He liked to act as though he owned the town, or at the very least that he could do whatever he wanted here and no one would stop him. My guess—and it really is only a guess—is that Neville didn't see the need to destroy your original papers once he had them in his possession and replaced them with forged documents stating he was the true owner of your property."

Wade narrowed his eyes, staring at her, trying to comprehend what she was saying. His brain, it seemed, was still asleep, because her words weren't making sense.

"I'm sorry," he said, shaking his head. "I just can't see what you're getting at here."

"What if your deed is still in Young's house? Even before you were sent away, no one questioned Young's taking over your ranch, did they? Other than you, that is."

"No."

"And Neville was just conceited enough to not feel any need to destroy the evidence that proved him a thief. He would never have expected anyone to question him about it, or to cross him even if they did suspect something. After all, you fought and defied him, but he didn't worry about it because he figured he could handle you."

Wade snorted. "Did a good job of it, too. But what about his son? Brady is running things now. He could have destroyed any authentic documents—if they still existed."

"Brady is just as bad as his father," Callie said. "Maybe worse, because he's not only arrogant but young. Which, in my estimation, makes him stupid. If Neville hadn't done away with your set of deeds, then I don't think Brady would even think to look for them. He's cocky and thinks that if he doesn't already own the town, he soon will."

"If you're right and there really is still proof of my ownership on the Triply Y, where do you suppose it would be?"

A muted whimper from upstairs caught their attention and Callie immediately rose to tend Matthew. "That, I couldn't tell you. Neville's study, maybe. Which is probably Brady's study now. Though they may very well have a better hiding place for that sort of thing."

"It's a start."

Wade pushed to his feet and followed Callie, watching the steady sway of her hips as she climbed the stairs. Taking the treads two at a time, he caught up to her and wrapped his arms about her waist from behind. She squealed as he lifted her off the ground and carried her the remaining distance to the second-story landing.

"What are you doing?" She sounded breathless and on the verge of laughter, just the way he liked her.

With his lips pressed to the soft skin just below her ear, he said, "Hoping you'll let me take that dress off of you again. It was such fun the first time."

She chuckled, swatting at his hands where they were locked like a vice beneath her breasts.

"Your son is awake and likely waiting for his breakfast, in case you've forgotten."

"I haven't forgotten. I was just hoping he'd wait a few minutes."

No sooner were the words out of his mouth than Matthew let out a caterwaul that ran down Wade's spine like the blade of a knife.

"Hungry babies don't wait," Callie told him needlessly, and broke away to enter Matthew's room.

Wade made faces at his son, tickling his belly and neck and pretending to bite at his tiny fingers while Callie changed his diaper. Then he carried Matthew downstairs for his bottle of milk, giving Callie the opportunity to clean up and dress in a different gown.

He was kind of partial to the purple one, frankly, but she seemed to be bothered by the wrinkles and wearing the same garment two days in a row, so he took over with the baby and let her go. Besides, new clothes would give him a chance to peel a whole different outfit off of her later.

Not too much later, though. Not if he could help it.

With that in mind, he made a mental note to play with Matthew as much as possible and tire him out so he'd be more inclined to take an early nap.

"I know you just got up, kid," he said to Matthew as he stoked the cookstove and began the process of heating milk for the bottle. "But your pa's got something going on here, and I'd appreciate it if you'd give me some time alone with Callie today. Sleep a lot, or at least find something to keep you happy and occupied. I'll be doing the same, believe me."

"Who are you talking to?"

He jumped at Callie's sudden appearance and felt his face heat, wondering how much of his father-to-son chat she'd heard.

"Nobody," he said, then quickly corrected himself. "Just Matthew here."

Her simple lavender day dress had been replaced by one of green gingham. The small squares drew the eye and created a beautiful backdrop for Callie's cream-colored skin and dark hair.

"It sounded a bit too earnest for a three-month-old," she commented, though he didn't think she was reprimanding him. Moving to the stove, she stood beside him as she tested the temperature of the milk and poured it carefully into the glass bottle.

"Well, a man talks differently to his son than to other people. Parents and children have serious issues to discuss."

"Such as . . . ?" With the lid on the bottle tight, she helped to rearrange the baby in his arms, then settled the rubber nipple in Matthew's eager mouth.

There was no distracting her, that was for sure. "Oh, manly things. Nothing you'd be interested in."

Her eyes twinkled and the corners of her mouth tipped up, as though she was struggling not to smile. "Ah, I see. Manly things. Well, since I certainly have no place in that sort of conversation, I'll go deal with the morning chores."

She headed for the back door, sticking her feet into the oversize work boots he'd noticed she sometimes wore out to the barn. He thought they were probably a pair Nathan had left behind when he'd taken off for California.

Before opening the door, she cocked her head to look at him over her shoulder. "Will you be taking care of breakfast?" she asked.

The hopeful note in her voice nearly made him laugh. He'd prepared meals so often since coming here, he thought his young lovely might be getting a bit used to it.

If it hadn't been for the fact that Wade never wanted her to be with another man, he might feel almost sorry for her future husband. The man would have to fend for himself if he ever cared for a decent meal. And aside from her tendency to burn things, Callie seemed to have gotten used to his handling the cooking; he wouldn't be surprised if it turned out to be a chore she demanded from her husband.

"Sure," he answered amicably. "What would you like?"

"Anything," she said, mumbling something else he didn't quite catch as she stepped into the bright morning light.

But he could have sworn the remark ended something along the lines of, *as long as I don't have to cook it.*

"Ouch." Callie pulled the sharp point of her embroidery needle out of the tip of her finger and stuck the sore digit into her mouth until it stopped stinging.

That was the third time. They'd been in the parlor going on two hours now, with Wade and Matthew rolling around on the floor while Callie attempted to sew a set of fancy blue initials in the corner of a handkerchief that now had tiny bloodstains on the thin white material.

All because she was trying to work up the courage to tell Wade something she knew he wouldn't like—that she wanted him to go to the Young ranch to look for his deed . . . and that she wanted to go along.

If she put it off any longer, though, blood loss might keep her from following through on her plan. And she hoped to go over there tonight, so she'd best circle her wagons and get on with it.

"Wade," she began, before she could once again talk herself out of it.

On his hands and knees on the floor, he looked up at her. He had Matthew situated just like him, urging him to crawl. She didn't bother telling Wade that the child was much too young for such a thing.

So far, Matthew had only managed to stick his diapered bottom in the air and wobble back and forth. He'd fallen on occasion but never cried. Instead, he smiled broadly, happy just to be having so much fun with his father. And Callie was having fun watching them.

She hated to ruin the lightness of the day by bringing up a topic sure to darken Wade's mood.

When she didn't continue soon after capturing his attention, Wade swept Matthew off the carpeted floor and took a seat in a nearby chair, placing the child on his lap.

"What's on your mind, sweetheart? You've got little crinkles between your pretty brown eyes." He reached out a long finger to brush the lines away. "Are you worried about something?"

"Only about how you'll react when I tell you the plan I've come up with."

Setting aside her sewing, she clasped her hands together, braced her shoulders, and faced him bravely. "But I'll warn you right now, Wade, I've made up my mind. You won't be talking me out of this."

237

His expression didn't change; he merely nodded somberly. "All right. But maybe you should tell me what's going on so I know whether or not I *should* try to talk you out of it."

"You won't, so don't even bother," she told him adamantly. Before he had to ask again for an explanation of her strange behavior, she continued. "I think we should go to the Triple Y tonight and search for the papers on your ranch."

He eyed her carefully and then said, *"We?"*

"Yes, *we.*"

"No."

"Yes."

"Dammit, Callie, I said no." He leapt to his feet, the baby clutched in one arm, chubby legs dangling in the air.

Callie jumped up to face him at eye level. "And I said yes. In case it's slipped your attention, this is my house you're hiding out in. I lied to Sheriff Walker about not having seen you around, and at this point, I'm the only one who believes in your innocence. I'm also the one who came up with the idea that a copy of your deed may still exist. So if anybody is going over there to look for it, that person will be me."

"The hell it will," Wade growled.

Arguing was obviously getting her nowhere, she thought with a resigned mental sigh. Fine.

"I don't need your permission, Wade," she said sternly. "I can come and go as I please. And you, being a wanted man, can do very little to stop me."

Wade arched a dark brow, and a menacing look came into his eyes that told her she'd gone one step too far.

"Is that what you think?" he breathed.

Callie licked her lips nervously, wondering if there was some way for her to worm her way out of the predicament she found herself in without giving up the fight altogether.

But he didn't give her time to answer or retreat. Faster than she could blink, he wrapped his free arm around her waist, hauled her up against the hard wall of his chest, and kissed her.

Chapter Twenty

It was a diversionary tactic. Kissing her both stopped her from going on with her ridiculous notion of breaking into Brady Young's house and gave him a moment to think.

Of course, with Callie's supple body pressed so close to his own, her warm mouth moving beneath his, all rational thought fled. There was only Callie and her heat, her softness, the passion that raged between them.

His fingers kneaded her back, his tongue dueling with hers. A groan rolled its way up his throat and he considered pressing her down to the sofa and raising her skirts . . . until Matthew took to squirming between them like a snake with its tail caught under a rock.

Wade broke away reluctantly, keeping his lips

on hers until he had no choice but to step back and open his eyes. His one consolation was that she looked as dazed as he felt.

"We could put Matthew down for a couple of hours and then . . . take a little nap ourselves," he suggested in a low voice.

"Somehow I don't think you have sleeping in mind," she retorted, and then moved even farther away. "Besides, we haven't yet settled our argument."

He shifted Matthew higher at his side before saying, "Oh, yes we have. You're not going, and that's an end to it."

"I was about to say basically the same to you. Yes, I am going, and that's an end to *that*. Wade," she went on, her tone changing from firm to almost cajoling, "please trust me on this; it makes sense. You can stay here with Matthew while I go over to the Triple Y."

He was already shaking his head, but she kept right on going.

"Brady spends most of his evenings at the Painted Lady, drinking and playing poker . . . among other things," she added with a derisive twist to her lips. "I'm betting the house will be empty and I'll have a chance to look around before he ever returns. And even if he does, I'll use the same excuse I intended to last time—that I was simply stopping by for a visit. It will be even more believable if I take along a loaf of bread or fresh pastry."

"I don't like it, Callie." His frustration was clear in the bite of every word. "Do you have any idea what kind of person Brady Young is? He shot his own father in the back, set me up for the crime, and put me in a hellhole state penitentiary for what was supposed to be the rest of my life. There's no telling what he might do to a pretty young thing like you, especially if he finds out you're up to no good."

She rolled her eyes. "That's exactly why I *have* to do this—because of the kind of man he is and what he did to you. And even if he does come home early, he won't figure out why I'm really there, Wade. He's not bright enough for that. Besides, I've told you before that he fancies himself sweet on me . . . or maybe I should say he thinks *I* should be sweet on *him*. Either way, with a few sidelong glances or girlish giggles, I can have him thinking I'm simply lonely for his company."

Wade glowered. Her argument infuriated him, even if she did have a good point—several of them. He had to think of something to talk her out of this asinine scheme.

"So you're willing to prostitute yourself for the sake of Brady Young not becoming suspicious?"

It was a vicious remark and he knew it. He was lucky she didn't reach out and slap him. But the look on her face stung more than a physical blow ever could.

"No," she said, and the word was brittle. "I'm willing to prostitute myself for *you.*" And with that, she turned and stalked from the room.

Wade didn't blame her; he'd acted like an ass. He couldn't seem to stop himself, though. The thought of her anywhere near Brady Young made him crazy. *She* made him crazy, even if she was only trying to help him.

He cringed. That smarted even worse. She really did have his best interests at heart. He owed it to her to at least hear her out. Which he'd done, for the most part, but he couldn't get past the image of her setting foot on the Triple Y— Brady territory.

With a sigh, he started for the kitchen, deciding he'd better unruffle Callie's feathers—and fast—if he expected to ever again get anywhere near relieving her of her underthings.

When he stepped into the room, Matthew still attached to his hip and happily gumming a fold of fabric from the arm of Wade's shirt, he found Callie packing several glass jars of various canned items into a wicker basket lined with a red-and-white-checkered cloth.

"What are you doing?" he asked automatically.

"Since you're being so stubborn, I decided not to take the time to bake something. I'll just take a basket of preserves with me in case he shows up, and act like I planned to drop them off all the while."

With that, she threw another checkered napkin over the jars and started past him into the other room.

He grabbed her wrist as she flitted by. "Callie."

"Don't try to stop me, Wade," she charged, yanking her arm free. "I've made up my mind and I don't care to hear any more about it."

"So I gathered. Did anyone ever tell you that you're a damn stubborn woman?" he muttered almost to himself.

A bit of the tension seemed to seep from her body. "My brother, upon occasion."

He chuckled. "I knew I couldn't be the only one." And then he took a deep, cleansing breath. "All right, so your mind's made up. But if you're going, then I'm going, too."

"It's not safe for you to leave the house," she pointed out. "Someone might see you."

A strange comment for someone who'd originally intended for the both of them to go on this little search mission, he thought. But all he said was, "I'll risk it."

She glanced at Matthew, her mouth turned down in a frown. A thin line of spittle connected his wet bottom lip to the soaked-through patch of material on Wade's arm.

"Who'll watch Matthew if we both go?" she wanted to know.

"Good question. Maybe we should give up on the idea altogether. Or you could stay home with him while I go over to Triple Y and have a look around."

He hadn't planned on trying to talk her out of her foolish strategy again, but since Matthew couldn't very well be left alone—and he wouldn't let Callie go off on her own, either—it gave him a good excuse for one final attempt.

Her eyes narrowed. "I have an even better idea," she said. "I'll take Matthew to stay with Father Ignacio for the evening. The padre won't mind watching him for a couple of hours."

His Callie was sharp, he'd give her that. She didn't miss a trick and wasn't going to be easily swayed from what she felt was right.

What other choice did he have? "Then I guess we're heading for the Triple Y come sunset."

She nodded. "I'll start out early so I can drop Matthew off at the orphanage first. If you're sure you want to chance going out, you can meet me there. Do you know how to get to the Young place from here?"

"Oh, I know how to get there." He knew the distance to Young's place from just about anywhere in or outside of town. He'd always intended to stop by, though in his mind, his visit had more to do with a confrontation and beating the ever-loving snot out of Brady Young than with taking the bastard a basket of blackberry jam.

"I'll meet you outside. Find somewhere you won't be spotted. When I arrive, I'll check to make sure it's safe before we go in. That way, if Brady or anyone else is around, you can remain hidden and we'll put the plan off until a better time."

"You've got it all figured out, haven't you?" he teased.

"Someone has to work at clearing your name," she retorted saucily.

"And I appreciate it. Provided this doesn't turn out to be the worst idea anyone's ever come up with."

"If we find the deed, you'll thank me."

"If we find the deed, I'll kiss you senseless, then drag you to the mission and have Father Ignacio marry us but good."

Callie's eyes widened at that, and he realized the nature of the words that had come out of his mouth before he'd really thought them through. They'd slipped out, certainly, but that didn't explain why Wade wasn't immediately scurrying to suck them back in.

He pictured the two of them standing before a preacher and didn't break out in a cold sweat. He imagined them coming home to this house, or the Circle M, with Matthew in tow, and setting to work making even more dark-haired, pixie-nosed babies and didn't get an urge to find the nearest whorehouse and prove he was anything but a one-woman man.

Because he wasn't sure exactly how he felt about the proposition that had unintentionally come up, he wasn't sure how to fix it. But Callie saved him the trouble and uneasiness of broaching the sensitive subject by pretending the words had never been spoken . . . or at least ignoring the impact he knew they'd had.

"Let me dress Matthew and get a few things packed for him before we leave," she said, reaching out to take the child into her own arms.

Wade watched her go, listening as she made her way up the stairs to Matthew's room and wondering what it would be like to live under the same roof as Callie if she wore his ring on her finger.

When Callie passed beneath the slightly crooked wooden arch of the Triply Y, the impressive two-story house was dark. The barn and bunkhouse several yards away were also unlit in the approaching darkness of evening.

She'd been hoping for this very thing. The hands got paid on Friday, which meant that most, if not all, of them would be in town, spreading around their newly acquired wealth.

Including Brady, who would go along with his men for a good time.

Walking with purpose instead of stealth, she made her way down the dusty lane and right up to the front door. Just to be safe, she knocked, both hoping and knowing no one would answer her summons. And when no one did, she wrapped her fingers around the handle, clicked the latch, and walked inside.

She didn't know where Wade was but suspected he was somewhere nearby, hiding in the trees or behind an outbuilding.

Leaving the basket of preserves near the door, she moved forward to find and light a lamp that she could carry through the house with her. She kept the wick low so as not to attract attention, knowing she would need the illumination to not only make her way about the house, but to conduct a detailed search for the deed.

Since Wade hadn't come through the front of the house, Callie carefully made her way to the back and opened a rear door most likely used by the housekeeper and other household help. She stood there for a long minute, letting her eyes adjust to the darkness and waiting for any sign of Wade's presence. Finally, she saw a figure at the top of a small hillock, coming out of the trees and hurrying in her direction.

Wasting no time, Wade reached the back door and ducked inside, and Callie quickly turned toward Neville's—and now Brady's—study.

"This way," she motioned.

The office was decorated in dark woods and fabrics. A mammoth, ornately carved desk took up most of the space in the room, with pine green drapes at the window, and book-filled shelves that stretched all the way to the ceiling.

Wade took a seat in the studded leather desk chair and immediately began riffling through drawers. Callie set the lamp on the flat surface in front of him and skimmed the book spines, looking for anything that might be a ledger or more than simply a novel for leisure reading. She pulled a number of volumes off the shelves, flipped through the pages, then replaced them when they revealed nothing out of the ordinary.

A clattering from the desk brought her around to see Wade yanking at an apparently locked drawer near the floor.

"Do you see a key anywhere?" he asked in a hushed voice. He rattled the handle again, at the same time searching the desktop with his free hand.

Callie came forward to help him look, glancing over papers as she moved them aside and rattling a small crystal saucerlike dish of coins.

"Forget it," Wade said, reaching past her for a pewter letter opener and ramming it into the narrow slit between the drawer and the desk frame. After working the implement against the latch for a few seconds, she heard a crack and the drawer flew open.

Callie returned the letter opener to its proper place while Wade shuffled through the drawer's contents. It was bad enough that Brady would probably know someone had been in his office by the broken lock on his desk; she didn't want anything else to be out of place.

"Hmph."

"Did you find something?" she asked in response to his snort, leaning across the desk to get a look at the books in his lap.

"No ownership papers for the Circle M, but they have two sets of books here. One shows they've been using my ranch for cattle and grazing, and turning a profit at it."

Deep lines of displeasure bracketed his mouth, and she felt a stab of sympathy for him.

As he continued flipping through ledger pages, she moved about the room, lifting rugs to feel for loose floorboards and running her hands over the lines of the wainscoting, searching for built-in hidden compartments.

"I'm going to check the rest of the house," she said finally, moving toward the doorway. "You keep that lamp; I'll find another."

His only response was a jerky nod.

As she started out of the room, she lifted the edge of a wall hanging and glanced behind it. She found nothing, but the almost unmindful action made her wonder if anything might be behind the other paintings in the room and inspired her to check.

At the last frame, hanging high above the mantel of a small hearth, she discovered more than flat, nondescript paper decorating the wall beneath. Standing on her toes, her fingers brushed across cool metal as she struggled to lift the painting from its hook.

"I don't suppose you could help me," she prompted when Wade didn't react to her huffing and grunting. "I think I might have found something. I just can't reach."

Before she'd even finished her sentence, he was beside her, lifting down the picture and setting it aside.

"I'll be damned."

They stood back a step, staring. Wade's curse summed up Callie's initial reaction precisely.

"It's a safe," she said, though she needn't have bothered.

"Deeds can be kept in a safe." Wade stated the thought uppermost in both their minds.

"There's only one problem: We don't have the combination."

Chapter Twenty-one

Wade's head was pounding as he turned around and hurried back to the desk. Holding the ledger he'd been perusing up to the yellowish glow of the dim lantern light, he said, "Try 15-38-7-24-19-4."

Standing on the edge of a small end table for better access, Callie spun the large dial in the center of the metal contraption. Right, then left, then right, and all over again. Barely auditory ticks accompanied her motions. When she was finished with all six numbers—only two of which she needed Wade to repeat—she wrapped her hands around the even larger pipe-like handle and yanked.

They heard a click and the vault door squeaked open.

"I can't believe it," Callie breathed. "How did you know that would work?"

"The idiot wrote the combination on the front cover of his business journal," Wade scoffed as he lifted Callie from her perch on the table and took her place, pulling out the contents of the safe and passing them to her.

When he was sure the vault was empty, he jumped down to the floor and joined her at the desk, where she'd spread out everything and was searching the pile.

His chest began to burn, and he realized he wasn't breathing. He shoved his shaking hands into his pockets, standing stock-still, letting her sort through the papers by herself. He was too afraid of what they might—or might not—find to touch any of the documents. He could only hope . . . and pray.

"Wade."

She said his name and his heart lurched. His eyes darted to hers and he swallowed hard.

"What? You didn't find anything, did you? I knew it was too good to be true." He took a deep breath, trying to dispel the cramping in his gut.

"Actually," she answered, sounding a bit too chipper for his peace of mind, "I think this might be what you've been looking for."

She held out a sheaf of yellowed parchment toward him, smiling her angel smile, but he was still afraid to look. Afraid it wouldn't be his deed to the Circle M at all, and he'd be right back where he started—on the run, with no prospects and no hope for the future outside of a dank, rat-infested prison cell.

Callie fluttered the papers beneath his nose and said, "Look."

He did, and he could have sworn he was about to swoon. He grabbed the sheets away from her and stared even harder.

It was his deed, the copy Neville Young had stolen from his house, and proof that he really did own his ranch.

"I can't believe it. I can't believe we found it."

"Neither can I. But now that we have, we'd best get out of here."

She gathered up the scattered contents of the safe and hopped up on the rectangular table to shove them back inside, slamming the heavy metal door after them.

Callie took the paperwork from him, and Wade re-hung the painting. They each examined the room, making sure nothing looked too noticeably out of place. He even thought he'd gotten the locked desk drawer closed again in such a way that Brady wouldn't necessarily notice it had been jimmied open. At least not right away.

He followed Callie into the hall and toward the front door, where she collected her jars of jam, hiding the deed beneath the checkered cloth. He snuffed out the lamp, and Callie returned it to what he assumed was the very spot she'd taken it from earlier.

"Are you sure you don't want to leave that, after all?" he asked, gesturing to the basket on her arm. "To thank Brady for returning my deed to me?"

One corner of her mouth lifted in response to his own grin, but she shook her head. "Since he didn't exactly *return* it to you, I doubt that would be wise. He'll figure out we've been here soon enough."

Wade peeked out the front door, checking that it was safe. "I don't see anyone, but be careful."

"*You* be careful," she warned him. "You have much more to lose if you get caught."

He nodded. "I'll see you at home," he said, waiting for her to slip outside before closing the door after her and heading for the kitchen.

Once on her way, Callie walked toward town, careful not to twist an ankle on the rutted dirt paths this late at night. But instead of going straight to the orphanage to retrieve Matthew from Father Ignacio's care, she stopped at the sheriff's office, where a light burned bright in the small window facing the street.

She hoped Sheriff Walker was still on duty. Although he often turned things over to his deputies in the evening so he could be home with his family, Friday and Saturday nights in Purgatory sometimes got a bit rowdy, so it was just as likely that he was working at this hour.

Callie wasn't sure she was doing the right thing. Her pulse picked up at the very thought of reciting to Sheriff Walker the speech she had worked to prepare her entire trek from the Triple Y to town.

Wade would kill her if he found out. If he'd had any idea of her intentions, he'd have dragged her home with him, and left Matthew at the orphanage until morning.

But he needed help, more help than Callie alone could provide. She'd tried to find the unidentified ranch hand Wade thought had witnessed Neville's murder; she'd come up with the prospect of trying to discover some proof of Wade's original ownership of the Circle M.

But even though she now had his deed in her possession, that didn't mean they would ever be able to use it or truly prove his innocence. Callie, for one, had absolutely no idea how to go about it.

Sheriff Walker seemed like a decent, honest man, however, and she couldn't keep from believing that if he knew the wrong man had been convicted of a murder, he would be willing to help set things right.

Callie realized she had to be careful, though. She couldn't let it slip—or even let the sheriff begin to suspect—that Wade might be hiding out at her place. Which was why she'd spent the entire distance between Young's ranch and Purgatory figuring out exactly how best to articulate her entreaty.

Taking a deep breath, she pushed open the door and stepped inside the sparse office containing a battered desk and chair, two heavily barred cells, and a wall of tacked-up WANTED posters.

"Miss Quinn."

Sheriff Walker, who had been working at his desk, stood as soon as she entered. Crossing the room, he picked up an extra chair from the corner and brought it forward for her.

"This is a surprise. What can I do for you?" he asked.

The sheriff returned to his seat, and Callie lowered herself gently to the solid pine chair he'd provided. She twisted her hands nervously, praying this was the right thing to do.

"You know that Lily, over at the Painted Lady, was Matthew's mother, don't you?"

He nodded. "I'd heard something of the sort."

"What you might not have known is that Wade Mason, the man you came to the house to ask about the other day, is Matthew's father. At least, that's what Lily led me to believe," she added quickly.

The sheriff's brow knit. "I'm not sure I'm following you."

Careful, Callie, she thought. She had to be so

257

careful. "Because Lily and I were rather close, she asked me to take care of Matthew when she realized she was dying. And confided in me probably more than she did anyone else. Before she passed on, she intimated to me that Mr. Mason was the father of her child, and that he wasn't guilty of the murder for which he'd been convicted. I don't know why she didn't come forward, but she seemed adamant about that man's innocence."

Taking a deep breath, she reached into the basket on her lap and withdrew the sheaf of papers they'd taken from Brady Young's study. This was the tricky part, the one she'd been most worried about.

"After you came to the house to warn me about Wade Mason's escape from prison, I went through some of Lily's things. I hadn't had a chance to look through them very closely before, but Mr. Mason's name sounded familiar to me for some reason, and I thought I'd try to figure out why. I found this."

She handed Sheriff Walker the deed to Wade's property and waited for him to read it.

"I'm familiar with the piece of land Wade Mason lived on and worked before being sent to prison," she continued. "He and my brother were friends. I also know Brady Young now claims ownership of that same area. Which is why, when I found these papers, I began to wonder—"

"If Lily wasn't telling the truth about Mason being innocent."

"Exactly."

He continued to study the papers in front of him as he said, "I don't know what to tell you, Miss Quinn. What happened with Wade Mason was before my time here. But I'd be happy to look into it, if you'd like. This deed certainly raises some interesting questions."

Refolding the deed, he passed it back to her. "If something unscrupulous occurred to put Mr. Mason in prison for a crime he didn't commit, that might explain why he supposedly headed back to Purgatory when he escaped."

"That's why I thought I should come to you," she said. "Nathan always liked Wade. He seemed to think he was a good man, and I remember how shocked he was that Wade had been accused, let alone convicted, of murdering a man."

Walker stood and Callie followed suit, slipping the basket back over her arm.

"I'll ask around, see what I can dig up. I can't make any promises, but if I find something, I'll come right out to the house and let you know."

"I'd appreciate that, Sheriff Walker," she said as she moved toward the door.

"Would you like me to see you home?" he asked, coming around his desk and hurrying ahead of her to the door.

"Thank you, but that won't be necessary."

"All right, but be careful. This town can get a little rowdy on a Friday night."

He swung the door open for her, then accompanied her out onto the boardwalk. Raucous voices and tinny piano music drifted out of the brightly lit Painted Lady, while tall, flickering lamps lit the rest of the street.

"I will. Good night, Sheriff," she said, starting for the mission. "And thank you again."

"My pleasure, Miss Quinn. You take care, now."

As she headed toward the church to gather up Matthew and his things for the walk home, Callie couldn't decide whether she was relieved at having talked to Sheriff Walker or even more apprehensive over the possibility of the lawman redoubling his efforts to track down Wade.

The only thing she did know was that Wade would be furious when he found out. And Callie must be a few blades shy of a hay bale, because she actually intended to tell him.

By the time he'd been home an hour, with no sign of Callie's and Matthew's return, Wade was ready to climb the walls.

He'd expected her to take longer to get back because she'd had to go the long way through town to retrieve Matthew. But she shouldn't have taken *this* long.

As he paced back and forth along the length

of the parlor, he couldn't figure out why he was this agitated. He should be concerned, maybe, sure. But his boots were pounding on the hardwood floor like Custer marching on Little Big Horn, and his gut was twisted tighter than a miser with a silver dollar.

These were not normal physical reactions for an escaped convict to have about his hostages. But then, they'd established pretty early on that Callie and Matthew weren't just hostages, and he wasn't just an escaped convict holding a gun on them until he got what he wanted.

He was a father . . . and had become a lover. He was a man awaiting the return of his son and the woman he was beginning to have very strong feelings for.

He didn't reflect any further than that, afraid to examine how he felt about Callie too closely. He just wanted her home now.

And if she didn't arrive soon, then WANTED poster or no WANTED poster . . . posse or no posse, he was heading out after her and Matthew.

Ten minutes later, just as he was seriously considering storming out of the house and searching every inch of ground between the farm and town, he heard footsteps on the porch and raced for the door.

Before Callie even had a chance to twist the

knob, Wade wrenched the door open and dragged her into his arms.

"Where the hell have you been?" he charged, squeezing her as hard as he dared without crushing Matthew between them.

"I was in town," she wheezed, and Wade let up when he realized his vicelike hold was impeding her breathing.

Pulling them inside, he shut the door behind them and propelled her toward the settee. Callie sat without any urging and arranged a sleepy-looking Matthew on her lap.

"What took so long?" Wade asked, attempting to tamp down on his uneasiness as he perched on the edge of the armchair adjacent to the sofa. "It didn't take you that long to reach Brady's place after you dropped Matthew at the church."

"Well, it's darker now than it was then," she said, not meeting his eyes. "I had to be more careful of stumbling or taking a wrong step."

He studied her quizzically. Why wouldn't she look at him?

"Is there something you're not telling me, Callie?" he asked softly. Reaching past Matthew's dangling leg, he cupped her knee through the layers of gingham skirt.

She lifted her head then. "There is something," she ventured slowly. "But you won't like it."

Wade sat back in the chair, bracing himself. "All right. What is it? Did you run into Brady

Young in town and invite him to Sunday dinner?"

Her eyes flashed at his attempt at humor. When Matthew began to fuss, she bounced her legs in an effort to settle him.

"Worse."

Worse? What could be worse than sitting through a meal with Brady Young?

"Spit it out, Callie. I'm not getting any happier waiting to hear what's going on."

She inclined her head. "Just remember not to yell; you'll hurt Matthew's ears."

It must be really bad for her to warn him ahead of time not to get loud. His fingers dug into the arms of the chair as he waited.

"Before I picked up Matthew, I stopped to talk to Sheriff Walker."

Chapter Twenty-two

To Wade's credit, he didn't yell. He also didn't breathe for a good minute.

Callie pulled Matthew closer to her breast, as though shielding herself from whatever onslaught Wade might throw at her. After all, he wouldn't throttle her senseless while she was holding a baby, now would he?

But he wasn't going to beat her. He wasn't even going to shout at her. At least not yet.

He felt too numb to do more than stare. She'd betrayed him. He'd confided in her, trusted her, let her "help" him try to prove his innocence, and she'd stabbed him in the back.

But it wasn't the first time, was it? Wade thought vilely. Oh, no, he'd been betrayed before. By Neville Young, who was supposed to be his friend and neighbor. By Lily, who had known all along he was innocent of murder but had said nothing; who had borne his child but never bothered to tell him he was a father until she was on her deathbed.

And now by Callie Quinn, who took such good care of his son. Who had shared his bed, writhing so beautifully beneath him, and possessed every single admirable quality he'd always wanted in a woman. In a wife.

There it was, the fact he'd been avoiding all night. Hell, ever since he'd kissed her. Callie Quinn wasn't just the guardian of his child but the woman he'd been waiting for all his life. The woman he wanted to marry and make a family with.

He hadn't let himself dwell on the idea often or for long because of his situation. Because he was even now being hunted and at some point would likely be thrown back into prison. But somewhere deep inside, he'd not only been thinking about it, he'd been mapping out their next fifty years together.

And it had all been a waste of time, a waste of energy and emotions, because she, too, had ended up betraying his trust.

"How long do I have before the sheriff gets here?" he asked in a shallow voice. "Or is he already outside, waiting for the right moment to take me into custody?"

Her eyes widened, and she sat forward abruptly. "Oh, no. Oh, Wade, I didn't mean that at all."

She shifted Matthew on her lap again so she could lean toward him and take his hand. "I didn't tell Sheriff Walker about you at all, I swear. I only thought that he might be able to help us."

She hadn't turned him in? Wade shook his head, struggling to absorb what she was telling him.

He narrowed his gaze. "I don't understand. You went to the sheriff. You talked to him about me. How can he not want to take me into custody?"

"I talked to him about the deed to your ranch," she clarified, but her eyes darted away before she went on. "I'm afraid I had to stretch the truth a little to protect you, but I couldn't think of any other way to convince Sheriff Walker to help us without putting you in danger."

Her gaze swung back to his, meeting what he knew was an intensely dark stare without flinching. "I told him that before Lily died, she confided in me about you. That you were Matthew's father, and that she somehow knew you hadn't killed Neville Young."

"What did he say about that?" he asked doubtfully.

"Nothing, really. He just listened. And then I

showed him your deed to the Circle M. I led him to believe I'd found it in with the things Lily left me when she died. He looked over the papers and agreed with me when I suggested it was odd for Brady Young to be using your land when you apparently still own it."

Wade raised a brow. "You told him that?"

With a nod, she said, "He promised to do a bit of checking around. I don't know if he'll find anything. We may end up in the exact same situation we're in now. But, Wade, we need help. We need someone who has the weight of the law behind him and can investigate in ways that we can't."

He remained silent, considering everything she'd said.

"Sheriff Walker is a good man, Wade. He would never make you pay for a crime you didn't commit if he could avoid it. I think if he finds anything to your benefit, he'll let us know, and he'll be one more person who can assist us in clearing your name."

Endless seconds ticked by in silence, and Matthew's eyelids began to droop as Callie watched Wade expectantly.

"I'm sorry, Wade, but I thought it was the best thing to do. Are you angry with me?"

"I'm not sure," he answered honestly. "I don't think so, but I can't say the idea of Purgatory's sheriff sniffing around in my past makes me terribly comfortable."

Meeting her soft brown eyes, he added, "You have to understand that I haven't had the best of luck with the law these past few years. It never would have occurred to me to ask Walker for help. But maybe it was the right thing to do. Maybe he'll come up with something."

"I hope so. I really do, Wade." Her hand tightened around his own. "I was only thinking of you."

Raising his head, he gave her a vague smile. "I know you were. Thank you, Callie."

Getting to his feet, he reached out to take Matthew from her, snuggling the drowsy child against his chest. "This little guy looks like he's about to drop." He held out his hand for her. "Care to help me put him down for the night?"

She gave an almost imperceptible nod, put her fingers inside his, and rose. "I'd also like to take a bath tonight. I thought you might help me heat the water and fill the brass tub."

He caught a glimpse of rose coloring her cheeks before she turned for the stairs, and Wade almost stumbled as he took a step to follow.

Why was she blushing over something as simple as asking for his assistance with heating water for a bath? Could it be that she had more in mind than just getting clean?

His pulse kicked up and every lick of sense in

his head slid straight down to pool in his groin.

He shouldn't get his hopes up in case he was reading her signals wrong. He shouldn't expect more than Callie might be willing to give.

But he'd damn sure be ready if those two pink spots on her cheeks meant what he thought they did.

Callie stood beside the large brass tub, letting steam waft all around her face. She was still wearing her green gingham gown from earlier in the day but had brought down a thin lawn night-dress and wrap to change into.

Wade had helped her carry bucket after bucket of water, including the last two kettles that had been set to boil on the cookstove. He'd been nothing but solicitous, questioning how he might assist her, doing anything she asked of him. And never once had he made an untoward move or suggested they do anything the least bit un-seemly.

Which was good, Callie reminded herself. Even though she had certainly thought about it when she'd mentioned the desire to bathe just as they were putting Matthew to bed.

She felt her face flame again now, as it had then. She hadn't meant for her request to come out the way it sounded, as though she were in-viting Wade to join her for a bath. But the second the words passed her lips, her brain had filled with all kinds of images.

The night Wade had first appeared, catching her completely nude in this very tub . . .

Wade stripping and scrubbing himself free of eighteen months of filth that same night, in the very water she'd been submerged in only moments before . . .

The two of them twined together on the cool sheets of her bed as Wade did wonderful, wicked things to her body . . .

How close the two of them would be pressed together in her brass tub if she did invite him to join her, how the warm water would lap around them . . .

Bathing together hadn't been her initial purpose, and she hadn't intended to imply anything of the sort to Wade, but once the thought took root in her mind, she couldn't seem to banish it.

With towels laid out, a fresh cake of soap on the decorative metal rack hooked over the rim of the tub, and a healthy dollop of lilac fragrance swirling around in the water, she began to loosen the buttons of her dress, first at her wrists and then down the front of the bodice. She slipped the material off her shoulders and let it fall to the floor. Next she untied the laces of her black leather walking boots, rolled down the sturdy material of her everyday stockings, and kicked both aside.

As she stood there in only her drawers and camisole, a shiver of modesty washed through her. Wade was in the next room and could walk in on her at any moment.

That thought should have had her grabbing for something to cover her state of undress. Instead, she found herself almost wishing for him to appear in the entrance of the pantry, march across the room, and sweep her into his arms, thus taking any decisions on the matter out of her hands.

But she knew the choice rested with her. She was a grown woman who had already made love with Wade once. Well, more than once, but all in the same night. If she wanted the same thing to happen again—and she strongly suspected she did—then she need only raise her voice and call for him. Or saunter to the doorway that separated kitchen and pantry and invite him to remove the rest of her undergarments.

But despite her boldness the night before, Callie couldn't find the courage now to do either.

With a sigh of regret, she slipped the lace-edged camisole over her head and undid the string of her drawers, dropping both garments to the floor. Now completely naked, she stepped into the still-steaming water and submerged her body below the surface.

Ahhh. The water felt wonderful. Warm and soothing and almost as good as being in Wade's arms.

If only he'd come into the room now and join her, she thought, letting her eyes drift closed. It was a terribly wanton notion, but one she mulled over all the same.

A few minutes later, as though in answer to her silent summons, she heard his masculine footsteps growing closer and his deep voice from just outside the pantry entranceway.

"Everything all right in there?" he asked politely. "Do you need anything else?"

When she opened her eyes, she saw only one worn workboot and the elbow of his plaid shirt peeking out from behind the wall. Out of respect for her privacy, he stood to the side of the doorway, facing in the other direction.

Her heart pitched and a bevy of butterflies took to batting their wings inside her belly. This was her chance. Now, before he moved away.

Lowering her voice to what she hoped was a smoky, sensual tone, she ventured, "Actually, there is something you could do for me."

Wade cocked his head around the corner, one brow lifted inquisitively. Catching sight of her arrangement in the tub, with no soap bubbles or wash rag to cover even a portion of her nudity, his gaze skimmed her from head to toe. Leisurely, his other brow rose in blatant male appreciation.

"What's the matter, sweetheart?" he asked in

a tone even deeper and more gravelly than her own. "Forget the soap?"

She reached for the homemade bar, holding it up for him to see. "No, I've got that. But there are some . . . places I can't quite reach."

She couldn't believe her ears, or that such words were coming out of her own mouth. But she wanted to be with Wade, and this seemed the only way to make him aware of that fact.

Eyes widening even more, Wade took a step into the room. "Are you asking me to . . . wash your back, Callie girl?"

"If you don't mind." Her response sounded weak, and she noticed the soap trembling in her hand.

Was she making a terrible mistake? Possibly, according to many people's standards, but Callie searched her soul and couldn't find a single hint of regret.

Slowly, a full minute seeming to tick by as he took each step, he moved around the tub until he stood at her back. She knew he had a clear, unobstructed view of her nakedness as he towered above her.

The floorboards creaked as he hunkered behind her and rolled up his sleeves. The warm flesh and rough hairs of his arm brushed her overly sensitized skin as he reached around her for the soap. She opened her palm and let him take it, their fingers brushing.

273

He lingered a moment, then dipped into the water up to his wrists. She heard the soft sounds of his hands working to build up a lather and sucked in a sharp breath when he touched the nape of her neck.

His slick fingers rubbed slowly, deeply. When the suds ran out, he dipped the soap again, then continued to stroke and circle. He washed her neck, her shoulders, the line of her spine. His ministrations took him lower and lower, until water covered his forearms.

"You may want to take your shirt off," she suggested, "so it doesn't get wet."

"Good idea."

He leaned into her to return the cake of soap to its metal stand and his entire chest—shirt and all—pressed against her back, indicating to them both that the condition of his clothes was of little importance. Their words and actions were merely a game, the building of tension.

Turning her head a fraction to the side, she watched out of the corner of her eye as he popped button after button free of its hole, dragged the tucked-in ends from the waist of his trousers, and shucked the shirt down the length of his sinewy arms.

"How's that?"

"Better. But what about your pants?"

One brow went up, making him look devilish and daring. "Afraid they'll get wet, too?"

She nodded and turned back around, retrieving the soap to begin a slow, luxurious once-over of her body.

"Whatever you say, sweetheart," he murmured, and started unfastening the front of his jeans.

She listened to the rasp of fabric, the thud of one boot after another falling to the floor. And then he was close behind her again, his warm breath stirring the hair at her temple.

One work-roughened palm curled about her shoulder, then slid over her arm to her wrist, covering her hand where it rested with the soap high on her chest.

"I thought this was my job," he said, twisting the slippery square out of her grasp.

She let it go and leaned forward slightly when he returned to massaging her back. His touch moved lower, in tiny intervals, to the small of her spine.

There, his motions stopped. His breathing sounded in her ear, matching the rise and fall of her own breast as the scent of lilacs enveloped them.

"That's as far as I can reach from here," he whispered, his lips gently brushing against the sensitive skin of her ear.

"Then maybe you should . . . join me. So you have better access," she suggested.

Chapter Twenty-three

He was already naked, wet, and throbbing like a thumbnail bashed by the head of a hammer. It would have taken a herd of stampeding longhorns, six mountain lions, and Callie's brother standing over them with a shotgun to keep him from climbing into that big brass bathtub with her.

"Slide forward," he said, straightening and laying a hand flat on her back.

When she did, he stepped carefully into the tub and dropped to a sitting position behind her. With one arm wrapped around her waist, he pulled her toward him until not even air could circulate between their two forms.

"Now *this* is what I call a bath," he murmured in her ear.

He felt her smile, a bit of the nervous tension running out of her limbs as she leaned against him and willingly let her head fall back on his shoulder.

"So you really aren't angry with me for talking to the sheriff."

It was more a statement than a question, but Wade answered, anyway. "I'm not angry, no. And even if I were, I don't think I could stay mad for long. Not with this luscious body fitting me better than my own skin."

His hands, soap and all, drifted up her torso to gently cup the swells of her breasts.

"You must think I'm terribly wanton," she said. "To let you take me to bed yesterday evening. To invite you into my bath tonight."

He crooked his knees, boxing her in even more securely. "Wanton women are my very favorite kind. Besides, I'm a bit of a wanton man myself," he said while his fingers continued to explore.

"Do you know," he intoned in a low voice, "that I've been dreaming of this since the first moment I saw you?"

"You did catch me off guard."

"Before you realized I was in the room, I just stood there, watching you. I couldn't help myself; you were glorious."

"I was naked," she corrected, slapping playfully at his upper arm. "You should have been a gentleman and covered your eyes."

Heidi Betts

"I was a gentleman . . . I didn't strip down and join you right then and there. And believe me, sweetheart, I sorely wanted to."

Sliding along his body, she twisted to face him. "Well, maybe this will make up for it."

Her spread fingertips molded to his chest. Soap falling forgotten to the bottom of the tub, he framed her face and said, "It makes up for everything."

Then he kissed her, letting his lips and tongue thank her. Telling her without words how much she was beginning to mean to him, how grateful he was for her faith and support and companionship.

When anyone else would have turned him in, or done their best to escape, Callie stayed. She'd stayed, she'd believed in him, she'd tried to help him clear his name.

She'd let him make love to her. Invited it, welcomed it, threw herself into the act with all the energy and enthusiasm of a woman in love. And that was just fine with Wade, because he was beginning to think he made love to Callie with all the energy and enthusiasm of a man in love.

They might have no future together, but they had now. A beautiful woman naked in his arms, a bath of warm water bound to have him smelling like a lilac bush by morning, and an opportunity Wade wasn't about to pass up—no matter what tomorrow might bring.

With his mouth still melded to hers, he ran his hands down her sides to her buttocks and upper thighs. Straightening his long legs as best he could in the squat tub, he urged her to open her legs and straddle him.

Tonight she wasn't nearly as modest as the night before. She not only let him arrange her limbs the way he liked but moved with him, leaned into him, rubbed her breasts with their pebble-hard nipples on his chest and dug her nails into the flesh of his back.

He moaned deep in his throat as Callie came up on her knees, causing his rigid shaft to brush against the downy softness at the apex of her thighs. Her water- and soap-slick hands moved over his chest, kneading the firm pectoral muscles and teasing the arrow-sharp nubbins that his nipples had become.

"You drive me crazy, do you know that?" he rasped.

"Good crazy or bad crazy?" she asked, arching her pelvis in such a way that his member became trapped between their bellies, adding pressure and heightening his arousal.

"Just . . . crazy-crazy," he nearly growled. "What are you doing?"

"Biting your neck."

"I feel that." Her teeth took tiny nips at the iron-tight tendons wending their way to his collarbone, followed by the silky slide of her tongue laving away the sting.

"Do you want me to stop?"

Hell, no. He wanted to see just how far she'd be willing to go. "Not on your life."

He felt her lips curve and looked down to find her grinning, her gaze canted up toward his.

While she was busy heating his blood from the outside in, Wade took advantage of her distraction to toy with the damp strands of hair that had come loose from her topknot. Trailing them over her bare shoulders and then letting the backs of his fingers drift down the milky white softness of her arms, her waist, then back up to her breasts.

Their fullness intrigued him, made him want to trace the contours, explore textures. With his thumb, he sampled the satiny smoothness of one round globe, then the darker, puckered circle of her areola, and finally the tiny pearl of her nipple. The stiffened bud contracted even more beneath his ministrations, and she gave a little moan of pleasure.

He repeated the motions with her other breast, leaning his head back on the rim of the tub as Callie's mouth found one of the bronze medallions that bisected his own chest.

"Where did you learn to do that?" he asked, eyes falling closed and hands clasping her rib cage for stability.

"I'm experimenting," she answered between licks. "Why, don't you like it?"

"I do like it," he said through his teeth. "I just didn't expect you to catch on so fast."

"You told me last night that I could do whatever I wanted to you, that I was in charge."

"That was last night. Tonight, I thought I'd take the lead."

She raised her head and gifted him with a dazzling smile. Part vixen, part innocent, it made Wade feel entirely wicked.

"But you weren't doing anything," she chastised lightly. "Just sitting there."

"And you wanted me to . . . *do* something?"

When she only inclined her head, he asked, "Like what?"

Her coquettish smile turned into a pale peach blush. "Like . . . what you did last night."

He arched a brow. "Such as . . ."

"Being inside me," she murmured quietly, avoiding his gaze.

Using the pads of two fingers, he tipped up her chin until her brown eyes stared directly into his. "You don't have to be shy with me, Callie girl. Remember? No matter what we do together, it's all okay."

The sides of his thumbs rubbed circles on her cheeks and jaw. "Do you want me to be inside you?" he asked softly.

Bottom lip pulled taut between her teeth, she gave a slight nod.

"Then put me there."

Her irises widened and turned an even deeper brown. She swallowed. But her obvious hesitancy didn't keep her from running a hand down the line of his chest, to his abdomen and lower, to the jutting hardness of his erection.

Below the water, her fingers closed around him, firm yet gentle. Callie the Curious, as usual, had to explore. She stroked up and down the velvety length a couple of times, which Wade endured by locking his jaw and praying for inner strength.

But when she dabbed at the tip of his shaft with one dainty fingertip, his hips arched, his lips stretched over his teeth, and he swore black enough to color the air around them.

At his sharp curse, she pulled back, her touch lightening on his member. "What is it?" she wanted to know. "Did I do something wrong?"

Wade let out a strained laugh, even as he silently castigated himself. She was too new at this, too skittish for him to be making any sudden moves or harsh noises as he just had. He needed to reassure her and give her space to discover her own sensuality.

Because, quite simply, she was *the* most beautiful, sensual woman he'd ever met. She deserved to realize and acknowledge that side of herself.

Of course, then she would know just how much power she held over the male of the species, and that could spell trouble. A woman who knew she could have any man in existence on his knees at the crook of one little finger was a dangerous woman, indeed.

"You didn't do anything wrong," he assured her. "Not only do you do everything right, but you do it too damn well. And I'm just not a strong enough man to take it."

Her nose wrinkled at that, but the corners of her mouth turned up. "So should I . . . go back to what I was doing?"

His head fell back as he groaned dramatically. "If you must," he sighed. "Only . . . be gentle with me."

With a grin, she returned a firm hold to his member and sat up on her haunches. Wade ground his teeth together to keep from moaning aloud and watched as she centered herself atop him, then lowered herself until he was fully embedded.

His hands went straight to her waist, just above the curve of her hips, but he only flowed seamlessly with her movements instead of encouraging or controlling them.

Callie's body rose and fell, riding him like a well-trained equestrian. Whether it was the water or her own feminine wetness, he was surrounded by moist heat. Encompassed by comfort and love and a serenity he'd seldom, if ever, known.

Water sloshed against the sides of the tub as their pace increased. The muscles in her legs and buttocks flexed as she moved against him.

He slid his hands up from her hips to her breasts as he leaned forward to take her mouth. And then back down while they kissed, pressed breasts to chest, abdomen to abdomen, pelvis to pelvis.

Her arms wrapped securely about his neck, hands gripping her own elbows, while the full length of his forearms pressed tight to her back and his fingers dug into the supple flesh just below her shoulder blades.

As much as he wanted to let Callie retain control, things were getting too intense. His blood was pounding too fast in his veins. His heart was beating too loud in his ears. Fire was blazing too hot in his groin.

No matter how hard he fought it, he couldn't keep his hips from moving. From meeting each of her downward slides with an upward thrust of his own.

In between kisses, Callie's breath started coming in short, shallow pants. Wade felt like heaven, filling her completely, holding her close. She'd never felt so safe. So cherished and wanted. The sensation of warm water flowing all around them, lapping at their bodies, only made the experience more intimate.

Her stomach flipped over as the muscles lining her feminine passage began to convulse. She gasped sharply, her head falling back, Wade's grip on her waist tightening as they climaxed together.

For long minutes afterward, they lay there, her head resting weightlessly on his shoulder, his arms looped loosely around her waist. The water turned cold, covering her arms with gooseflesh, and still Callie lacked the strength to move.

"You're going to catch a chill," Wade mumbled.

She moaned in reply, too tired and spent for coherent speech.

His chin bumped against the top of her head as he chuckled. "Since you seem to be in such a charitable mood, there's something I want you to think over."

She waited, concentrating on nothing more than his warm, solid body making such a wonderful bed beneath her.

"I've been mulling it over, and I think you should marry me, Callie girl."

Chapter Twenty-four

For a moment, she didn't react. When his words finally did sink in, her eyes popped open, but even so, she remained still.

He couldn't be serious. They'd only known each other a matter of weeks.

A small voice in her head reminded her that a few weeks had obviously been long enough for her to be lured into bed by the man, but she quickly tamped down on the too-late bout of conscience.

Besides, making love with someone and marrying that person were two different things. Especially when the man was on the run, being hunted, with no clear sign of regaining his freedom on the horizon.

She would be crazy to say yes.

And yet she wanted to. So badly, her heart twisted with the effort of not accepting.

"I know it's sudden," he said, breaking into the cacophony of her thoughts. "I know there's no reason in the world for a woman like you to agree to marry a man like me. An escaped convict, a man with a price on his head and no prospects beyond being sent back to prison."

Lifting her head from the soft pillow of his chest, she saw his lips twist. It made her want to reach out and smooth away the small lines bracketing his mouth.

"But I do have something to offer." He sat up in the tub, bringing her with him. "I told you once before that the reason Neville Young was so eager to get his hands on the Circle M was because he thought there was a mine hidden somewhere on the property. A gold mine."

When Wade made a motion to stand, Callie stood up with him. Beads of water rolled down their bodies as he reached for a towel and shook it open. Wrapping it beneath her arms and around her torso, he overlapped the edges and let her hold them in place over her breasts.

Not bothering to cover himself, he lifted her into his arms, stepped out of the brass tub, and headed for the stairs. He didn't speak again until he'd carried her up the flight of steps and deposited her in the middle of the wide bed, settling himself above her. His long, nude frame rested against her, her towel soaking up the excess moisture from both their bodies.

"You probably ruined my floor, you know, tromping up here without drying off first."

"Do you want me to go back and clean it up?"

"Yes, I do," she said, tipping up her nose primly.

"All right," he answered slowly, "but I'm going to need your towel." And with a quick twist of his wrist, he pulled the thick nap out from under her.

Callie squealed, but he ignored her, stalking from the room completely naked, dragging the towel behind him. She watched the flex and release of his taut bottom as he moved and was glad he was facing the other direction so he wouldn't see her appreciative grin.

He was all lines and planes of hard-packed muscle that hadn't been there when he'd first arrived. But with his own handiwork in the kitchen, his gaunt face and weak limbs had filled in nicely. He looked healthy now. And, judging from their latest bout of lovemaking, his stamina had certainly improved, she thought, her mouth curving into a satisfied smile.

For several seconds after he disappeared, Callie stared at the empty doorway, awaiting his return. Then she scrambled over the mattress, loosening the covers and climbing under.

She pictured a nude Wade, bent over the

stairs, sopping up the water they'd tracked through the house, and smiled. She hadn't actually meant for him to go back and clean up but was rather amused that he'd jumped so quickly at her complaint.

Maybe he was good husband material, after all.

Of course, he hadn't mentioned marriage again since carrying her up here. Maybe it had been merely a passing fancy, not a sincere proposal.

In which case, Callie still didn't know how to feel.

Stark naked and as confident as though he were fully dressed, Wade strode back into the room, the used towel balled up in his hand. He tossed it aside and headed straight for the bed.

He joined her under the covers, snuggling up next to her, sliding his hands along the mattress until they wrapped around her and pulled her flush against his warm, hard length.

"Now, where were we?"

"You were sopping up the water you dripped when you carried me upstairs."

"But I finished that," he returned. Smiling crookedly, he added, "You're a damn hard lady to impress, do you know that? Any other woman would find it romantic if I swept her into my arms and carried her off to the bedroom."

She cocked a brow. "And just how many other women have you carried to bed?"

Turning serious, he said, "You're the first. You're also the first woman I've ever asked to marry me."

Her stomach clenched at that, all the same wants and worries and arguments playing through her head once again.

"Neville Young thought there was a gold mine on my property, and he was right," he announced, his fingers curling in at her waist. "What he didn't know is that the deed to the mine is separate from the deed to the Circle M."

She frowned, trying to absorb what he was saying.

"It's a little complicated, but suffice it to say that I inherited ownership of the mine from my grandfather a few years back, then bought the adjoining property when I decided to raise cattle. The opening of the mine is hidden, and I've never told anyone exactly where it can be located. But even if Young finds it, even if he starts digging, with the counterfeit deed he has, he can't lay a true claim to anything but the ranch land."

"So Neville didn't know they were two separate properties, with two separate sets of documentation."

"Right. And when I realized he'd stolen the deed to the Circle M, I hid the deed to the mine where he wouldn't find it. Where no one will find it, believe me," he said vehemently.

"But if you marry me, Callie, I'll sign the mine over to you and tell you exactly where it's located so you can hire men to work it, if you want. That way, I'll know you and Matthew are taken care of, no matter what happens to me."

Callie swallowed, blinking back tears. "You don't have to marry me for that," she said softly, stroking his stubbled cheek with one hand. "You can tell me where the mine is now, or simply sign it over to Matthew for when he gets older."

"I know I don't *have* to marry you. I want to. I've never met another woman like you, Callie. Taking responsibility for a child who's not even yours, believing in me when no one else in this world has. . . . I know I turned your life upside down by coming here. I've put both you and Matthew in danger, and taken advantage of you in more ways than I can count. But I'm also falling in love with you, Callie. I have feelings for you that I've never felt for anyone else."

She didn't bother holding back her tears now, and they ran past her temples and into her hair. Wade's own eyes were deceptively bright, and she leaned over to press a light kiss to his lips.

"If things were different, you're just the sort of wife I'd look forward to spending the rest of my life with. But we both know I can't promise you anything, Callie. Not happiness or forever or even my being around much longer. There's a good chance I'll be caught and sent back to prison. But if that happens, at least I'll know you and Matthew will be taken care of. At least I'll have a couple of really nice memories to think back on whenever things get too tough and I don't think I can stand one more day of being locked up in that hellhole."

His teeth ground together, and Callie ran her fingers through the hair at his nape, trying to draw his attention away from such dark, discouraging thoughts.

"I think I love you, too," she all but whispered. "And if you're sure, then the answer is yes, I'll marry you."

His eyes closed and his face went out of focus as he closed in to kiss her. She savored the heat of his mouth, along with all the emotions his lips and tongue conveyed. And in return, she tried to show just how much she cared for him.

The kiss was long and slow but intense, and full of passion and joy. Callie couldn't remember anything ever feeling so right.

When he lifted his head, he was grinning like a greenhorn who'd just broken his first bronco. She couldn't help but smile in return.

"I want to get this done as soon as possible. Make sure things are in order for you and Matthew."

In case something happens to me. The words

went unspoken, but she heard them clear as cut crystal. She swallowed, not wanting to think about the danger Wade was still in, what could happen to him if the posse managed to track him down.

"We can sneak into town and have the priest you left Matthew with perform the ceremony," he continued.

And then he cupped her face, caressing her cheeks with the sides of his thumbs. "I'm sorry I can't give you more, Callie. A woman's wedding should be the most special day of her life, with a beautiful dress, and flowers, and friends and family at her side. Not some clandestine event." His mouth turned down in a frown. "You deserve better."

She didn't know what to say to that. True, she'd always dreamed of a lovely, romantic wedding. A long, lace-edged gown for the bride, a dark suit for the groom. A church decorated with flowers and ribbon, pews filled with smiling faces.

But she'd never imagined walking down the aisle toward a man like Wade. He was caring and kind and made her feel more special than anyone ever had before.

"It doesn't matter," she said, and meant it.

"It does matter. I've got to be crazy to even ask this of you. Even so, I can't find it in me to try to change your mind.

293

"But know this, Callie: if something happens to me, I want you to marry again. Find someone worthy of your devotion. And use the money from the mine to do it, to buy and do anything you want."

Keeping her tone upbeat, even as sadness and worry clutched at her chest, she said, "We're not even married, and already you're trying to get rid of me."

His fingers feathered through the long strands of her hair. "Never. Never, Callie. If there's any way for me to clear my name, to come back and spend the rest of my life with you, I will. But that's not something we can hang our hopes on. We have to be realistic. I'm going to stay with you and Matthew for as long as I can, Callie, but I won't put either of you in danger.

"We'll go into town and get hitched, hope the padre doesn't get suspicious," he added with a weak half-smile, "and then I'll sign over everything I still own to you. That way, no matter what happens, you and Matthew will be set."

Keeping her eyes locked with his, she wished he would tell her again that he loved her. Or thought he did, at any rate. She didn't want to think about him being caught and sent back to prison. She didn't want to think about him rotting away in that penitentiary in Huntsville. She only wanted him to love her, and to love him in return. For him to stay here with her and Matthew, and for them to build a life together.

Of course, none of that was possible as long as his face still adorned WANTED posters all over the south of Texas.

"Let's not think or talk about any of that right now. Let's just . . . be happy. For as long as we have together."

"For as long as we have together." He rested his forehead against hers and nodded solemnly. "I wouldn't have it any other way."

Early the next evening, Callie dressed in a pure white shirtwaist and a royal blue skirt, then bundled up Matthew while Wade changed into one of Nathan's Sunday suits.

Butterflies flew around in her stomach. She was really doing this. She was getting married.

Nathan would skin her alive if he knew. Not only for agreeing to marry a convicted felon, but for not warning or at least alerting him of her plans.

But she didn't have time to send a message all the way to California, let alone wait for her brother's response. She'd already made her decision. She believed in Wade and was willing to put her name, her reputation, her life on the line for him.

The plan, as they'd ironed it out, was for Callie and Matthew to walk into town while Wade did the same, making only a small detour past the

Circle M to retrieve the deed to the gold mine.

That was the part that frightened Callie the most. She didn't want Wade setting foot on the Circle M. She was afraid that if Brady or any of his men caught him there, they would kill him, or frame him for another crime he hadn't committed. And she couldn't let that happen.

Carrying Matthew into the sitting room, she lifted the lid of her sewing basket and took out the Colt revolver Nathan had left with her for protection.

Chapter Twenty-five

When Wade came down the steps and walked into the parlor, he found Callie standing in the middle of the room, one hand balancing Matthew on her hip, the other holding a pistol pointed directly at his belly.

"You weren't planning on making yourself a widow before you even became a bride, were you?"

She jumped as his voice filled the silent room.

"This is for you," she said, ignoring his teasing question altogether and marching forward.

With the gun barrel pointed at the floor, she held it out to him. "I want you to take it with you when you go back to the Circle M. For protection in case you run across someone who wants to do you harm."

"Like the posse?" he asked, taking the revolver, checking to see that it was loaded, and tucking it into the waistband of his pants, where it would be covered by the overlapping sides of his suit jacket.

"If it comes to that, though I was thinking more of Brady Young or any of his hired men."

"I don't expect trouble, Callie. No one knows where I hid the papers to the mine."

"There's a posse on your trail and Brady Young has not only been working your land as though it's his own but has offered a reward for your capture—dead or alive. I'd say you have plenty to be cautious of. Do what you have to on the way to the church, but *be careful.*"

He caught the alarmed edge in her tone and took a step forward to put a hand on her arm. "Are you having second thoughts, Callie? Because if you are, I'll understand."

"About marrying you? No." Her head moved back and forth vehemently. "About letting you go exactly where the law and Young both expect you to go and your possibly getting killed in the process? Definitely."

"I'm doing this for you, Callie. For you and Matthew. Without the proof of ownership to that gold mine, I won't know the two of you are taken care of."

"You don't understand, Wade. We don't want your money or possession of your mine. We've been fine up until now and will continue to do well, no matter what happens. What we *want* is for you to be safe."

A lump formed in his throat, and it took a minute to dissipate so he could speak.

"Thank you." The words came out hushed and intense. "You don't know what that means to me. Really. But I need to do this. Let me do this so that if the worst comes to pass, I will know I left you at least a bit better off than I found you. All right?"

She remained silent for a moment, her mouth set in a thin, flat line. And then she nodded. "If you feel this is what you have to do, then do it. Just know that it doesn't matter to me. It isn't necessary."

"Agreed," he said, shooting her a quick, reassuring half-smile. "Can we go get married now? I've got a hankering to hurry through the formalities and hightail it back here for the honeymoon."

As he'd hoped they would, Callie's lips lifted. Matthew blew happy little spit bubbles, as though he followed what was going on around him and found their adult problems highly amusing.

"I'll see you there," he said, pressing a soft kiss to her cheek.

Callie left the house through the front door, carrying Matthew, while Wade sneaked out the other way. She'd made the trip into town numerous times before, but that didn't keep him from worrying for her and the baby's safety. Especially when it came to meeting up with him at the mission.

If anyone saw him . . . if anyone saw them together, both she and Matthew could be in danger. His hand ran over the shape of the pistol in his belt, and he was suddenly glad she'd thought to give him the gun. He hoped he wouldn't need to use it, of course, but it eased his mind at least partially about his ability to protect Callie and Matthew if anything untoward occurred.

Making his way into the woods a short distance from the house, he moved as fast as he could toward his old homestead.

When he'd discovered the deed to his ranch missing, he'd known instinctively who'd taken it and why. He'd also known that Neville Young didn't really want his land, but the mine rumored to be hidden somewhere nearby.

Just as he'd explained to Callie, the ranch and the mine were actually two different properties, with two separate sets of ownership papers. That didn't mean Brady Young wouldn't work the mine if he discovered its location, thinking it was all part of the land his father had stolen from Wade. But Wade was the full legal owner. At any time, he—or Callie, once they were man and wife—could come forward and take possession of the mine back from Young.

All he had to do was retrieve the deed.

After finding the other documents missing, and before he'd stormed over to Neville Young's to confront the man about the theft, he'd moved the rest of his important legal papers from the previously locked storage box in his office to the hollow of a loose stone in the well behind his house.

It was risky to go even that far onto the Circle M, but not quite as dangerous as if he had to actually go inside the house.

Making himself as small as possible to remain unseen, he crouched at the edge of the tree line on the east end of the Circle M.

As far as he could see, no one milled about behind the buildings. No cowboys rode watch along the fence lines. He hoped any hired hands still working would stick to the area around the barn out front so he could slip around back, collect what he needed, and escape again into the woods without being spotted.

When he felt the situation was as safe as it was likely to get, he cut across the pasture at a run, heading straight for the round stone well. It took him barely a minute to find the secret stone, remove the battered tin hidden behind it, tuck the mine papers into the inside pocket of his jacket, and return to the protection of the trees.

Now all that was left was for him to get to the church and make Callie Quinn his wife.

Twisting her hands together at her waist, Callie paced back and forth behind the two rows of polished wooden benches in the vestibule of the Purgatory mission. Seated at the end of a nearby pew, Father Ignacio bounced baby Matthew on his knee, playing with the child and casting sidelong glances in her direction.

She'd arrived at the church more than half an hour earlier and had been nervously awaiting Wade ever since. Chances were, he was fine. But the possibility existed that he had been hurt or captured, and she didn't think her heart would stop pounding until he arrived safe and sound.

"You are agitated, child," Father Ignacio finally commented. "What is it we are waiting for?"

She shook her head, not answering that particular question. "I need a favor, Father. You'll understand soon enough. We just have to wait . . . wait for something."

Instead of pressing for further details, the padre returned his attention to Matthew, addressing her over the baby's shoulder. "You know I will help you in any way I can. I only wish you would confide in me about what has you so upset."

She jerked her head again in denial, then spun

around at a sound from the front of the church. Entering through a lesser-used door at the side of the building, Wade stalked up the aisle toward them.

Callie met him halfway, wrapping her arms around his waist and reaching up to press her cheek against his own. The hard metal outline of the Colt she'd given him dug into her torso through the layers of their clothes, reminding her of just what a dangerous mission he'd been on.

"Are you all right?" she asked. "How did it go?"

"Fine. Everything's fine." His glance skimmed past her to Father Ignacio. "Does he know what we want? Will he perform the service?"

"No. I didn't want to tell him too much, in case something went wrong. I'm sure he'll agree, though."

His fingers linked with hers, he hooked her arm over his elbow and led her toward the priest.

Father Ignacio rose at their approach, lifting Matthew from his lap to his chest.

"Father, this is Wade Mason," Callie began. "He's asked me to marry him, and I was hoping you'd perform the ceremony for us."

The priest considered Wade, sizing him up, Callie saw.

A gentleman down to his toes, Wade offered his hand to the holy man. "Padre," he murmured politely.

Father Ignacio's gaze moved from Wade to her. "Callie. Child. I have never heard you mention a male suitor before. You are sure about this?"

"Very sure, Father. Wade is a wonderful man."

She almost told him, too, about Wade being Matthew's father, but was afraid he might have somehow heard that the man who impregnated Lily had also been sent to prison for murder. She didn't want him to realize Wade was on the run from the law.

"He and Nathan are friends. And he loves Matthew. He'll make an excellent father," she added for good measure, giving Wade's hand a squeeze to keep him from correcting her.

"You love him, then?" the father asked pointedly.

Callie felt a little flutter in her stomach and lifted her head to look at Wade. Their eyes met and his warm coffee-brown gaze washed over her.

Oh, yes, I am sure. She might have her doubts about some parts of this plan, about what their future would hold, but she had no qualms about loving this man and wanting to spend the rest of her life with him, God willing.

"I do," she told the priest, her gaze still locked with Wade's.

"And you, young man," he addressed Wade.

"Your intentions toward this woman are honorable?"

"Absolutely," Wade answered without hesitation.

After another lengthy pause, the padre inclined his head. "Very well, then. I will marry you. We will need a witness, however. I will get one of the sisters."

He handed Matthew back to Callie and bustled off toward one of the doorways leading to the orphanage attached to the church.

When he returned, a petite young nun in tow, Callie and Wade were waiting for him at the pulpit. They smiled appreciatively and thanked the sister for taking the time to witness their wedding, then waited while the father gathered his Bible and special vestments.

"Before he comes over here," Wade said, leaning close so that only Callie would hear, "I want to tell you where the mine is located on the Circle M."

In a whispered voice, he described what the overgrown area would look like, and how to count paces from the southwest corner of the house. Callie hoped she'd remember his instructions when the time came.

Better yet, she hoped she would never need to go looking for the mine on her own. She prayed Wade's name would be cleared and he would be free to mine his land himself.

Reaching into his pocket, he pulled out the deed to that particular portion of land. "Here, take this. Keep it somewhere safe."

Carefully folding the parchment, she balanced Matthew's weight on her chest and forearm and slipped the papers into her reticule just as Father Ignacio came to stand before them.

"Are we ready to start?" he asked.

"Yes," both Wade and Callie responded at the same time, moving closer together. Their arms brushed, and the heat of Wade's body seeped into hers.

The priest began to speak, intoning the merits of faithfulness and the importance of keeping promised vows. To love, honor, obey, and cherish.

Well, maybe not obey, Callie thought, but she was pretty sure Wade knew that already. She hadn't exactly been the most agreeable in his short stay with her. And now he got to put up with her through all eternity.

"Do you, Callie, take this man to be your lawfully wedded husband?"

Her pulse sped up at those words. For a second, she couldn't speak, too caught up in the fact that she was actually getting married, that Wade would be her husband from this day forward, and she would soon be Matthew's mother both by choice and by law.

It was almost all she'd ever wanted. Certainly

her main goal since Wade's arrival had been to secure her place in Matthew's life. And now she would never need to use the adoption certificate she'd been in such a lather to have Father Ignacio sign for her. A fact for which she was almost pathetically grateful.

The only thing better than knowing Matthew would never be taken from her was to be married to Matthew's father.

And the only thing that could make this moment more perfect—aside from perhaps Nathan being present—would be the knowledge that Wade would be cleared of his conviction and able to stay with her forever.

But she pushed that thought and the fear that accompanied it aside, determined to wring every ounce of happiness from this moment, regardless of what tomorrow might bring.

Finding her voice, she softly but firmly answered the father's question. "I do."

"And do you, Wade, take this woman to be your lawfully wedded wife?"

Wade's eyes met hers. "I do."

"By the power vested in me . . ." Father Ignacio intoned, but Callie barely heard him. Before he'd even finished the end of the haphazard ceremony, Wade had pulled her into his arms, baby and all, and begun kissing her.

His mouth moved over hers like sunlight over a field of daisies. Warming her, comforting her, making her stretch up on tiptoe and lean into his intensity.

"Yes, well . . ." She heard the padre mumble and clear his throat uncomfortably when finally they broke apart. "All that remains is to sign the marriage certificate."

He moved to the side of the altar, returning with a sheet of vellum. Using the communion rail as a writing surface, Callie and Wade both scrawled their names, followed by Father Ignacio and the nun, who added their signatures as celebrant and witness.

"Thank you, Sister. You may return to the children now."

With a nod, the young woman wished them well, then turned and left the chapel.

"You should keep this, too," Wade said, folding the marriage certificate into quarters and handing it to her.

Her fingers lingered over the thick paper a few seconds longer than necessary before tucking it into the reticule at her wrist, next to the deed he'd given her not half an hour earlier.

While her purse was open, she removed several doubled-over bills she'd taken from the hidden stash at the bottom of her wardrobe at home and held them out to Father Ignacio. "Thank you again, Father. We really appreciate this."

The priest took the money. "*Gracias.* This will go directly into the poor box. And it was my pleasure, child. I wish you many years of happiness together."

"I wouldn't count on that, Padre."

Callie and Wade both spun around at the low, dangerous voice behind them. She gasped at the sight of Brady Young standing just inside the large double doors of the church, flanked by four other men. They all had guns, and all five barrels were pointed directly at Wade.

Chapter Twenty-six

Acting on pure instinct—and more than a healthy dose of fear—Callie practically threw Matthew into Father Ignacio's arms and stepped in front of Wade. The baby immediately began to squall, and Wade tried to shove her out of the way.

"No," she hissed, holding her ground.

When she refused to move, refused to put him back in the line of fire, she felt him take advantage of the barrier she made with her body to reach under his jacket for the Colt revolver.

"Move out of the way, Callie," Brady growled. "Your friend there is coming with us, and no one wants you to get hurt."

"Listen to him, Callie," Wade whispered above her left ear. His fingers flexed around her upper arm. "We knew this moment would come. I'll be all right."

But he wouldn't, and she knew it. Brady Young wasn't here to take him into custody and turn him over to the law. If Wade left with Brady now, he likely wouldn't make it to morning.

Without considering the consequences, she reached behind her for Wade's arm—the one holding the six-shooter—and brought it up so that the gun rested against her breastbone, aimed at her heart.

"What are you doing?" Wade breathed frantically just above her ear.

"They won't shoot you if they think you're willing to shoot me. And they can't take you anywhere if you drag me off first."

"I won't use you as a shield," he argued.

"You already are. Now shut up and threaten to kill me."

"I hope to hell you know what you're doing," he muttered, and then wrapped his free arm around her waist to hold her tight against his body and look more like he was controlling her movements.

"Don't come any closer," he barked at Brady and his men.

Callie saw Young hesitate, the bead of his firearm faltering, just as she'd hoped. Now if only they could escape.

Father Ignacio would care for Matthew; she

wasn't worried about that. He had already backed into a corner, blocking the child with his body.

"Take him out of here. Please," she begged the padre.

Matthew might have been only a baby, but she didn't want him witnessing whatever might take place in the next few minutes. And she certainly didn't want him to be in danger, or to be used as a pawn in Brady Young's hateful games.

Father Ignacio looked as if he might argue but then gave a sharp nod and slipped through an entranceway beyond the altar that would take him into the connecting orphanage. Maybe he could even send someone for help.

With Matthew away and safe, her mind returned to Wade's well-being—and her own. She realized that even if they managed to get out of the church without Brady putting a bullet into Wade, she had no idea how much farther they would get, what they would do, or where they would hide.

Wade moved them a step to the side. "Drop your guns."

Brady's mouth curled in an arrogant smirk. "Drop yours, Mason. In case you haven't noticed, you're outnumbered."

"Yes, but I've got a badge, and the authority to back it up."

The voice came from even deeper in the shadows at the back of the church and echoed into the rafters.

Seven sets of eyes whipped in that direction to find Sheriff Walker standing just inside the door, his gun drawn and hovering at waist level. Callie took heart in the fact that the sheriff hadn't added his revolver to the four others already pointed at them and could aim just as easily at Brady and his men as at Wade.

"Sheriff Walker," Brady said, "I'm glad to see you. This man is an escaped convict. He's the one who was sent away to prison for shooting my father in the back. We spotted him over on a piece of my land and followed him here. You can take him over to the jail now, if you like. See that he finishes paying for his crime."

"That's a fine idea," the sheriff drawled, "and I'll do just that as soon as we have a little talk ourselves, you and I."

"Excuse me?"

Even from a distance, Callie saw Brady's brows knit.

"There are some things we need to discuss."

Two deputies entered the church through the over-large doorway and came to stand on either side of Sheriff Walker.

The sheriff gestured with his revolver. "I'd appreciate it if you'd hand over those six-shooters, boys. We don't want anyone to get hurt."

"What's going on, Sheriff?" Brady asked, in no hurry to give up his gun.

Walker motioned with his head, and his deputies started down the line of men, relieving them of their weapons.

"Just a few things we need to iron out."

Once the firearms were in the lawmen's possession, Sheriff Walker motioned Brady's group toward a pew at the back of the church. They sat, placing their hands in plain sight on the back of the bench in front of them as the sheriff ordered.

"Now for Mr. Mason." Sheriff Walker turned in Callie's and Wade's direction. "I don't think you actually have any intention of hurting Miss Quinn, so if I could have your gun as well, I'd feel a mite more comfortable."

A long, tense minute passed while Wade seemed to consider. Then his hold on Callie loosened, the revolver falling away from her breast as he let the sheriff take it from his grasp.

"Take a seat," Walker commanded, waving toward the front pew.

Callie sat, her legs barely able to hold her any longer, as it was. Wade took a place beside her, his hand resting protectively on the curve of her waist.

She wondered why Sheriff Walker didn't drag Wade off to jail immediately. After all, he was an escaped convict and a reward was being offered for his capture.

But the sheriff's delay at taking Wade into custody, his disarming of Brady's men, gave her hope that—at the very least—Purgatory's sheriff wasn't one to assume a man guilty simply because his face appeared on a WANTED poster.

Sheriff Walker stood in the middle of the aisle, halfway between Callie and Wade and Brady and his men. He wore a double gun belt but kept only one weapon out of its holster. Wade's was tucked into the front of his trousers.

His two deputies hovered behind the men sitting in the last pew, legs spread and hands on hips, ready to go for their guns if necessary.

"Wade Mason did escape from the Huntsville Penitentiary a few weeks ago and will have to be held accountable for that. But what I find even more interesting is the crime Mr. Mason was tried and convicted of."

Callie glanced up at Wade. His eyes were dark and somber, his teeth clamped so tight, a muscle jumped in his jaw.

"As you all know, I haven't been sheriff here in Purgatory for very long. Jensen Graves was the law in these parts before I came along. I have always known he and I approached the job very differently. But I seem to be constantly amazed at just how differently."

With the hand that wasn't holding his revolver at the ready, he dug into the inside pocket of his vest and withdrew what looked to be a book.

Bound in brown leather, it was beaten and worn around the edges, the pages crinkled and starting to yellow.

"After Sheriff Graves died," Walker continued, "they boxed up most of his personal effects and brought them over to the jail. They've been sitting in a corner, collecting dust, ever since. That is, until Miss Quinn came to see me yesterday. She got me to thinking about some things. Like how this town was run before I came along."

He re-holstered his Peacemaker and began flipping through the battered volume in his hands. "Turns out Sheriff Graves was involved in some rather shady dealings. In fact, it looks like he pretty much had a hand in all the questionable activities going on in town. And he was kind enough to keep track of it all.

"Interesting reading, this book," he said, tapping a finger against the page he'd opened to. "It's filled with notes on exactly who in Purgatory was doing what—and how much he got paid for not stopping them."

Raising his head, he fixed Brady Young with a steady glare. "Your father had quite a handle on this town," he told the young man. "Seems he liked to get his own way, and he wasn't above paying people off . . . or muscling them out, if need be."

Callie's gaze shifted to Brady. His eyes narrowed to slits beneath the short-cropped bangs of his blond hair, his lips pulled back in a near snarl as his nails curled like claws, digging into the wooden bench in front of him.

"I don't know what the hell you're rattling on about, Sheriff." He spat the words, as though Sheriff Walker was barely a step above a belly-crawling sidewinder. "My father was a fine, up-standing citizen, and *this man* killed him in cold blood."

Brady jumped to his feet, shaking a finger in Wade's direction. Wade's grip on her waist tightened, and she reached down to cover his hand reassuringly with her own.

"Sit down." Walker's voice maintained a normal pitch, but his tone left no room for argument.

One of the deputies stepped forward to place a warning hand on Brady's shoulder. Brady looked none too happy about it, but he sat.

Sheriff Walker stepped closer to Brady. "As I was saying, Mr. Young, Graves mentions your father in this book. I'm not so sure you'd appreciate his opinion of your family, but I'm inclined to believe just about everything the late sheriff wrote. After all, this was his personal diary, nothing he expected anyone else to read. It appears to be a complete accounting of the numerous pies he had those pork-sausage fingers of his dipped into."

"I don't know what you're talking about," Brady replied, a mutinous tilt to his chin.

"I think you do." The sheriff pulled some loose papers from the journal and began to unfold them. "This, for instance, is the deed to a piece of land owned by Mr. Wade Mason."

Callie gasped and Wade's hand tightened so hard around hers, she thought the bones might break.

"I think you're familiar with the land I'm talking about. It's that acreage Mr. Mason called the Circle M but which you're currently working and claim to own."

"I do own it," Brady charged. "I don't know what those papers say, but I have a deed for that property, too, and mine, at least, is real."

"Actually, it isn't. According to Sheriff Graves, your father didn't want Wade Mason's ranch so much as he wanted access to the gold mine he suspected was somewhere on the property."

"Gold mine? What gold mine?" Brady's head swiveled from side to side as he scrutinized his hired hands. "There's no gold mine on that land. Is there?"

"Maybe you should ask Mr. Mason. It *is* his ranch, after all."

Wade's arms looped around Callie's waist and he pulled her back against him. His heavy, rapid breathing sounded in her ear as he pressed a scratchy, beard-stubbled cheek against her neck and face. She felt his grin and couldn't help smiling herself.

Sheriff Walker was on their side. He held in his hands proof that Wade *did* own the Circle M. Perhaps even some evidence that Wade was innocent of the crime for which he'd been sent to prison.

Her heart jolted beneath her rib cage, but all they could do was wait and see what else Sheriff Walker would reveal.

"You see," the sheriff went on, "whatever papers you have claiming ownership to that stretch of land are fraudulent. Your father had the originals stolen from both Mr. Mason's home and the registrar's office here in town. He just didn't know that instead of destroying the extra copy, Graves kept it for himself. As a bit of a safeguard, I suppose, against your father."

"That's a lie," Brady snarled.

Both deputies moved their hands to rest on the butts of their guns in case Young made any sudden moves.

"It's not. What's more, Graves made an interesting entry about your father's death. It seems Mr. Mason only went over to the Triple Y that night to confront your father about the stolen deed. And that he was disarmed almost the minute he stepped onto the property. In which case, he couldn't have shot your father at all, let alone in the back. Graves claims *you* shot your father," Walker slowly disclosed. "Out of greed, he suspected. And he never said anything—went along with your plan to frame Mr. Mason—because you paid him even better than your father had. Apparently, Sheriff Graves's loyalty was available to the highest bidder."

Sheriff Walker's eyes flashed to his deputies, and he nodded. In a smooth, synchronized movement, the three of them drew their weapons and trained them on Brady Young. One of the deputies removed a heavy set of wrist irons from his belt band.

"Brady Young, you're under arrest for the murder of your father—among other things." The sheriff sent the men sitting on either side of Young a meaningful look. "Your men are welcome to go with you, if they like."

Almost in unison, the four ranch hands began shaking their heads and easing away from Brady.

"Nope. No way," one of them said, hands in the air as he sidled away from his soon-to-be former boss. "He pays us good, but not that good. I ain't goin' to jail for nothin' he did."

"I'm glad to hear it," Sheriff Walker said, sounding almost amused. "I'll need to speak with the four of you about what you know of Mr. Young's shady dealings, but as long as you don't give me any trouble, you can walk to the jailhouse without the shackles."

With a more pronounced nod to his deputies, he said, "Cuff him. And don't give them any trouble, Young. I wouldn't lose much sleep over putting a bullet between the eyes of a man who would shoot his own father in the back."

Brady tensed but struggled only moderately as the deputies locked the dark metal manacles about his wrists and led him away. With a gesture from the sheriff, Brady's men followed.

And then he turned toward them.

Callie and Wade got to their feet. She wrung her hands in front of her nervously.

"I'll question them," Sheriff Walker said. "Find as much evidence as I can against him. The journal will help." He tucked the book back inside his vest.

"Wade has a letter from Lily, written on her deathbed," Callie said. "She was there that night, watching from one of the upstairs windows. The letter tells what she saw that night, and may be even more help in convicting Brady."

Walker inclined his head. "I'll be needing that letter, then. The judge will probably find it real interesting."

"It's back at Callie's house," Wade put in, his voice scratchy and low. "I'll see that you get it."

"What happens now?" Callie asked Sheriff Walker, almost afraid to hear the answer. Her fingers dug into Wade's flesh like a vice.

Gaze locked on Wade, the sheriff said, "I'm

going to have to take you with me. Not because I don't believe everything I just said. . . . There's not a doubt in my mind that Neville Young stole your land, or that Brady took advantage of the situation to kill his own father. But you were tried and convicted of the crime, and then you broke out of prison. Until we can get things straightened out, I need to keep you in custody."

Callie's hopes plummeted, and her emotions must have been clear on her face because the sheriff turned to her and laid a reassuring hand on her arm. "It'll be all right. We know the truth now, and I'm going to do everything I can to clear his name."

His glance shifted to the altar beyond. "I take it the two of you got hitched. Congratulations. I'll do my best to see he's returned to you as soon as possible," he added, lips quirked in a grin.

"Thank you, Sheriff." Wade extended his hand and the two men shook. "Other than Callie, no one really believed I didn't kill Neville Young."

"Well, I had my fair share of trouble with Sheriff Graves when I first came to Purgatory. It doesn't surprise me in the least that he played a part in wrongly sending you to prison. I'm only sorry I didn't go through his box of things sooner, or know what was going on so I could retrace Graves's steps, based on his past actions alone. To be honest, though, it's Callie you should thank. If she hadn't come by the jail yesterday and piqued my curiosity with her questions about you, we might never have figured out what really happened. Now, at least, we have a chance of setting you free."

Wade drew her snug against his tall frame. "Believe me, I know just how lucky I am. And as soon as all this is cleared up, I'm going to see to it she's thanked good and proper."

Heat flooded her face at Wade's undisguised innuendo, and she knew she was blushing like a new peach. Worse yet, a hint of red began to climb Sheriff Walker's neck, as though he knew exactly what Wade was implying, making Callie wish she could melt through the floorboards and disappear.

"We'd better start over to my office," the sheriff prompted, ushering them down the aisle of the church ahead of him.

"I have to check on Matthew," Callie said. "I'll see if Father Ignacio can keep him a while longer, but I want to make sure he's all right."

Wade nodded. She started toward the door separating the chapel from the orphanage, but he didn't release his grip on her hand until he absolutely had to.

As she moved away, she heard the sheriff say, "There is one more thing that I'd really like to know."

"What's that?" Wade asked.

"Is there really a gold mine on your property?"

Wade chuckled. "You'd have to ask Callie," he replied in a low voice. "It's her gold mine now."

Chapter Twenty-seven

In the weeks that followed Sheriff Walker's taking Wade in to custody, Callie did her best to keep her and Wade's spirits up.

She visited him at the Purgatory jail at least once a day, taking him home-cooked meals, books, a change of clothes, or even just giving him time to play with Matthew.

And Sheriff Walker had been wonderful. He'd investigated even further into Neville and Brady Young's crimes and sent for the circuit judge, confident Brady would be found guilty of his father's murder.

Until such time as a judge overturned Wade's conviction, however, he was considered a felon and had to remain behind bars. Sympathetic to Wade's circumstances, Sheriff Walker kept him in Purgatory for as long as he could, but eventually Wade had to be transported back to the State Penitentiary at Huntsville.

The day the guards came to get him, Callie stayed with him until the prison wagon rolled away. She'd kissed him, hugged him past the shackles once again binding his ankles and wrists, and told him that she loved him. She promised to care for Matthew and the Circle M and even the mine she'd heard so much about but had never seen.

But as soon as enough dust from the road had been stirred up to keep him from seeing her features clearly, she'd broken down in sobs that had shaken her to her very soul.

Since then, she'd thrown herself into doing everything she could to make his homecoming a happy one. And he would be coming home. She didn't know when, she only knew he would be.

One week later to the day, in a trial everyone but Callie clamored to attend, Brady Young had been found guilty of his father's murder. He'd been sentenced to hang, which she found a rather fitting punishment for someone who would go so far as to shoot his own father in the back out of nothing more than greed.

While the townspeople looked on in awe, a gallows had been constructed in the center of town, and three days after his conviction, Brady was hanged.

Once again, Callie refused to attend. She hated Brady possibly more than anyone else in Purgatory for what he'd done to Wade—which was why she hadn't wasted one moment sitting through his trial—but that didn't mean she wanted to actually see him put to death. Simply knowing it had been done was peace of mind enough for her.

Besides, she had plenty of other chores to keep her busy. In addition to the daily care Matthew required, Wade's ranch had been returned to his possession and she'd been spending a good chunk of time cleaning the house, hiring new hands to handle things until Wade could see to the running of the ranch himself, and getting rid of any and all signs that Brady had ever set so much as one foot on the Circle M.

If nothing else, it helped her to work off her own simmering fury at both Brady and Neville Young and all of the horrible, nasty, back-stabbing things they'd done to Wade. As well as making her feel she was preparing something homey and welcoming for when the man she loved returned to her side.

She'd just finished washing the last inside pane of glass on the first floor of his house with an ammonia-soaked rag and was wiping beads of sweat from her brow with the back of her arm when a knock sounded at the front door.

Sighing, she shuffled forward. She looked like

something the cows had just rolled across the pasture, with myriad stains on her skirts, splotches of water on her bodice, and ragged tufts of hair straggling from the bun at her nape.

When she opened the door, she found Clay and Regan Walker standing on the other side, arms linked and wide smiles on their faces.

"Good afternoon," Regan offered brightly. Her hair was a riot of curls, held back by a yellow ribbon that perfectly matched her gabardine skirt. Only a slight swell was visible beneath her garments, hinting at the condition Sheriff Walker had revealed to Callie several weeks earlier.

"We stopped by your place first, but when we didn't find you at home, Clay suspected you might be here. He says you've been fixing the place up for Wade's release."

"That's right," Callie replied, weary from a full day of backbreaking work but glad for friendly faces to disrupt the solitary monotony of dusting and scrubbing. "I don't think Brady paid much attention to anything but the ranch, and I thought it would be nice for Wade to come home to a clean house."

"Absolutely," Regan agreed, smiling even wider. "Though I imagine when Wade finally makes it back to Purgatory, he won't care about a little bit of dust on the mantel. Not as long as he has you warming his bed."

"Regan," Clay warned in a low voice, an embarrassed grin tugging at the corners of his mouth.

Ignoring him, Regan threw Callie a woman-to-woman glance. "It's obvious the two of you love each other deeply, so I don't think it's any great secret that Wade will be coming home to *you*, not this house."

She leaned forward to look past the doorway. "Though it is a beautiful place to raise a family. Maybe your brother will return to run your family farm after you move in here."

Callie and Wade hadn't spent much time discussing where they would live once he was a free man again; she only knew where they put down roots wasn't nearly as important as being together. The three of them, just as it had been while Wade was still hiding out, but without the threat of discovery hanging over their heads.

To keep Regan Walker from bringing up any more sensitive, emotional subjects, she stepped back and ushered them inside. "Would you like to come in? I can put on a pot of tea."

"No, thank you," the couple answered quickly and in unison.

"Actually," Clay put in, "we came over to ask a favor of you."

Callie raised a brow.

"We were wondering if you'd walk with us. Just a little ways," Regan added. "There's something we'd like to show you."

She couldn't imagine what the Walkers wanted her to see and didn't know whether to be worried or curious. "I'm sorry. Matthew is napping upstairs. I couldn't leave him in the house alone."

"I'll stay with him," Regan piped up immediately, sidling her way past Callie. "I love children, as you well know, and it will do me good to get used to holding a baby again." With a gentle pat to her belly, she flounced across the room and up the steps to the second floor.

Feeling like her world had been tipped upside down, Callie glanced at Clay, eyes wide. "Whatever you want to show me must be pretty important. She seemed rather eager to have me gone."

He chuckled. "You can't sway Regan once she's got an idea in her head, and she really wants you to see this." Offering his elbow, he half turned toward the porch steps. "Shall we?"

She was hot and tired, but she had a feeling that if she didn't go with Clay Walker willingly, his wife would breeze back into the room and drag her off by her hair.

"I guess I don't have much choice."

Clay smiled. "It will be worth it, I promise."

Taking his arm, she let him lead her down the porch steps, around the house, and through the back pasture.

Careful to keep the hem of her skirts above the

330

ground and to watch where she put her feet, she asked, "Where is it that we're going? I didn't know there was anything back this way."

"It's my understanding that this has been one of Purgatory's best-kept secrets for going on several years now."

Her brow crinkled, wondering what in heaven's name he could be taking her to see. The farther they walked, the more it occurred to her that this was the same general direction Wade had told her to take to reach his hidden gold mine.

Could that be where Clay was leading her? But why? If she wasn't even certain of the mine's exact location, how could Sheriff Walker know?

As they climbed to the top of a small hillock, she thought she spotted movement in the bushes. And then she was sure of it.

Slowly, a human form appeared. A pair of dusty, well-worn boots. Denim-clad legs. A man's brass belt buckle and light blue chambray shirt. Callie's breath caught. It couldn't be, could it? The figure pushed bushes and branches aside to reveal the boarded-up opening of a cavelike den.

Finally she saw the most important feature of the man clearing the entrance of the mine—his face.

His handsome, strong, tan face, with its chiseled jaw and deep brown eyes.

Heidi Betts

The air caught in her chest and tears prickled the backs of her eyes as she dropped her hold on the sheriff's elbow and raced forward, throwing herself into Wade's waiting arms.

He hugged her close, lifting her off the ground and spinning her in circles. She squeezed him back, kissing him over and over all along his cheekbones, his jaw, his chin and nose and brow.

"Oh, Lord. Oh, Wade, I missed you so much," she murmured between kisses. "When did you get back?"

"Just a couple of hours ago." Lips and nose nuzzling her neck, his words vibrated against her skin. "I asked Clay and Regan to bring you out here so I could surprise you."

"It worked," she whispered in a shaky voice. The tears that had threatened to fall only seconds before now dampened her lashes. "I'm very surprised. And so, *so* happy. Are you home for good?" she asked. "Is everything taken care of?"

"Everything is fine. I'm free as a bird, sweetheart."

"And you flew straight home to me."

He threw back his head and laughed. "It was more like a good day's hard riding, but I definitely made a beeline for my sweet Callie girl. That's not the surprise, though. There's something else."

"Something better than my husband coming home to me? Not possible."

Grinning that wicked grin she'd missed so much while he was gone, he bussed her on the tip of the nose. "Maybe not better than that, but still good." He ran his hand down her arm to grasp her hand. "How's Matthew?"

"Wonderful. He's taking a nap back at the house. Regan stayed with him."

He led her a few steps away, toward the cave opening. "I can't tell you how much I missed you two these past few weeks. I thought about you every minute. I dreamed of your lips, and your touch, and the way you smell of lilac after a bath. I even missed having the kid wet on my lap."

They were still laughing as he pulled her to a stop beside the low-riding hollow dug into the earth.

"This is the mine," he told her. "It's not nearly as important as it was before. Provided you intend to stay married to me," he added on a teasing note.

"You'll have to get yourself sent back to prison if you hope to get away from me," she shot back. "You asked me to marry you, I said yes, and I have a priest, a nun, and a signed certificate to prove it."

"I was hoping you'd say that."

He leaned in to kiss her again. This time his lips moved hungrily over hers, until she swayed into him and forgot all about Sheriff Walker standing behind them, likely watching their every move.

Except that he wasn't. When she turned around, blushing, to look, she saw only the back of his brown leather vest as he headed back toward the house, leaving them in privacy.

"Since you've decided to stay married to me, at least for a while," Wade went on, "I think it's only fair that I finally get around to giving you a ring."

"Is that my surprise?" she asked eagerly, wrapping herself around his arm as he moved scant inches into the overgrowth beside the mine opening.

"Not quite, Little Miss Eager. It's this."

Leaves rustled as he pulled a large wooden sign out of the bushes and propped it up for her to see.

" 'Callie's Claim,' " she read.

"It's yours," he explained. "I gave the mine to you before I left, and I mean for you to keep it. Which is why I named it after you. I've never worked the mine before, but I was thinking we could start. And the first nugget we find, I'm going to have made into a ring for you. What do you think?"

"I think the day you broke into my house was the luckiest day of my life," she said, laying her head against his chest.

"Not half as lucky as it was for me. I love you, Callie girl."

"I love you, too, Wade. I'm so glad you're home."

"I'm glad to be home."

His mouth captured hers again, and for several long seconds the world disappeared. There was nothing around them but blue skies and a soft summer breeze. His lips and tongue moved on hers, his hands spanning her hips as her fingers toyed with his silky chestnut hair.

When they finally broke apart, he tipped back her head so he could meet her eyes. In a low voice, stroking her face and hair, he said, "As nice as the Walkers are, what do you say we try to get rid of them so we can start on that honeymoon? We got a little sidetracked last time around."

"Mmm. I think that sounds like a delightful idea. If we're lucky, Matthew will sleep a while longer."

Wade temporarily secured the wooden CAL-LIE'S CLAIM sign against the opening of the mine, then looped his arm around her waist and started for the house.

"I think we've already established that our luck is going strong. Nothing can stop us now, sweetheart."

The corners of her mouth lifted as she gazed up at Wade. Her husband. The father of the baby she'd always considered her own. And she hoped the father of many more children they'd have together.

"Wade."

"Yes, darlin'?" He drawled the words, his lips curling in a self-satisfied half-smile, their hips bumping together as they walked over the uneven ground.

Her cheeks colored at what she was about to say, but she charged ahead anyway. "I know Matthew is awfully young, but what do you think about having another baby?"

There was only a slight hitch in his gate as he tipped his head to study her. "With you? It would be my pleasure." Pulling her even closer to his side, he said, "What do you say to a little girl this time? We can get started as soon as we reach the house."

"As soon as we get rid of the Walkers," she added impishly.

He grinned and tugged at a lock of her hair. "Yeah. As soon as we get rid of the Walkers. We'll probably have to make it up to them later, but I think they'll understand."

"You can invite them over for dinner and fry up those steaks you've been promising me."

Eyes twinkling, he said, "I see I'm going to have to watch what I say around you. You remember everything."

"Yes, I do."

"Well, steaks it is, then. A woman should get a honeymoon, after all, no matter what the cost."

"And a man should get his," she put in.

"Oh, he will. Believe me." And then he brushed his lips against her temple and whispered, "Little Callie Junior, here we come."

WALKER'S WIDOW

HEIDI BETTS

Clayton Walker has been sent to Purgatory . . . but it feels more like hell. Assigned to solve a string of minor burglaries, the rugged Texas Ranger thinks catching the crook will be a walk in the park. Instead he finds himself chasing a black-masked bandit with enticing hips and a penchant for helping everyone but herself. Regan Doyle's nocturnal activities know no boundaries; decked out in black, the young widow makes sure the rich "donate" to the local orphanage. And the fiery redhead isn't about to let a lawman get in her way—even if his broad shoulders and piercing gray eyes are arresting. But caught in a compromising position, Regan recognizes that the jig is up, for Clay has stolen her heart.

___4954-6 $5.99 US/$7.99 CAN

Dorchester Publishing Co., Inc.
P.O. Box 6640
Wayne, PA 19087-8640

Please add $2.50 for shipping and handling for the first book and $.75 for each additional book. NY and PA residents, add appropriate sales tax. No cash, stamps, or C.O.D.s. All Canadian orders require $5.00 for shipping and handling and must be paid in U. S. dollars. Prices and availability subject to change. Payment must accompany all orders.

Name_____
Address_____
City_____ State_____ Zip_____
E-mail_____
I have enclosed $ _____ in payment for the checked book(s).
☐Please send a free catalog.
        CHECK OUT OUR WEBSITE! www.dorchesterpub.com

Heidi Betts
ALMOST A
Lady

Pistol-packing Pinkerton agent Willow Hastings always gets her man. Until handsome, arrogant railroad security chief Brandt Donovan "gallantly" interferes in an arrest, costing Willow a collar and jeopardizing her job. And now she is supposed to collaborate with the dashing, distracting bachelor to catch a killer? Never! Brandt is shocked yet intrigued by this curvy, contrary, weapon-wielding brunette. Willow's sultry voice, silken skin, and subtle scent of roses make him ache to savor her between the sheets. But go undercover with the perplexing Pinkerton? Chastely pose as man and wife to entrap a killer? Such unthinkable celibacy could drive a bachelor to madness. Or to—shudder!—matrimony. . . .

___4817-5 $4.99 US/$5.99 CAN

Dorchester Publishing Co., Inc.
P.O. Box 6640
Wayne, PA 19087-8640

Please add $2.50 for shipping and handling for the first book and $.75 for each book thereafter. NY, NYC, and PA residents, please add appropriate sales tax. No cash, stamps, or C.O.D.s. All orders shipped within 6 weeks via postal service book rate. Canadian orders require $2.00 extra postage and must be paid in U.S. dollars through a U.S. banking facility.

Name_____
Address_____
City_____ State_____ Zip_____
I have enclosed $_____ in payment for the checked book(s).
Payment <u>must</u> accompany all orders.☐Please send a free catalog.
   CHECK OUT OUR WEBSITE! www.dorchesterpub.com

A Promise of Roses

Heidi Betts

Spunky Megan Adams will do almost anything to save her struggling stagecoach line—even confront the bandits constantly ambushing the stage for the payrolls it delivers. But what Megan *wouldn't* do is fall headlong for the heart-breakingly handsome outlaw who robs the coach, kidnaps her from his ornery amigos, and drags her half across Kansas—to turn *her* in as an accomplice to the holdup!

Bounty hunter Lucas McCain stops at nothing to get his man. Hired to investigate the pilfered payrolls, he is sure Megan herself is masterminding the heists. And he'll be damned if he'll let this gun-toting spitfire keep him from completing his mission—even if he has to hogtie her to his horse, promise her roses . . . and hijack her heart!

___4738-1 $4.99 US/$5.99 CAN

EXTREME MEASURES
RENEE HALVERSON

NEW HISTORICAL VOICE CONTEST WINNER

If André DuBois were a betting man, he would lay odds that the woman in red is robbing his dealers blind. He can tell the beauty's smile disguises a quick mind and even quicker fingers. To catch her in the act, he deals himself into the game, never guessing he might lose his heart in the process.

Faith O'Malley depends on her wits to succeed at cards, and experience tells her the ante has just been raised. The new gambler's good looks are distracting enough, but his intelligent eyes promise trouble. Still, Faith will risk everything—her reputation, her virtue—to save the innocent people depending on her. It won't be until later that she'll stop to learn what she's won.

Dorchester Publishing Co., Inc.
P.O. Box 6640
Wayne, PA 19087-8640

_____5062-5
$5.99 US/$7.99 CAN